# UNTYING THE MOON

## STORY RIVER BOOKS

*Pat Conroy, Editor at Large*

# UNTYING THE MOON

~~~~~~~ A NOVEL ~~~~~~~

## ELLEN MALPHRUS

*Foreword by Pat Conroy*

The University of South Carolina Press

© 2015 Ellen Malphrus

Published by the University of South Carolina Press
Columbia, South Carolina 29208

www.sc.edu/uscpress

Manufactured in the United States of America

24 23 22 21 20 19 18 17 16 15
10 9 8 7 6 5 4 3 2 1

Library of Congress Cataloging-in-Publication Data
can be found at http://catalog.loc.gov/.

ISBN 978-1-61117-610-0 (cloth)
ISBN 978-1-61117-611-7 (ebook)

This book was printed on recycled paper with
30 percent postconsumer waste content.

For Mom and Big Jim Dickey—and Andy, of course

Elsewhere I have dreamed of my birth,
And come from my death as I dreamed;

Each time, the moon has burned backward.
Each time, my heart has gone from me
And shaken the sun from the moonlight.
Each time, a woman has called,
And my breath come to life in her singing.
Once more I come home from my ghost.

JAMES DICKEY, "INTO THE STONE"


To the dolphin alone, beyond all others, nature has granted
what the best philosophers seek: friendship for no advantage.
Though it has no need at all of any man, yet it is a genial friend
to all and has helped many. . . . it is the only creature who
loves man for his own sake.

PLUTARCH, "DE SOLLERTIA ANIMALIUM"

# CONTENTS

# FOREWORD

The novelist Ellen Malphrus and I were both students of the otherworldly poet James Dickey, who taught us poetry at the University of South Carolina. Though Ellen is younger than I am, we both consider ourselves Dickey-shaped and Dickey-transformed and there are echoes of his magisterial world in all that we write. He was not merely a teacher, but a compendium of technique and knowledge, an atlas of milky ways, a bridge to a universe unknown. He made you quiver with joy at the many noises the English language could make. He forced you into offering yourself in covenant to become a Knight Templar of that language, an avowal of blood and passion, and set you in voyage to discover whatever formed you and to find if the hunt for the Holy Grail was within you. In his class, I discovered to my dismay that I was not a poet. Ellen Malphrus found that she was one.

Ellen and I met by accident, but in a fashion that was Dickey-esque in all of its particulars. She was, and will probably remain, the only South Carolina poet I've ever met in Blue Hill, Maine. I had just hit and killed a deer on the road from Brooklin to Blue Hill in a violent collision that had left my wife and me both shaken and trembling. Cassandra was certain we had killed a man, but I was sure that a deer had flashed out of the forest that came to the edge of the road before I could hit the brakes. When I found a road on which to turn around, we drove back and I saw some boys from Maine hauling away freshly killed venison in their pick-up truck. The Buick had incurred three thousand dollars worth of damage and a brand new source of nightmare for me. Cassandra was getting our prescriptions filled and I was still wobbly when a lovely woman with amazing hair approached me and said, in a rich southern accent, "You're a long way from James Dickey's class, aren't you, Bubba?"

"How in the hell do you know that?" I asked.

It was during that summer that Ellen and her husband Andy Fishkind became friends with Sandra and me. Ellen and I bored our spouses with Dickey stories, which are not boring the first hundred times you've heard them. But all devotees of the great poet tell these stories with the combination of awe and inspiration that must have once enlivened the reminiscences of whalers who had put to sea with Ahab. Ellen had become a lifelong friend of James

Dickey while I had passed through his stormy, illuminating classes unnoticed. But the fires he lit burn brightly in all I write. In Maine, I began to badger Ellen Malphrus for this remarkable novel *Untying the Moon*.

Because she was a poet, I entertained no fears about the quality of language she would bring to this effort. You can thump all the sentences in this book and set them to ringing like a row of wine glasses. Her writing is impeccable, gorgeous, precise. I always look for poets who turn to novels when poetry becomes too contained and refined to express the immensities within them. I watched it up close when I took my class with Dickey right before they began to film his first novel *Deliverance*. His novel is splendid and classic because Dickey's prose is polished from the same silver service as his poems and he writes about rivers as well as any writer who ever lived. Before he began his greatly honored career in the short story and novel, Ron Rash was writing some of the best poetry in the language and I was one of the few to know it. If the thunderheads are not gathering in their western horizon, the poets remain our pearl divers. They tell us all the secrets of refinement as poetry will always reveal the deepest shine of our words made bright in their depths. The poets send encoded messages to the stars. The novelist sends messages to us. So it is with Ellen Malphrus.

Like many first-rate novels, *Untying the Moon* begins with a prologue that is both artful and secretive, yet it tells us the whole tale in miniature and lets us in on the themes and undertones the novel will roll out for us. It is also a love note to the green marshes and tidal rivers of the South Carolina Lowcountry. Ellen makes you smell its richness, describes its remoteness and the starriness of his dark skies, and shares with you the magical birth of Bailey Martin, an astonishing girl born in a tiny, mother-rowed boat between two islands. Dolphins observe the birth and a black midwife, Henrietta Simmons, wades out into the shallows of the Jericho River, holding her toddler son, Ben, to help her friend Merissa deliver her child by moon and dolphin-light. I have written often about the Carolina Lowcountry and believe it has served as the central metaphor of my own attempt at art. But Ellen Malphrus writes about it with the osprey-eyed vision of a native, where I came to it late as a passionate outsider. Her descriptions of this infinite landscape achieve an ardor of completeness like none other. Ellen possesses a raw genius for nature writing.

Motion is the word that sets this novel across America toward Bailey's troubled, unfixable past as she hits the road for parts unknown more than any character I've encountered in modern fiction. For the first hundred pages of this book, I thought I was in the middle of a road novel, but behind the wheels of her indomitable machine, "a 1967 Blue Skylark G-S 400 cream puff of a

girl" that Bailey has christened Blue Ruby, this wild child of the eighties takes
to American highways with such recklessness that she makes Jack Kerouac
seem like a homebody. Bailey, an artist with a sublime gift, is running away
from herself and her past and even her future as she tries to supply mortar to
the gaps in herself by changing her life on a weekly, if not daily, basis. Forcing
the reader to ride shotgun, she drives us to the coast of Maine and takes us on
a cruise to the edge of Old Sow, the largest and most dangerous whirlpool in
North America. With her artist's eye aglitter, she describes the spectral, van-
ishing coast of Maine as though she were born a lobster fisherman in Castine.
Nor does she ever allow us to escape from the twisted coils of that whirlpool
as we feel the immensity of its power throughout the headlong pace of Bailey
Martin's frantic search for her deepest self. Like *Don Quixote*, it becomes a
novel of quest and heroic self-fulfillment, but with far more demons to con-
tend with than the Man from La Mancha ever considered.

Whenever Bailey grows restless or dissatisfied or uncomfortable in her
skin, she obeys the most authoritative voice inside her and unties the moon—
that is the call of the road, the cry of moving on, to load up Miss Ruby with
her few belongings and set out for the unknown. Always, she maintains a strict
adherence to all the laws of escape. Yet, the Self, that most insufferable and
absurd element of modern life at its most authentic, keeps asserting the raw-
ness of its needs and congeries on Bailey's tender yet unsinkable psyche.

Like many southern novels, the most mordant whimper is always the ancient call of home. In any quest, only the return to Ithaca will satisfy the
wanderlust. Though Bailey can help rescue whales trapped beneath the ice
of Barrow, Alaska, and clean the clotted oil from the wings of seabirds and
wildlife murdered by the Valdez oil spill, and lament the devastation of the en-
vironment wherever Miss Ruby takes her, she and the novel spring to amazing
life whenever she returns to Kirk's Bluff and that river that was her birthplace.
Her resistance to that cry of home is heroic but futile. She was born beneath
the eye of a white dolphin and though her memories of that home are com-
plex, it is where the central action is always flowing toward. It is the one moon
she cannot untie.

In the middle of the book, Ellen Malphrus presents us with a love story
that is as moving as it is disturbing. Already, she has demonstrated that the
pretty Bailey Martin often has execrable taste in men. This is neither a surprise nor even a worry in modern fiction, but the Vietnam vet Padgett Turner
is as appealing to the reader as he is to Bailey and her falling in love with him
seems a natural finish to Bailey's life of constant voyage. Her childhood friend
Ben Simmons sounds enough alarms and warnings to set off fire bells in the

reader, but the love is the real thing and when Bailey brings Padgett home to meet her laconic father, introduce him to Henrietta and George Simmons, and take him to visit the island cabin which matches all of her reveries of paradise, we learn something about love that is all too painful to bear.

But enough. I've told too much already. Bailey Martin is a magnificent creation. Henrietta and Ben Simmons are two of the strongest characters I've come across lately and demonstrate Ellen's intuitive and imaginative feel for the Gullah-Geechee culture she grew up around, a world she captures with certainty and devotion. The story begins and ends on the same river. It forms a perfect coda, a connection of a thousand dots in the circle, and it completes the restless journey of Bailey as though in fulfillment of a great prophesy— thunderstruck and dolphin-haunted and a significant work of art. Perfectly, the moon is tied at last.

PAT CONROY

# Prologue

Come in to the water and listen, child.
Come into the water and sing.

*S*he wakes in the night. Nothing has startled her—she simply finds herself awake, looking into the same ice blinked sky she has taken into her dreams. The world pauses untroubled around her and she drifts in silence hearing the warmth of him nearby.

Her wandering question is what has brought her to the surface, but whatever it is Bailey doesn't mind. It's good to lie there untethered in darkness.

The sound. She feels it more than hears. Different, delicate, as if she is listening with something other than ears. Movement in the water, she knows that, but slow, so slow and entirely apart from other sounds of the abiding woods around her and the meandering river below.

She tautens to hear it, but then the sound is gone.

While she lies there opening herself to what it could have been, there it is again. She pictures someone standing in the water, barely waist high, completely still, except that she—it has to be a woman, for a child is too impatient to make such movement and a man too forceful—is trailing one arm slowly, slowly, ever so slowly, through the current, front to back, with the almost imperceptible sound of forever.

As she listens, Bailey hears as well the starry voice of her mother Merissa sing of the fair curved skiff she rowed across the Jericho River that warm March morning when the moon drew all the earth into balance and Bailey was born to the coaxing hands of Henrietta. Henrietta, more than midwife, beyond neighbor and friend, beckoned from her garden by the silent calls of the young mother. Henrietta, who swooped her toddling son Benjamin in her arms and strode through the two yards and down to the boat landing. Who climbed into the skiff with her boy and told him hold onto me and don't let go 'til I tell you, full aware there was no time to travel, the baby nearly there from the thrust of each stroke Merissa had rowed as she calmly crossed from May Isle, determined to surround this child with water as she made her way from the womb.

*The boy Benjamin, stunned, mesmerized, held tight and watched in wonder and fear and confusion. In years to come the fear and confusion fell away, but the wonder remained steadfast. Bailey was magic, otherworldly. Ben knew it as a child and knows it as a man.*

*Now Bailey rises, as slowly as the sound, and walks to the water's edge. And there she sees her—the magnificent dolphin shining alabaster in the moonlight, partly on top of the water, partly submerged, like a stray timber adrift in the flood tide. The sound is of her poised body suspended in the gentle flow toward the headwaters of the Jericho River, as measured as the moon itself.*

*Entranced, she watches the dolphin pass through the channel of moon wake in the water. And when the light of the moon catches in the dolphin's eye, Bailey sees herself and knows this ineffable creature is somehow connected to her now, that she is somehow bound to the drifter as well.*

*She lies wakeful through the night, hoping the dolphin might surface once more when the tide changes, hoping to hear her again as the current carries her along in motionless repose.*

*But all of it flies as she listens, as she comes from the water and sings.*

# PART I

# Daughter of Motion
# (1988)

# High Tide and High Time

**M**otion. Bailey wakes from a liquid dream but can only glimpse water through slits of high rise buildings. What a joke. New York is a city that does not need her. Or anyone. Click. She doesn't belong here. Click. Has never belonged here. Click. Will never belong here. Click. Click. Click. The simplicity of it shuts out everything else and shoots adrenaline through her in a wave of delicious resolve. Motion. Sweet motion. There has to be motion— and today by god is the day. Untie the moon and walk on. Drive on. Swim on. Go. That's what Ben would tell her, and she could hear him all the way from Philadelphia. Bossman.

She paces the train from Grand Central to the depot in Old Saybrook, doesn't breathe from her belly until she reaches her friend Jack's rambling Connecticut barn, puts the key in the ignition, and folds herself into the power of three hundred and sixty horses, all raring to get the hell out of Dodge and onto the smooth southbound highway—a civilized and soothing direction— away from a city and a man and a life she's pretended for long enough.

But the glog of traffic.

Maybe head north then, skirt around the glog. Hell, why not shoot up to Maine, take it to the tip, stare into the eye of Big Sow, that colossal whirlpool—see what the oracle has to say. She sweeps her long brown hair into a pony tail, stuffs it under a Galapagos ball cap and rides the northbound wave, making time, marking miles, music cranked and singing loud about living life in chains.

And then they're gone. The key in your hand where it's been all along. The doorway appears and you simply walk through it and head on down the highway, out to the deep blue sea. If perspective is everything then motion is its all-star catalyst.

Her treasure box and clothes are in the back half of the trunk and her pal Raymond the doorman will send books and music, artwork and desk to Ben's place. Give away what he can't use of the rest. Stuff. How easy to be shed of it all in a day.

Crossing into New Hampshire she takes another long belly breath and blows a kiss to the disappearing state line. The time has come she says to Blue

Ruby, the 1967 Buick Skylark GS 400 cream puff of a girl that has carried her many ten thousands of miles toward freedom in all directions, often on the way to Anywhere Else. Miss Ruby, her constant companion and means of motion through the highways, byways, and dirt tracks of North America.

On to Maine, the great land of lobster, a state where there's room to exhale. If it weren't the weekend she would take a hard right tack straight for the coast. But it is the weekend, and hooking into the inch worm of traffic that crawls up US 1 each Friday afternoon doesn't remotely interest her. It's movement she needs, smooth sailing. That and a real deal lobster roll—a gem of American culinary creations. The properly prepared lobster roll is a glorious assemblage, and in Maine there is no shortage of them. She glides up I-95 to Augusta and cuts over on Highway 3, leap frogging the inch worm when she turns toward the sea. The sea.

She had searched for The Perfect Lobster Roll during the better part of a summer she'd spent there, and her mental map of favorites lies shimmering before her. First stop would be that roadside stand just north of Camden, which involves a slight detour southward at Belfast but is still out of the worm's reach. When she passes by the little road to Liberty Tool, that astounding menagerie of implements and treasures, Miss Ruby instinctively slows to turn but Bailey knows that even if she tells herself ten minutes she'll in fact spend the afternoon smutty fingered from obscure tools and weathered books in the endless ramblings of dusky alcoves. Another day, when she isn't so buzzed with the thrill of escape.

Just now her taste buds are set to flower, and when they wheel into the shingle strip parking lot of the lobster pound the guy at the window recognizes Miss Ruby and then Bailey and turns out to be a kid she'd sailed with in another life. She orders two rolls and asks him to time the second one for five minutes after the first. When the first one is ready she leans her willowy body against the convertible to study the bay and makes ridiculous attempts at savoring each bite. Who am I kidding, she says aloud to the big blue sea and walks over for the second course. There's been too much self control these last months—never her strong suit anyway.

It's tricky business, the lobster roll, a cunning balance of simplicity and timing. The easiest way to ruin one is to complicate the matter. There's no such thing as jazzing up a lobster roll. No such thing as a "company" lobster roll. Nothing more than mayonnaise—the right mayonnaise—and a dash of salt and whiff of pepper should be ever-so-gently tossed with the nuggets of sweet meat from a pounder.

Then there is the important consideration of the bun, a square bottomed hot dog bun that when properly buttered and toasted becomes as crucial to the overall flavor as is the unearthly delicacy of perfectly steamed lobster meat that someone else picked out. The butter must be rich and creamy and it must be applied to the interior of the bun before toasting, lovingly so as not to smush said bun—toasted such that the butter golds and each bite has one moment of subtle crunch between the lobster and the warm puff of bread that vanishes as the bite continues, offering the palate an exquisite union of noble flavors. Celestial.

She pulls over again at Searsport, and as night wears on stops at Cherry-field Crossroads too. At Roque Bluffs State Park she showers, opens a bottle of wine, picks the meat from a now soggy roll she ordered just in case, snugs down in the back of Miss Ruby beneath her Morning Star quilt from child-hood and stares long into the true sky, the one Manhattan will never know again, listening to Lyra and Cygnus and Aquilla and Delphinus, the star cluster her mother gave her on her seventh birthday. She dreams off into the sea . . . drifts . . . wakes with the urge to keep moving, so she and Blue Ruby swing off US 1 and swoop into Jonesport where Tall Barney's will open at 5 am with the daily influx of seafaring locals, the clatter of cups, the smell of fresh coffee and warm sugar.

The talk of lobstermen. Those in Jonesport, the Allens and the Beals, have a dialect that remains decidedly locked into ancient ancestry. They assemble themselves over strong brew and jaw about seals and Canadians, useless regu-lations and poor markets. They speak of tides and rigging and lines, just as sea reapers have gathered in thousands of ports for thousands of generations while the big earth slowly tilts oceans out and in to the beckoning moon.

And though the talk is hushed, spoken mostly in the clipped and par-tial sentences of the indigenous that is encoded to the outsider, there is also laughter, hearty laughter. It is this long ago language that brings her to Tall Barneys, to the outstretched table where lobstermen come and go in freeform clusters through the day, but the rhubarb pie is also a draw—the best she's ever encountered.

As she passes the marina at the edge of town the naughty Norton fel-las, Barna and John, are boarding *Chief* with the fifteen passengers they haul twenty-seven nautical miles every day out to tiny Machias Seal Island to clam-ber onto the rocky outcrop where thousands of puffins and auks and terns screech and scrabble and dive bomb interlopers en masse. Barna has been making the run since 1939 and his boy John has now marked decades himself.

Boundary dispute with Canada has yet to be settled, so they share—one boat-load per country per day.

Bailey took a 10 mg valium when she made the trek years ago, aware she'd get wiggy once they got to Machias and everyone was cooped up in the minis-cule clapboard blinds scattered around the rocky island. As one of the few who have set foot on Machias, she proudly keeps her souvenir patch in her bag of treasures, knowing she'll not be making that journey again. It was an amazing adventure, but to be hemmed in that tightly, locked in a box where elbows had to be tucked in order to turn, was the stuff of nightmares. "Don't Fence Me In," Willie Nelson trills, and she sings right along with him.

During her first conversation with Barna Norton she'd called to sign on for the trip to Machias and ask how long the drive would take to Jonesport from the Wooden Boat School in Brooklin. After a long silence he asked, "You mean by land? I have no idea." Nautical miles are the miles he knows and Bailey was smitten from the start. Now she stops for burly hugs from both boys, happy to see Barna looking spritely, but she doesn't tarry.

In Lubec, one of the bitter-end clusters at Canada's edge, she hires the captain her friends in Jonesport approved for safe passage into the vortex. Old Sow, created in part by 70 billion cubic feet of the Atlantic pounding into Passamaquoddy Bay where an underwater mountain is flanked by two great slashes in the ocean floor, each several hundred feet deep. A deadly shape-shifter, edging this way and that, depending.

Old Sow is the star attraction in a hinterland where travelers happen along on occasion to view this oddity of nature from the irrelevant vantage point of land. They perceive only a bit of churning water, so they move on to collect a commemorative tee shirt, a sticker that reads "I Survived Old Sow." Rarely do they venture into the water itself. Yet calamitous persons and vessels have been drawn in perpetuity to the monstrous abyss never again to be looked upon in this world. Less hapless souls have been spewed out once more by the onerous deep, ever to remain dry-landed.

There are daredevil captains who will ferry those desirous to the scalloped edges of the surge before turning back to safety. Bailey herself had once rid-den the insistent roiling of Old Sow with a foolhardy captain, whooped at the electric sea pumping through her as he fought to control the rudder while Old Sow tossed them like matchsticks in an eighty foot trough. As a child she never understood why no one else was thrilled in an undertow.

This temperamental place rivets her—tingling skin, drumming heartbeat —the possibility to spiral down a sea wall of rushing water and be spirited to another world, antediluvian. She's always fantasized about the lost kingdom of Atlantis. Poe's "Descent into the Maelstrom" beguiled her, as had Odysseus' high adventure with Scylla and Charybdis. To happen across Old Sow like she did years before was auspicious, and since then she's made pilgrimages from time to time to this source of boundless energy. A seeker. Of what she isn't certain.

The offshoots of Old Sow, the "piglets," mesmerize her equally. While Old Sow boils and thrashes, roils and churns, the smaller whirlpools form glass sided funnels that clearly bespeak the strength of each downward spiral. And, unlike Old Sow, they allow themselves to be closely seen. The whirlpools turn up again and again in her paintings. Since she first witnessed them, Bailey has believed the chaos of Big Sow, coupled with the order of each smaller whirlpool, forms an oracle—if she could only learn to read it.

She comes to witness and marvel, to toss questions into the eddies and watch them get sucked under, thinking maybe the answers will spring forth and she can catch them. Unlikely, since the questions themselves are thorny and blurred. Who she is. What she is. Where she is. Why.

At least, standing on the bow of the boat, in a long red slicker against the drenching splashes and spray, the coils of Manhattan unwrap, the suction marks of an outworn lover begin to fade. She's been given no answers to cagey questions, but what she can do—what she's done before—is clear a path to search for them anew. Right? Wrong? Runaway? Who can say? She spreads her arms wide and, utterly tethered to the almighty moon, for a fleeting moment the powers of all oceans rise through her.

~

On the return through Jonesport she chooses a dozen two pounders—fine fresh lobster—and arranges them in Miss Ruby's custom refrigerated bait well in the trunk. At Tall Barney's she collects the still warm pie, noshes on a lobster roll, clam fritters, and a blueberry popover, then eases across the street to gas up and call ahead.

"Hey Boss," she says when Ben answers. Friend Ben, Bossman, Brother Ben, Pal. There since the day she was born. Always there, no matter her vagabond ways.

"Hey Boo," he says in return. The salutations they've used since their Carolina childhood when he forever tried to tell her what to do and why. In high school he quit bossing, but she knows what he'd say anyhow.

"Room in the inn?"

"Oh, lord." The voice that sounds like smooth deep water.

"Yes, ladies and gentlemen, Bailey the Blitz has once again pulled her renowned disappearing act."

"Give me the gories when you get here. Where are you now?"

"Top of Maine. Thought I'd bring you some lobster but maybe I'll take them to the home folks and bring you a mess of fish back."

"We've got fish in Philadelphia."

"Not the same, Boss."

"Well come on. I could use a good story."

"I'll be there after while. Just making sure the coast is clear."

"Always is, Boo. I'll fluff your pillows."

"Alright then. Watch for Miss Ruby's wake when we sweep the Seaboard."

In adolescence, when their bond gravitated toward the path of the physical, Bailey shut the gate. Not worth taking the chance. Not then. Not now. Loss— that loss, even the possibility of it—is a depth she cannot fathom. Whatever the out-of-sorts something is in her soul, there will be no risk of safe harbor. Safe harbor that will never deny or forsake. That will always be home. If she unlocked the gate he would come running, and if he really wanted he could hurdle the fence—but he won't.

And it's not as if he's sitting around waiting. He's been through three "special" ladies in the time it's taken her to quit kidding herself about this last guy, Kerret. Jesus, even the name sounds fake to her now.

As she stands there pumping gas she catches a whiff of inevitable empty and debates a ride to the docks. Some sturdy, no frills guy whose boat bunk she could share for the night. Just a little catch and release fun. Sweet temptation, but she's restless for motion.

On the southbound highway she turns to tidal thoughts instead. In the Bay of Fundy where she's just been, not only do the tides go in and out every six hours, but around Eastport the boat you looked at six hours ago is now 26 feet higher or lower. At the mouth of the bay the shift can be fifty feet. Five stories of a building. It is the most profound tidal change on the planet. Change. Yes.

By midnight she's backtracked through Maine and dozes in some benign state park across the New Hampshire line. At sunup she grazes a breakfast buffet, loads her bag with fruit and cheerios. Never mind the live ones in Miss Ruby's trunk, the stinging truth is there will be no lobster rolls this day.

The next hours blur through Massachusetts, a bit of Connecticut, a corner of New York, then the Pennsylvania mountains. A string of junctions and a stream of cars, but nothing like I-95, and she takes child pride in notching off the states to Miss Ruby as they roll along with Billie Holiday and Patsy Cline, Pink Floyd and the Supremes, unsettled thoughts shifting song to song. The sky shades outside Worcester, Massachusetts, but she smells no rain, and by Hartford the sun bellows once more.

Somewhere in the thick of Pennsylvania a man walks the roadside, a grizzled burnout shuffling along at the unmistakable pace of contrition, insensible to passing traffic. She slows to offer him a ride but he says he'd just as soon walk, has no interest in talk. I've got nothing much to say myself, she tells him, and he gets in.

He's wearing two different shoes, one dilapidated loafer and one white laced sneaker, a second loafer strapped to his pack, sole flapping like a puppet as the old man moves. A sneaker is a comfortable thing he says when he sees her looking. You'd be surprised how many end up on the side of the road. Blowouts mostly. She considers this. I'll be able to wear my good shoes when I stroll into the Waldorf one day he says. She elects not to mention the hotel is a long way in another direction but he sees her eyes in the mirror. The path's not always where it looks to be, he tells her, and she considers that as well.

"Can you take some music?"

"What you got?"

"Most anything," she says. "You name it."

"Willie Nelson singing Stardust Memory?"

"Sure."

"Okay," he says. "Let's hear it."

He folds himself into the back seat and sleeps for a while, wakes with a start and weeps in quietude, then softly sleeps once more. When he wakes again he asks what state they're in and she says Maryland. That's good he says, could you let me off here and she says don't you want to get to a town first. No, he says, I'm ready to walk now, so she stops and when he flat refuses money she insists he take the rest of the pie that's been warming in the floorboard, that she's caught him lusting after, telling him she thought it was blueberry when she bought it, that she doesn't much care for rhubarb. With it she gives him the contents of the coffee thermos in a big styrofoam cup and wishes him well and drives on as he disappears into the wayfaring world she knows so well. You can overthink a thing is what he says when he leans in to shut the door.

Deep in the afternoon she brushes past the panhandle of West Virginia into Virginia itself and the lush promise of the Shenandoah Valley opens before her. Though she's taken a route that only grazes the congestion of the megalopolis northeast, it is nevertheless with gratitude that she turns onto the hundred mile stretch of Skyline Drive, devoid of most motorists, and watches the sun nestle toward the ridges on her right as Miss Ruby curves forth and back along the crown of the Blue Ridge Mountains.

By twilight she and the day are done, and after a belly full of road snacks she's ready for fresh mountain trout. At Big Meadows she takes a room on the lake and is so pleased to have slipped in before the dining room closes she orders crab stuffed trout almandine, a smoked trout Caesar salad, and a bottle of Montrachet to celebrate the getaway. The easy part. Then there's the What Now. She can outrun it, though, until the answer comes. Or a better question.

Fully aware she's the last patron of the evening, she strikes a deal with Verna that she'll finish her wine in the taproom if Verna will be kind enough to box two orders of smoked trout with crackers and capers and onions and dill sauce for tomorrow since she'll likely be gone before the breakfast doors open.

In the taproom she falls in with a foursome of sag-bellied fishermen, swaps them tale for tale with her own repertoire of angling adventures, but declines the offer to come up for poker and instead sweet talks the bartender into a piece of the chocolate torte she missed at dinner. With that and a split of champagne she climbs the stairs to her room for the hot bath she's prospected for hours.

That night in the clean covers there's sleep for the weary. She rolls and fades again and again, through to the morning knock of housekeeping, blinks her way to the sliding door and is taken aback by what lies beyond—one of those startling blue days that bar the door of despair. A Bossman kind of day. She brews coffee, sits in the slatted porch rocker with both hands around a stout mug and drinks big before the mountain air can brisk it.

Alright then, she says to the gloss feathered raven on the porch rail, prompting him to hop and flap once as she rises. She fills the coffee jug, warms Miss Ruby, cruises the camp store, and hits the road, a hot blueberry muffin in one hand, scattering bars of bluegrass onto the southbending highway. After Loft Mountain she stops at the next overlook, spreads the quilt in a grassy spot, props on one elbow, and reads aloud the opening pages of Steinbeck's homage to the open road, her voice spreading the gospel of wanderlust across the studded valley.

It's Monday so most of the weekenders are already home sorting laundry, but every now and then a Winnebago pulls in, gawks, and grinds back onto the incline, satisfied that Bailey hasn't sighted a bear.

At the end of the chapter she drives another stretch, this time choosing an even more capacious viewpoint before she spreads the quilt, pulls out her sketch pad, opens a bottle of Beaujolais, and feeds herself a cluster of red grapes and slabs of hoop cheese on Ritz crackers. On the hood of Miss Ruby she sets a Hershey bar to soften and returns her attention to the wanderings of Charley and Steinbeck.

Her eyes heavy after only a few pages into the sun so she closes the book and licks her supple chocolate from its foil wrapper, considering the migratory journeys of warblers that chorus among the hardwoods—how far they've come, how far they still have to go. The squawks and trills of all the flittering birds will quiet as summer lengthens, but for now the Appalachians are alive with the parlance of wings.

She gathers the quilt and drowsily follows the red clay path to a small meadow the sun hasn't chosen. Mountain laurel blooms in hushed pink along the dense trail and the tall grass is sprinkled with tiny bluets, cow parsnip, wild columbine, and Indian Paintbrush nodding red and yellow. Here she lies and drifts, sweet scented honeysuckle somewhere nearby, an occasional engine rounding the mountain above her. At the edge of sleep she feels a twitch on her arm, tries to ignore it but finally cannot deny its movement, knows it to be a tick before she looks, then finds two more crawling up her jeans, the signal to move on.

Through the afternoon she weaves the Blue Ridge, reads a chapter here and there at wildflowered turnouts that catch her fancy, and surveys the rolling ranges as one atop a towering lighthouse, sketching the ones that call out to her. With a fiery sunset kindling the westward sky she leans on the windshield of Miss Ruby and toasts the day, a fine day of unclouded vistas, while she relishes the smoked trout, disregarding entirely that the bread has gone dry and that the rest of the world exists somewhere outside the shadow of that particular shoulder of mountain.

By full dark the warmth of Miss Ruby's 360 horse hood has long cooled. She buttons her canvas jacket, pulls on a felt hat and thin leather gloves and drives on with the notion of finding an inn, but as she curves past one sign and then another she's uninspired to stop. The night's too clear, the road too agreeable, so she holds a course toward the bottom of the Blue Ridge backbone. Orange eyes of occasional critters shine on the roadside, beacons to mark the passing miles, and the nocturnes of Chopin drift among them.

On a particularly high and distant ridge she stops to find Delphinus, the dolphin, her mother Merissa's constellation, breathing deeply the pleasure of disconnection, her whereabouts unknown to all others on the planet. The sky here isn't quite so legible as in Maine, but not bad, not bad at all.

Delphinus is a small arrangement of five stars, four that form a diamond—the dolphin's body—and a fifth for the extended tail. It is often overlooked by the uninitiated, but even those who can't envision the dolphin itself can easily see the kite-shaped framework. Like Piscis Austrinus, it belongs to the Heavenly Waters family of constellations.

There are stories of the dolphin as Poseidon's messenger, others of how she rescued the poet Arion from drowning. In the earliest years of childhood Bailey herself couldn't see what her mother saw in the stars, no matter how earnest her efforts, but then one evening there it was, the gift was finally received. Since then her fascination with all things Delphic and cetaceous has been passionate and ever present.

Now, as she gathers night vision Bailey looks to celestial landmarks, echoing her mother's ritual, her mother's words, trying to hear something of her mother's voice in the sound of her own.

There's the Big Dipper and the Little Dipper. There are the ladies, and brave Orion the hunter. And there, my darling, is my gift to you. Delphinus, the dolphin stars. When I'm no longer here, look for me there. And when you see stars in the water, I'll be there too. Stars rose into being from the sea itself, so the sky is but a reflection of the real light that shines beneath the water.

It is their special secret, and Bailey has used it as a litmus test for people all her life. Did you know that starlight comes from under the sea she would ask—a game, rather like St. Exupery's little prince with his drawing of an elephant being eaten by a boa constrictor. Most people, of course, see only a hat, just as most people only find her question about the stars droll.

Now the elegant solitude of the Appalachian night enfolds her and she hears her mother's delicate voice sing across the waves of echoed mountains.

Down in the valley,
    valley so low,
        hang your head over,
            hear the wind blow.
Hear the wind blow, dear,
    hear the wind blow.
        Hang your head over,
            hear the wind blow.

Roses love sunshine,
    violets love dew,
        angels in heaven
            know I love you.
Know I love you, dear,
    know I love you.
        Angels in heaven
           know I love you.

That her mother has been dead three years is an unfathomable fact for Bailey. She knows every dancing callous on her mother's tiny feet, every crease around her velvet blue eyes. She sees the aquarium fish dart each time Merissa jerks and she jumps up to hold her, feels every convulsion of those last eternal hours. Hears the hiss of death zing in its little machine each time another surge of morphine runs through her mother's tired veins. Ugly, unmerciful death that hovers around the white pillowed bed extracting pounds of flesh and misery before finally concluding the grim business as Merissa thrashes in the arms of her brokenhearted daughter.

Loss.

Gone. Not without avowal, though. Not like Alaska.

But there you are. It's what was given them to brook and that's what they did. All her life Bailey has held a belief in the imperfections of destiny, a notion that there are simply glitches in the great scheme of things. Fuckups of fate.

That affairs of the universe occasionally go awry she feels profoundly, but the torment is whether the lapses are benevolent or malevolent—or simply random miscalculations, blunders that may or may not ripple out to ruin. Cantankerous questions that perpetually nag and gnaw. Though she usually comes around to the attitude that things simply get off kilter sometimes, in the case of her mother she rages at the cosmos for the cruelty of timing.

Now, though, she forces herself away from deathbed memories and into her mother's arms, rocking with the lullaby of low valleys and angel love. Against the falling temperature she cloaks herself with the quilt and sets off again. As the lullaby fades, she slips Santana into the tape deck and settles back into the highway.

Just past Craggy Flats tunnel two white tailed deer, doe and fawn, leap into the road then turn long synchronized necks straight into the headlights where they freeze in disbelief. Tires screech in time-suspended lengths across a patch of hell that echoes through the mountains, but as Bailey veers left the deer bolt to safety, released from the onerous beams.

Three hearts and Bailey's fists pound as she wails through the blazing pain of her mother's death and all that came after. For long minutes she cries and curses, gets out of the car and walks the quiet highway. When breath comes she looks once more at the heavens, across the indiscernible valley, says alright then, cranks Led Zeppelin and checks her map for the next campground, one with a hot shower and strong coffee.

~ ~ ~ ~ ~ ~ ~ ~ ~ ~ ~ ~ ~ ~

## BAILEY
### (1962)

*They, fair haired Bailey and her beautiful deep skinned mother Merissa—half breed to many—arrived in Anchorage after a long day of travel, several long days of travel, and made their way along the docks so Merissa could arrange passage to the small village of her family. Her husband, Bailey's dad Cecil, was back home in the thick of shrimping season. That Merissa would arrive sometime that week her family was aware. That she had brought four year old daughter Bailey from South Carolina to Alaska for the first time would be a joyful surprise.*

*They walked onto a pier to watch a family of seals, and as they rounded the corner of a packing house that jutted into the harbor they saw a woman carrying a large tray. Her hair was stuffed under a black net and she wore a long white apron with pink red stains. She'd come to the edge of the walkway to dump a pile of fish guts, and as she hoisted the load she lost balance and fell into the cold cold water.*

*Without stopping to take her handbag from her shoulders Merissa dove after the big woman. The woman flailed and fought Merissa off, sleeves of her dark flowered dress flashing in every direction, and there was time, it seemed like a very long time, before anyone noticed the commotion, then mayhem began. Bailey, unnoticed, kept getting pushed farther and farther back. Each time she found another way around all the legs, but there wasn't much room on the walkway and the crowd quickly grew.*

*When Merissa first dove Bailey was unworried because her mother was always in the water. Bailey could see the big woman needed help and she knew her mother would help her, but the woman fought against her mother, hit her and hurt her, so Bailey began to call, Momma, Momma. The woman fended Merissa off with wide-eyed thrashes until she took them both down. Merissa didn't come up and she wasn't there, over and over she wasn't there.*

*The crowd watched and grew quiet but for Bailey's small voice calling Momma, Momma. The whole world splashed and there was so much hair. Merissa's black hair and the big woman's yellow-white hair that had loosened around them—arms and hair and the woman's pink face. And then the woman was gone and Bailey knew it. Merissa burst from the water, gasped, and plunged again. Twice more she did this before she rose near enough the dingy to be caught by two men and hauled into the tipping little boat. Merissa kept saying I have to find her. I have to get to her. Then she went to sleep.*

*Bailey called and called, Momma, Momma. But no one noticed in the continued chaos as Merissa was covered with stacks of rags and aprons and carried to the bed of a green truck that took her away. Bailey watched the water where the big woman had disappeared and couldn't understand where everyone was. Her mother would return for her but Bailey didn't understand what happened to the woman in the water, was transfixed by where she had gone.*

*Finally the shift boss was made aware of the child and assumed her to be the daughter of the Swede. Who knew?*

*When the officer told Bailey she had to come with him she screamed and tried to run. He jerked her arm and said Stop it. Pipe down. But someone else stepped past him and held her and stroked the crown of her head and said it will be all right. We'll find your mother. She had Juicy Fruit and offered Bailey a stick. I need to stay here, Bailey insisted. She knew she should wait for Merissa but they assumed her to be the child of the drowned woman and wouldn't listen when Bailey said her mother wasn't drowned, that she flew away but would come back. She pleaded for her father Cecil and for godmother Retta and for Ben—for all of them until the lady with the chewing gum asked her to please be quiet so she was.*

*They took her to a place where the rooms smelled like licorice and rot, and everyone talked at her, over her, around her about what to do. Words like foster care, next of kin, orphanage, social worker swirled. But then a soft lady with dangly earrings knelt in front of her, asked if she'd like some hot chocolate, and listened to her story, that her mother dove to help the big woman with the apron and almost didn't come back, but that she would. Bailey answered questions that described a woman like the one at the hospital, not the drowned woman.*

*The soft lady took her to a sad room with other children and said for her to play with them but she didn't want to play. Then she looked up and there was her mother in a funny chair, and her mother smiled but it was not her mother's smile. And in that long moment before Bailey could call Momma, Momma and run to her, their eyes met and the excitement and need, the certainty and joy were blocked by a void from her mother that turned instantly in Bailey to panic and terror and fear beyond bones. Her legs froze, and no matter how hard she tried to call out, her voice would not sound.*

*It didn't matter. For in that moment, in the tender clarity of her innocence, Bailey came to know full well and forever that when it matters most, words can do nothing.*

*She let them take her away, and when they gave her food she ate it and when they showed her where to sleep she got in bed and cried. Goodnight they told her, but there was neither good nor night. She pulled her coat around her, licked the salt from her Happy-as-a-Clam shell, and thought about the other half of the shell in Ben's treasure box. The next day the soft lady helped bathe her and gave her clothes that smelled like somebody else, and she asked for nothing until Retta came and the nightmare finally ended.*

~ ~ ~ ~ ~ ~ ~ ~ ~ ~ ~ ~ ~ ~

No, not a campground with Murphy this close. Somewhere in the wee hours of the North Carolina night Bailey turns off the crest of the Blue Ridge and begins the spiral that will unwind mountains into hills, hills into flatland, flatland into coast, and she tastes the pull of tidal waters. Miles slow as the fog settles, and while some other time she would thrill with the uncertainty of where the road ends and the side of the mountain begins, tonight she is weary and ghosts gather in the void.

Nearing the turnoff for Cruso she calls from a lonesome booth outside the one pump filling station, and within the half hour she drives into the hollow and echoes her way along a steep gravel road toward the cabin where a popping fire is no doubt waiting.

Murphy opens the door with arms wide and enfolds Bailey before she can even knock.

"Look at you, river girl. A sight for sore eyes, that's what you are."

"Hey Murphy."

They lean into each other and laugh. Lean and laugh.

"Could you use a cup of coffee?"

"I'm here for the full treatment, Murph. Road worn and hungry."

"How hungry?"

"Hungry enough to wait."

He stokes the fire, takes her by the hand, and leads her upstairs to the hemlock paneled loft.

"You haven't seen this. I built it two summers ago and when the weather's right I've been sleeping up here. It's got a surprise to it."

"Well?" she says. "Show me."

"You'll see."

Though each can only haze the shape of the other in the half light he says, again, "You're a sight for sore eyes, Bailey. It's good to see you."

"Shhh," she says. "Show me."

And he does, with the gentle gestures of a strong man who seldom entwines himself with a woman's body, especially a woman he holds with such earnest devotion.

She edges toward sleep as he strokes the length of her and kneads the road knots from her shoulders and neck, then whispers and points.

"There's your surprise, river girl" he says. "Look at it before you nap. There."

Through a tiny circular window in the pitch of the cabin roof shards of sunrise cast themselves upward over a faraway peak.

"Why is it so much more beautiful like that?"

"Because for just a moment you're convinced you could hold it in your hands. Now sleep while I cook you some breakfast."

"Not just yet," she says and spoons to him in the sweet hush of daybreak.

When she wakes it is to that most exalted of all morning smells—bacon frying—made even more tantalizing when cooked by someone else, someone who knows just how crisp you like it and would do that for you.

She lifts onto her elbows and watches him, barefoot and shirtless, whistling to himself with the ease of someone accustomed to his own kitchen. Follows his taut movements, the long hard back of a working man always a particular pleasure.

"You ought to get yourself a girl, Murphy."

"Let me know when you're ready to give it another whirl."

"I'm serious. Why don't you get yourself a girl?"

"I do from time to time. Now get your lazy bones down here. I've got sweet potato pancakes and bacon, and the best honey you've had in a while."

"You're the best honey I've had in a while. Honey."

"Yeah, yeah. Tell me more than once a year or two and I might start to believe it."

They eat in unspoken satisfaction at a table Murphy's great grandfather hewed from hickory for the cabin that his own father had built. Murphy now in buttoned flannel. Murphy who would never come to the table without a shirt. One of a long line of lean scrapping people who bore pride and sons that began to walk off the mountain two generations back. Until Murphy came of a mind that a weekend here and there at the old home place was not justice to his forbears and so had returned to reclaim the fruits of their labor, the pleasure of their customs.

"Wait a minute. Shouldn't you be gone by now?" She reaches for more pancakes and honey. "And you're right. This batch is incredible."

"Thank you, ma'am. I've got a case of it for you. And yes I should be gone, but I called and switched runs with Jake. It's the Five Falls section of Chattooga—come go with me."

"White water sounds great, it really does. But I'm gonna pass. I've got lobsters that need to get to Kirk's Bluff."

As she rises he too stands to pull the chair for her.

"Lobster you say. Where've you been?"

"Maine, but that was Sunday. Those boys will soon need a pot."

He rinses the plates, stacks them on the right side of the deep farm sink, and they walk outside into the crisp mountain air. He picks a blue morning glory bloom from the fence vine and places it in her open hand. To match her eyes.

"You heading back this way?"

"Come on, Murphy. Don't start."

She sets the flower on Miss Ruby's dashboard and opens the refrigerated cooler that takes up half the enormous trunk.

"I'm leaving you two big daddy lobsters," she says. "Invite one of these pretty little mountain girls over tonight."

"Thanks coach," he says but kisses her with a hungry heart.

He loads the honey and an apple basket of picnic, tugs her pony tail when they hug goodbye.

"So long river girl," he says when she shuts the trunk. "Hold it in the road."

"You got it, Murph. See you when."

~

Into the Pisgah National Forest, Vanderbilt legacy. There are too many cars at Whitewater Falls, but she can't resist Sliding Rock—a place that has enchanted her since girlhood when she first slid down the glassy side of worn-down mountain and plunged into the heart attack pool at its base. Then climbed the stairway blasted out of rock and slid back down again, squealing and waving her arms wide while her bottom numbed in the cold. As she parks and gathers bathing suit and towel she thinks of long ago native children whooping down this same geological playland, and the children of settlers, and now the children of many scattered tribes.

Three slides later the top of her head is blasting and she changes back out of her swimsuit, exhilarated by the snow melted water, wraps her fingers tightly around a mug of honeyed coffee from the thermos Murphy filled, and drives on along the fern feathered Cradle of Forestry Road. Even the sound of it—Cradle of Forestry—whispers primal comfort, green and encompassing.

It will be the last stretch for a while with no traffic, no billboards, no buildings, nobody, and she wanders and weaves and stops to listen to Looking Glass Creek, savoring the emerald embrace of the antique forest. At each slow curve the world rounds into cascades of sunlight pouring from the mountains. She's traveled this rain forest road dozens upon dozens of times since childhood, but never has it offered such angles of tender beauty.

The course she follows is the way of spring snow and ice that thaws in the ancient Appalachians and sifts toward the grand Savannah, the mighty Congaree and all their tributaries, gathering minerals and detritus along the way to nurture the shores. And as these vital waters flow toward the coast, summer flounder and blue crabs and brown shrimp migrate in from the cold ocean depths in a ritual of renourishment that has patterned spring through the ages.

Across the Continental Divide and into her Carolina homeland, she snakes down through Caesar's Head dodging patches of rain and eats a Murphy sandwich on the side of Highway 11, the Cherokee Foothills Parkway, imprinting the last view of the distant mountains she has just traversed.

At I-26 she pulls onto the eastbound express, ready to make time toward the coast. The bottom falls out near Columbia in a blinding rainstorm and hazard lights flounder in the muted glow of six lane traffic around her— hydroplane hell for lightweights. Beneath an overpass she secures Blue Ruby's stubborn top and opens the sack of sop-up rags that lives under the front seat. By Orangeburg the front has passed but she lets the vinyl top dry until she stops for gas.

Charleston is a thought—and out to Seabrook Island where she'd summer camped as a kid, but rattling her brain for someone to phone in a clearance pass for the now-gated community she decides never mind. Besides, Miss Ruby has never been fond of interstate highways, so at the Summerville exit they swing over and down Highway 165 to 17 to 174 toward Edisto, an earnest island not yet neutered by gentrification.

The drive out to Edisto is a passage of moss laden tunnels, plantation chapels and shaded cemeteries, shotgun shacks and markers noting only bits of better stories that are still passed down on porches, balustraded or not. The Carolina Lowcountry. Hallelujah.

State road 174 is a direct path to the ocean. In the shade of a rustling palmetto she slips into her still wet bathing suit and dances across the warm beach, kicking up sand with every footfall, through the foamy surf and into the blue brown sea. The sea. For four days she has relished the thought of precisely this, taking in big mouthfuls of the Atlantic, her Atlantic, the warm swaying Atlantic of the south, and tasting the briny deep that is her life blood.

A long swim later she lies in the sand watching dolphins feed and lets the sun seep into her skin, heat the long body that plied those cold cold waters only hours before. Amused with the notion that she herself has come down wet out of the mountains carrying even the slightest particle of nutrient for her beloved coast, she drifts for a while in that half sleep that comes so easily at the beach, then knocks the ground-in sand off as best she can and heads to Docksides for a cold beer and fish tacos. No one minds the beach grit there.

She walks to the back deck, sees the tide has turned, and can't resist—climbs the rickety rail and dives. When she rises to the air again she sounds Whitman's barbaric yawp and spins. Nothing could be finer, indeed. To be in these river-rich waters listening to the crunch and crackle of life below the surface. Surrounded by marsh grass and pluff mud, crowning glories of the Southern coastline. Oh yes, she thinks, waving to people on their docks and herons on the flats, sated in the sunshine of Carolina June, afloat in the Edisto and not adrift in the city.

This is it—one of those often wished for and seldom won moments of well wrought bliss. On a nice slick bank with no oyster shells she wallows in the slippery mud like the dolphins of Jericho, and the interval of contentment is complete. By god, she thinks, I may not know where I'm going, but at least I know where I'm not.

At the last dock before river turns to sea she climbs a swim ladder, bums a towel and a ride to Miss Ruby, stops for a tall iced tea and a bag of boiled peanuts and, unshowered and salt crisped, takes to the journey renewed.

Driving Highway 17 in the back yard between Charleston and Savannah she imagines the roadway as arms extended between these comely sisters. And where the hands clasp is a broad green expanse of beauty and pain, ten thousand acres of rice hammocks fed by waters of the Combahee River. Canals remain, many of them miraculously straight, others as swayed as the backs that strained to dig them—the bold engineering vision of aristocratic planters made real by the toil of slaves. Channels dug with the impetus of bondage and bondage alone, for no other enticement, neither love nor greed, could have mastered such marsh.

Containment. Consider trudging and mucking and shoveling hour upon hour, day after month after year, in a ponderous drive to defy God. To reroute the river, retell the tides. To mound and mound and mound the mud that was meant not to be there and make dry land on which oxen could groan to haul wagons around the murky fields of Carolina gold rice, renowned for the delicacy of its honeyed flavor. Consider the whelps of mosquitoes and the whelps of deer flies. Consider the whelps of refusal.

As the highway threads these miles of salt flats, red-winged blackbirds flock in sheets that billow luminous curves across the gathering darkness, and the moon posts itself in the turning sky while Bailey crosses the last of the marshlands and drives onward into the now forested twilight.

Toward home.

Jericho River. Kirk's Bluff. Just west of the village, their place on a high bank of oaks and magnolias, cedars and palmettos, that had been Martin land only before the war but for these more than hundred years has been Simmons land too. When Cecil Martin and George Simmons, current patriarchs, returned from service in the Pacific each had skills enough to earn a fatter money roll in the farther world but neither was of a mind to seek it. Once they found themselves wives—Cecil's Merissa in Alaska, George's Henrietta in the West Indies—Cecil came home to work the sea, just as George came home to work the land.

The truer story: Merissa's Cecil, Henrietta's George.

Tiny Merissa, delicate child bride. Tall Retta, exotic older woman. Each dauntless in her own spirited way.

Bailey Martin and Ben Simmons, children of the bluff.

Neighbors.

Friends.

Family.

More.

As she drives, Bailey's thoughts turn to childhood, Ben's and hers, where laughter tosses above the drone of outboard motors. Where offshore charter boats hustle to the Gulf Stream and sailboats tack this way and that. Where pendulums of slalom skiers swing past party cruisers and old timers wet a line toward the trout. Where diesel trawlers chug out to big waters and in again with their catch. Always the coming back, the pull of homeport. Wakes and cross-wakes slosh the shore—dolphins and herons, egrets and barking dogs fill the marsh flanked memories. The occasional yelp from some kid with a crab-pinched toe.

They were part of it all, she and Ben. If it moved in, on, or around the water it was a portion of their realm. In the lingering years of their youth they created each of those wakes, over and over—as skiers, fishers, and pleasure crafters, on rafts and trawlers and boats of all size and purpose between—sailboats, runabouts, kayaks, and canoes.

Most of their wake was made swimming, though. So much swimming that if every ripple could be harnessed from every jump off a pier head, every race to the buoy, every shrivel skinned hour treading water or lapping dock to dock—if all that energy could be contained in one swell it would surge over the high banks of Kirk's Bluff.

Then there was the tender wake that only the river knew, the wake of them drifting. How many hours had they spent suspended in a slow sweep of tide. Sometimes upriver, other times down. Maybe in one of their rafts, maybe on inner tubes—sun blistering rubber that made for constant cupping of water to cool thighs and shoulders. With inner tubes they mostly wandered along with their heads inside the rings, teasing one another into fear that something might get them—namely a shark. They maintained diligent respect for sharks.

Many times they simply floated along with their scrawny little selves, then adolescent selves, teenage selves, other selves. They brought oranges or tangerines to float alongside them and studied what path the fruit might take through the current. Sometimes they tossed the orange balls ahead and lunged underwater in attempt to surface dolphin-like exactly where the citrus bobbed. Once in a while the dolphins themselves would play the game, nudge the oranges with their long curved rostrums. Groovy, the dolphin with the double nicks on her dorsal fin who often hung out around the oyster factory, was especially keen to join the game if there wasn't much boat traffic. Fast boats don't make for friendly dolphins.

When the tide turned or they edged out-of-bounds, Bailey and Ben peeled the sweet fruit and slaked their salty thirst with each ambrosial section. Spit seeds at each other and watched as shingles of citrus peel meandered on, maybe attracting gulls, maybe not.

If there wasn't time to ride the tide home they'd climb out at somebody's dock and walk back wet and dripping, a salt and pepper staple to everyone around the village. And if the day called for it, they'd leave their boat at somebody's dock as casually as other kids leave their bikes in a neighbor's yard. Of course they left bikes too, and fishing poles, and cast nets. But it all came home to roost—when they needed it and remembered or were scolded and remembered. Around the Bluff everything eventually comes home to roost.

They knew every board on every pier head, every ramp on every dock, which boats had their bottoms painted and which boats needed it. Attention was paid to that kind of detail because over the years they operated small busi-nesses offering various maritime services, from scrubbing guano to chipping barnacles to varnishing teak to baiting crab traps.

During high school when they weren't striking for Cecil or working Mis-ter George's fields they catered a fair share of shrimp boils, crab cracks, and oyster roasts. Always had money to go where they wanted to go, do what they wanted to do. When her parents told her they'd spring for college Bailey said thank you very much and bought herself Miss Ruby, the convertible land yacht that has cruised her these years through waters calm and stormy.

Now, as she drives south along the inland perimeter of home territory, Retta and Mister George would be in their house watching *Matlock* and her father Cecil, across the field at her own house, would soon climb the stairs to bed, past the gallery of wedding and baby, recitals and swim meets, shrimp boats and trophy fish, birthday parties and graduations. An empty house without Merissa. If Bailey turns toward home she'll be there before Retta and George or her dad, before any of them turn off the last light. Maybe. . . . Maybe not. Hard to say if either of them—she or Cecil—is ready for it. Hard to know if they ever will be.

~ ~ ~ ~ ~ ~ ~ ~ ~ ~ ~ ~ ~ ~

## MERISSA
### (1962)

*Merissa was so very tired and wanted only to let go and sleep, but she kept hearing Bailey's small voice calling Momma, Momma. There was such a pull to let go, but she had to get to Bailey. She was confused because the voice seemed to come from above and below and she didn't know how to reach her, to reach Bailey. Merissa could hear her everywhere but didn't know where she was. I have to find her, she kept calling as the colors folded in on themselves. I have to find her. And then she could find nothing, not even herself.*

*There were people everywhere, none of them known to her. She looked at her hands and feet but they were unwilling, and the touch of her skin was not a touch she knew. Every sound was excruciating ricochet and there were distorted faces, mouths moving but disconnected from the noise. It was cold and there was no air and the smells burned acrid and unnatural.*

*Then she was in an empyrean place of childhood—mossy rocks jutting up from the bay and her mother calling. The pounding stopped and she tried to reach but had no arms and the pounding began again and she was lost.*

*And then Retta was there and found Bailey. This time the water settled and Merissa could tell where her voice was. They went home to Merissa's family on the Kenai Peninsula and there she found pieces of herself as well. Cecil waited for them in Carolina and Retta never minded the time for miles so they drove east from Seattle. Merissa and her beautiful fragile daughter nested in the back seat under Retta's Morning Star quilt and meshed their hearts once more in the shelter of Retta's safekeeping.*

*Two years later, on that odd feeling Good Friday, the eleven o'clock news broke with announcement of a megathrust earthquake near Anchorage measuring 9.2 on the Richter scale. Cecil was sound asleep and Merissa rose from their bed and went into Bailey's room. There she sat watch over her child through the night and hummed silent prayers to her loved ones. All weekend intermittent broadcasts brimmed with news of aftershocks and tsunamis, ground fissures and rock slides, collapsing structures and death tolls.*

*On Easter morning Cecil filled the sweetgrass basket Retta had made for Bailey, but Bailey hid it in the back of her closet and returned to her mother's vigil. It was Tuesday morning before Merissa heard her own mother Adèle's sweet voice on the other end of the telephone line. The call was brief, but her parents were alive. They had been in the hills looking for a missing dog when the earth shook and a wave nearly thirty feet high washed Chenega into the sea. The only other survivors had outrun the wave to higher ground.*

*For weeks details of this most powerful earthquake in North America unfolded. On that Saturday between Good Friday and Easter eleven shocks over 6.2 were recorded. Tsunamis were reported not only in Alaska but also in British Columbia, Oregon, California, even Hawaii and Japan. Land around Kodiak was raised thirty feet and other land southeast of Anchorage dropped eight. Major aftershocks registered for three weeks and evidence of motion directly associated with the Great Alaska Earthquake was felt all over the planet for a full year. A full year for mother earth to settle.*

*Bailey flat out refused to leave Merissa's side and missed so many days of school she was placed in first grade once more that fall. When Merissa began planning for the trip home to see her parents Bailey stopped speaking again—to anyone but Ben. It never gets dark so the moon can't follow me there, she told him. Merissa overheard and at bedtime assured her the moon will come with you wherever you want. You simply untie it and take it along. Just because you can't see it doesn't mean it's not there.*

*Cecil went with them to Alaska that summer, and the three of them spent a month in efforts that were miniscule—the child's and the parents'—given the work to be done. The myriad ways in which we are deficient.*

~ ~ ~ ~ ~ ~ ~ ~ ~ ~ ~ ~ ~ ~

Now, at the Yemassee train station, Bailey sits in the far corner of the parking lot and debates going home, wishes she could face Cecil, but her uncertain thoughts vanish when the tracks rumble news of the leviathan's approach.

Every train thundering into every depot is a brief apocalypse, deafening and deadly massive, and this one has just let up from a pounding 70 mph to the slow coast that allows a gaggle of recruits bound for Parris Island and a few locals home from visiting family up north to disembark as Bert Simmons with lightning efficiency offloads the ladies and luggage. Before the last bag touches the platform the clacks resume and off the beast roars toward Savannah. Bert's smile widens at the sight of Bailey, but she knows well to step aside the flurry until he's done.

Within five minutes the passengers have cleared and she follows Bert into the antique but air conditioned office where he'll wait for the next train, sometimes playing chess or his harmonica or the radio. Most days some fellas stop by to play checkers and shoot the breeze, and he's forever selling raffles for the church ladies. Crocheted baby blanket, gift certificate to LaWanda's House of Beauty, toaster oven. If you're in the market for a raffle ticket, Bert Simmons is the man to see. Always with a smile, always light on his feet, never without a pressed white handkerchief in his back pocket, a custom he's passed on to his nephew Ben. Bert is taller than his brother George but they both have that small rangy frame that belies the strength and stamina within.

Bert has only been manning the station for four, going on five years since he retired, under considerable pressure, from his duties as steward. Seventy-five, said the folks at Seaboard Coastline, was time to quit riding the rails. Bert didn't see it that way.

He'd lapped the east coast so many thousands of times, and the west and midwest, in his 58 years on board he hardly knew. No, he didn't know how to stop moving. But he learned, and although his instinct when every single train pulls in is to hoist himself onto it instead of hoisting baggage off, he's come to appreciate the quiet times between arrivals. Tells himself he does, anyway. It's nice when people stop by.

"Lobster, eh? Where've you been?"

"Maine," Bailey says. She and Bert have walked into the parking lot and stand before Miss Ruby's open trunk. Tops of the battery cooled bait wells open with rubber grips like the soda machine.

"You hauled those boys from Maine?"

"Yessir," she says.

He lifts a lobster, pronounces it sure enough still alive, and says he's never seen such a rig as the trunk of Miss Ruby.

"Mister Bert," she says, "whoever designed the refrigeration system for this beauty of an automobile is a genius, flat out."

It's a conversation they've replayed many times. Bert Simmons paced train corridors since he was 17, but there was a time in his twenties, newly married, when his bride had borne down on him to go to tech school and get a trade, one he could ply closer to home. He dutifully attended classes in electrical engineering that included heating and air conditioning and refrigeration. He compliantly got his certificate then he thankfully resumed his full time duties on the train once more. By that time his wife had seen the light and eased up on the bearing down.

"I was about to call and see if anybody at home might be coming this way." She squints in speculation.

"You need me to call?" He cocks his head and his eyes dance a smile. They all—Retta, George, Ben, and Bert Simmons—do what they can about the standoff between Cecil Martin and his daughter Bailey. Step aside when there's nothing to be done. Stubborn lays its own tracks. Anger too. And grief rides along the top with a schedule all its own.

"Would you?"

"You know it."

"You're a sweetheart."

"Can't help myself."

"When Mister George gets here, please tell him to cook them tonight," Bailey says. "I dawdled on the way down so they're pushing it."

"I'll do it."

"Keep one for yourself, Bert. Oh, and there's fresh mountain honey too."

"I appreciate it."

"Alright. It's always good to see you." She hugs him and walks to the driver's door. "Tell Mister George I'll get that way soon."

He sidesteps before her and opens the door.

"I'll tell him," he says. "They sure would like that. Your daddy too."

"Yessir. I'm heading on now."

"Lord, you got that wandering bone, girl."

"Well, it's just—"

He puts his hands in his pockets and laughs.

"I've told you before, missy—roll when you've got to roll. There's plenty of slowin' down time when you're six feet under."

~

28

Long day and time for rest, but not this close. Not yet. Past the turn off for home, past Coosawhatchie and Ridgeland, she considers a late night drive, then crosses the Talmadge Bridge into Savannah and thinks better of it. The sky has clouded again and Miss Ruby is humorless in the rain so Bailey sheers down Bay to the River Street Inn, places Miss Ruby in the good hands of the valet guys, and checks into a room overlooking the river where cargo ships crawl up and back.

A hot tub soak, a stop at Spanky's for a chilly crown with the gang, then a walk over to Vinnie Van Go-Go's for the best white pizza around—thick slathered with pesto, sweet mounds of sun dried tomatoes, and freshly steamed artichoke hearts. Yes indeed. Dylan twanging ballads in the background, cold Moretti beer.

An assemblage of art students front her a slice while hers bakes. They're mired in philosophical debate concerning Nostradamus and his influence on Camus, coaxing goatees from their baby faces, profound in their draft beer buzz. She flips through stacks of albums piled at the end of the bar until the pizza arrives and she repays the slice, then eats in time with big band and show tunes she's chosen for the record player. After all, this is Johnny Mercer country.

When she can eat no more she boxes the last of it and is ready to watch the ships. Her room is on the third of a four story building, one of the old warehouses where planters brought their goods to be loaded on boats bound for the islands or Europe. The ballast that steadied these vessels on the way to fetch cotton or rice or indigo has been used to pave streets that cars and people now tenuously pick their way along. Bay Street on top, then Upper Factor's Walk, Lower Factor's Walk, and River Street edging on the Savannah itself. There's a river balcony too small for chairs that she makes cozy with pillows, but the ships are already docked upriver. She admires the bridge and listens to revelry on the street below, but it's too muggy to sit still.

Driving into town she'd caught scent of magnolia blossoms on Oglethorpe Street so she sets out walking through squares that James Oglethorpe laid out in 1733 when he first dropped anchor from his good ship *Anne* and climbed the steep bluff to make camp in the pines and peace with the Indians. Lucky for him Tomochichi and Senauki, the Creek chief and his wife, made the colonists welcome.

Bailey wanders the common spaces of these small parks filled with live oaks that drape scores of genteel structures, late night music and late night people drifting in and out of coffee houses and bars. Oh the trouble she and Ben had skirted in this town on college weekends home. But they'd done it. Without fail they've always skirted the Big Issue. The place there's no point going.

Carefully now, she chooses four magnolias, two of them tightly closed, makes her way back to the inn and calls it a night.

~ ~

And when she wakes the air is intoxicating with that most southern of scents— on the verge of excess, but not quite. She wallows in it. Wallows in the cool white covers, then pulls off the top sheet and stands on the balcony fanning the fragrance of magnolia across the river and onto a freighter bound for Ceylon.

I could swim out to them she thinks, spend the season at sea. It's something she did two years before. Rode a cargo ship halfway round the world and back, port to port to port, many thousand miles of colossal oceans. Another world, another subculture—of captains and mates and deck hands, and the occasional tourist fortified by wherewithal and time that books passage for long seafaring weeks or months—wandering souls who can't quite bite the full time vagabond bullet.

But no, she'll not hop a freighter today. Not today. Instead she calculates the approach of another gargantuan vessel escorted downriver in the snug embrace of tugboats as she sips a bottled coke, the real breakfast drink of the Deep South in summer.

On the walk to Clary's for breakfast she's overwhelmed with hydrangeas unnoticed the night before. Magnificent blues and lavenders. Alright then, she'll have to check on Granny.

Mid morning she calls for Miss Ruby and follows the squares of Bull Street past the fountain and out to Bonaventure, that regal burial place on the banks of the Wilmington River where the air is even more scent-laden, not only with magnolias, but also with gardenias, both white and yellowed.

"Hell of a view you've got there Granny," Bailey says, as she's always heard her father say. And it is. A walled garden overlooking the river, sprinkled with sculpture and bird baths, tumbling with vines and blossoms and stories, told and untold. One of those places where everything's somehow more intense— like Old Sheldon church or the rice fields she drove through yesterday. Places that prick you into contemplation. But contemplation is precisely what she's trying to bypass. Time to roll.

The dew has long dried even here in the shade of widespread oaks, and the day's coming on hot. She snaps as many gardenias as she can place on the floor boards and passenger seat without them touching and stops by St. Joseph's on the way out of town.

~

Back in southbound motion she pictures the islands off to her left as she drives, a string of them that front the Atlantic and back the mainland as barriers of protection. The road parallels the coast and though they are miles away, in her mind's eye she sees each of the Golden Isles, pretends to be in a boat navigating the Intracoastal, slipping through Ossabaw Sound to Ossabaw, St. Catherine's Sound to St. Catherine's, Sapelo Sound to Blackbeard and Sapelo, Doboy Sound to Wolf Island, Altamaha Sound to Little St. Simon's and St. Simon's, St. Simon's Sound to Jekyll, St. Andrew's Sound to Cumberland. Then comes Florida and she hooks onto A1A and into Fernandina. Miss Ruby needs an oil change and it looks like rain.

~

On a bicycle borrowed from the service station she pedals the blocks of Old Town Fernandina, past Steamboat Gothic and Queen Anne houses, up Centre Street and over to Standard Marine where her father has bought his shrimp nets from the get-go. Fernandina is where the very first fleet of commercial trawlers set out from the downtown docks, and to these stalwart docks they continue to venture forth and back, hauling home hard earned fruits of the sea.

At the Palace Saloon, Florida's oldest, Bailey enjoys a cold beer and two songs for a quarter on the jukebox. Arlo Guthrie sings "Highway in the Wind" and Louis Armstrong follows with "It's a Wonderful World." So it is, she nods, and keeps the tune as she pedals Atlantic Avenue toward the ocean. The rain begins at Fort Clinch and by the time she gets to the beach she's a hundred fold soaked.

What a wonderful world. Cool, wet. If Miss Ruby had drain plugs and Bailey could see to navigate, she'd travel in the rain any old time the sky felt like singing.

On an empty stretch of beach she strips, drapes her clothes on the handle bars, and runs into the rain dappled ocean, shooping and splashing. A merman, she thinks, that would be the ticket right now. To slip up behind and say nothing. Ride in the waves for a while, then swim off to frolic elsewhere.

The sun comes out blazing and she hears music, no doubt a hump-day party at Slider's. She dresses and bikes toward the guitar and cackling, buys her all-you-can-eat-and-drink bracelet and steps into the roped off entertainment zone. Brown girl-bodies lean into brown boy-bodies. Waitresses and

31

shrimp strikers, golf caddies and paper mill shift workers—in cut offs and tube tops, t-shirts and tattoos. Flip flops haphazardly slung left and right.

Beach volleyball, open mic, banner trailing airplanes, an oil drum grill on the spit of lawn between the back of the restaurant and the ocean's edge, kegs of beer steadily flowing. Plastic cups of it, set down for someone to dance, are long forgotten and flat. Others, propped against the low concrete railing, collect cigarette butts in the brown juice of disintegrated tobacco.

Through it all the beer keeps coming, the occasional dose of tequila shots limed and salted. People dance and sing and lie in the grass with dirty feet, everyone's scant clothing damp from the rain that starts and stops, starts and stops. They all flocked under the awning when it began, but few even bother now.

There's a muddied puddle in front of the DJ where a group shuffles and sways without rhyme. Volleyball players rotate in and out as the tide eases toward Africa, leaving strands of tiny treasures for those in hunt of a prize shell or shark's tooth.

By mid afternoon the talent has exhausted their repertoires of Lynyrd Skynyrd, Marshall Tucker, but mostly Jimmy Buffet, and a grassroots call for karaoke begins to circulate.

There comes that split in the path where you either catch the crowd or veer off and wonder what the hell you were thinking anyway, and Bailey is nowhere near buzzed enough to witness lighters flicked in demand of karaoke. Karaoke for godsake. When there's the beach.

She walks as the tide continues outward, sandpipers with their impossible little legs skittering along the wrack line. A star fish has missed the ride back to sea but is still alive so Bailey walks it waist deep and sends it on its way. Just up the beach is another that she walks out, and not far beyond that yet another. These she takes only knee deep before casting them into the surf—and then there's another. Then three more, then two. Some already dried out and dead, but some that appear dead then make the slightest movement as she lifts them. When she realizes that an upward slope of beach has stranded hundreds more she gathers armfuls and simply pitches them seaward from the water's fringe, but the more she collects the more they seem to multiply.

Each is surrounded by the heartbreaking design of its powerless attempts to free itself from the heavy wet sand. Some have been able to drag themselves a few feet, some a few inches. Some merely pivot their five points nowhere, stuck, dancing in place.

The music fades, the buzz fades, and the whole world fills with stranded starfish. The dead ones Bailey doesn't grieve, but the ones that struggle fill her with mercy and dread.

In the corner of her eye someone else bends and walks to the edge again and again, a tall guy in red running shorts. As they labor they gravitate each toward the other, and as the starfish dwindle she becomes more aware of his lanky stance, the longish brown curls. They comb the beach once more and step together to the water's edge with the last few.

"I watched you earlier," he says. "Out here by yourself." When she doesn't resist his words he says, "Can I tell you what I was thinking while I watched?"

"No," she says, and moves away from him, farther into the water.

He shrugs, says sorry, but when he turns to leave she voices two more syllables.

"This way."

They move together in the easy roll of waves, sea creatures coupling in the warm sway of the Atlantic. But afterward, as he caresses her outstretched body, seawater dripping from his wet curls, she's unable to silence him before the chatter begins, questions about plans for later. Squeezing his hand she whispers her need for the ladies' room and walks to Sliders before he thinks to follow.

The world fills in again with the most godawful rendition of "If I Said You Had a Beautiful Body, Would You Hold It Against Me," one of Bailey's all-time favorites when it's done right. Godawful rendition or not, the revelers, now several notches nearer totally trashed, cheer the karaoke singer and the dizzying antics of his entertainment.

A fresh batch of burgers is coming off the grill, so Bailey grabs one and a long neck Bud, slips out of the party zone, and pedals up the sand scattered road past boxy beach cabins decorated with driftwood and clotheslines sagging with bright colored towels, laughing at ludicrous life.

While the bun is still warm and the beer still cold she pedals to Fort Clinch and looks across to the dunes of Cumberland where horses descended of thoroughbreds saved from the glue factory by Lucy Carnegie roam the island wanton and unbridled.

In Fernandina proper she fetches the freshly tuned Miss Ruby, treats herself to a hot fudge sundae on the way out of town, and at Mayport queues for the auto ferry and reads another chapter of *Travels with Charley* while she waits.

Two hours later Bailey rounds the corner into Saint Augustine with its coquina history and kitsch, a city occupied and flourishing in 1565—more than half a century before the famed pilgrims Mayflowered into Plymouth Rock. A town of many marvels.

Another day, she tells Miss Ruby and crosses the Bridge of Lions over Matanzas Bay. Then again, why not an order of fritters at the Conch House? Under a palm frond canopy she watches a foursome play "Pigs" and drink blue margaritas as they laugh in the sunlight and share camaraderie that can't be forced or bought. She ought to call Boss.

Back on A1A she drives south past Marineland, where she'd interned one summer of college. She'd made good friends there, all of them cetacean, and is still haunted by the lonesome echoes of their yearning for the sea. How the world loves a cage.

That was sophomore year. After her junior year she landed a job across the state as a Mermaid at Weeki Wachee Springs. That was fun. Ben couldn't be convinced when it came to synchronized underwater ballet, but Bailey and her cousin Sessy were mermaid naturals and spent long hours of childhood choreographing their glamorous routines in Sessy's salt water pool.

Bailey's official marine biology internship that summer focused on manatee populations in the springs, fascinating as well, but that required only sixteen hours a week and left plenty of time for mermaid shifts. The costumes, the bubbles, the clear fresh spring water—she loved it all. From time to time she's driven down for reunions, the enchantment never waning. Once a mermaid, always a mermaid—that's the official Weeki Wachee motto.

Now, past quiet stretches of beach, she catches a glimpse of the ocean here and there as evening colors settle across the vast plain of the Atlantic. Pelicans flap in deep Vs, sometimes along the water's edge, sometimes directly overhead, and she marvels at how much glide they get per flap. Such a big unlikely bird and yet the movement seems effortless. She feels this way swimming—but to fly. Now that would be something.

Through traffic around Daytona Beach the pelicans make better time than the Skylark, and then the kingdom of condos rears up in full force to block the beach. The pelicans adjust accordingly and fly on, unaware of Bailey's disappointment to see them go. At sunset the temperature eases and when she stops in Titusville for a coke and boiled peanuts she pulls on a thin sweatshirt that lives under the passenger seat.

At the marina there's big talk of fish running in Sebastian Inlet, so she buys beer and live bait for trade and by midnight is angling the north jetty with a set of ball-capped cronies, listening to their no-doubt oft told stories of ship-wrecks and close calls, learning from their fishing rigs, noting the nuances of their customized dock carts—each a different setup of pvc rod holders, tackle boxes, and coolers. Coolers steadily filling with mangrove snapper and jacks, blue runners and permit—and, though not for the cooler just now, still the prize of the inlet—sweet daddy snook. That's the one. Spawning and hungry, crazy for the greenies.

If it hadn't been a beach day, she'd have sat with them through the night, but it has been, so she showers, pitches a quick tent, stretches onto the sleeping bag, and listens to the chuck-will's-widows while she crunches Cheerios out of the box and swats mosquitoes that have invaded her sanctuary. She's done a good job of wearing down to weary and the mosquitoes don't have much of a target once she nestles into the sleeping bag and covers her head with a towel.

~ ~

Tern cries and gull ruckus wake her and she rinses yet again to help stop the itch, breaks what little camp there is and sets off, ready to cover some serious territory.

When the cramp of development is too much she veers to Highway 27 and drives through the middle of scraggly nowhere, on the lookout for ca-racara and burrowing owls, special birds in the Florida scrublands. At Lake Okeechobee she grabs an egg salad sandwich to go, extra pickle, and some-where along the New River Canal she finds shade and climbs into the back of Miss Ruby for a sweaty nap made brief by the bugs.

After Homestead she hooks into the backside of Miami traffic and within the hour is on the US1, the Overseas Highway that leads through the Florida Keys. Whoops at the prospect of the glorious drive ahead. One hundred and twenty-six miles of skipping across the archipelago—plenty of distraction to quell her unquiet mind. Muzzle your brain, she hears Boss tease—there's no cause for cerebration.

Caravans of cotton ball clouds move sporadically across the sun, slowly gathering steam for the probable afternoon squall, pleasant but brief shelter from the searing heat. As each cluster passes, an outburst of sun amplifies the astonishing shades of tropical blue waters. Grand, she thinks, and toys with how her translation of the scene to canvas would be unrecognizable to most. That's just how it happens.

A beach towel covering the car seat has been sweat-soaked for hours, but a perspiry towel is better than your back and thighs, in shorts and a halter-top, stuck to leather. Miss Ruby's air conditioner cranked at full blast is pure decadence with the top down on a 98 degree day. But hey.

Signs for Marathon are the signal Bailey needs. Siesta. She's sleepy and hungry and the time has come to do laundry. The Seven Mile Grill, home of the ultimate fried grouper sandwich, calls her name. The restaurant looks much like a concession stand at a little league game and perches at the foot of the famous 7 Mile Bridge, America's longest. Locals are kind enough to make a few phone calls and set her up with a little yellow cottage on the water, one that catches the cross breeze and even has a carport. As soon as she showers she wraps herself in a sheet, grabs a pillow, and climbs into the hammock for a real nap beneath placid coconut palms that rustle in the sea breeze.

Laughter and reggae and charcoal come to her as she wakes to a party next door. She laughs to hear their laughter and rolls side to side in the hammock, making it swim in big waves of motion—a favorite trick from childhood, a scolding offense that has yanked more than one hook from wall or post. For this reason she unfailingly and without thinking assesses the sturdiness of all hammock hardware before climbing into one.

The neighbors, a bevy of Cleveland optometrists and their wives, insist that Bailey join them, and by midnight most of the crowd is dancing in the sand and howling at tequila shots. As the tempo of the party peaks but before it begins the downhill slope she takes her quiet leave to the moonlit ocean.

Out past the breaking waves she floats in the shaft of light, gradually blocks the party noise, and edges into tranquility, salt crystals slow crackling in her ears. It is the most peaceful thing she knows how to do—and nobody needing to know her whys or whereabouts. Well, Boss. Tomorrow she'll call the Bossman.

When she comes out of her trance she's drifted a fair distance off shore and humps to get back, just fine since she's gotten next to no exercise these last days. Come morning, though, she'll skin dive Coffin Patch.

~ ~

Isabella, the guide recommended by her old friend at the Pigeon Key Marine Lab, is energetic and accommodating. She's studying eagle rays around Coffin Patch and takes Bailey to a section of reef that's haven not only for rays, but also an entire prismatic world of undersea life—yellow tangs and blue tangs, banded butterflies and four eyes, angelfish and chromis, darting wrasse and stoplight parrots, blue-rimmed doctors and box-like filefish, grunts and schoolmasters, jacks and snapper, bright orange squirrels and snaggle toothed barracudas. The coral is stout and healthy and shelters swarms of juveniles.

Isabella is the perfect dive buddy—easygoing and curious. Bailey likes it that she double kicks when something really catches her eye, but when she mentions it later, Isabella has no idea what's Bailey's talking about. They explore lobster crannies and watch puffer fish, follow a green turtle from a distance and swim through a swarm of synchronized silversides so thick the water darkens with flashes. Out of nowhere an immense tarpon, scales the size of roofing shingles, surges past, followed by another, then two more—at least a dozen of them, traveling with, dining on the silversides in that strange symbiotic pairing of miniature and massive.

Nearly three hours later the women make themselves break for lunch. With shriveled fingers they eat cheese sandwiches and Bailey fields unexpected questions about her own research, offering the standard answer she's given the past few years. Yes, she'd been involved with cetacean studies, specifically the sleep patterns of bottlenose dolphins, but life had taken other turns and she isn't sure if she'll get back into it or not. She'd burned out on the politics of research but loved the fieldwork. Who knows, maybe someday.

As if on cue to help change the subject, a pair of eagle rays shoot from the azure deep and linger in long seconds of suspension before continuing on their watery way.

"That's precisely what inspired my research," she tells Isabella. "A fascination with dual identity organisms—birds that take leave of the sky and dive underwater, rays that fly upward from the same water and are creatures of the air, even if momentarily. Amphibians are one thing, but birds in subsurface flight—cormorants and dippers and auks and shearwaters—now that's something. And of course there are the penguins and seals, otters and walrus. So many creatures that have it both ways."

She shakes crumbs over the stern and folds the waxed paper wrapper.

"When I learned that dolphins evolved from a species that was once terrestrial, I was hooked." Bailey says. "I found, and still find that to be one of the most remarkable bits of information in the history of existence. Dolphins—the most graceful, most agreeable, arguably the most intelligent of all animals, are descended from beings that over the course of millennia adapted themselves out of the water to walk on dry land."

She drains a cup of cooler water, pours it on top of her head, and combs her hair back with her fingers as she continues.

"That's fascinating enough," she says. "But even more mind boggling is that, relatively speaking, they didn't stay long—twelve million years or so—before they evolved into sea creatures again. As if they came up onto terra firma to give it a go but decided never mind, let's get back in the water. Last one in is a human being."

They both laugh, but Bailey stops short and looks at Isabella.

"But you know all this," she says. "Sorry for the spew."

"Not at all," Isabella says. "Can't say I've ever thought of cetacean evolution in quite those terms, but I like it." She smiles a playful smile and Bailey returns it.

"Turns out," Bailey says, "the bottlenose dolphins in my home river still go both ways, come out of the water—and not just to leap in the air."

"Oh?" Isabella squints and cocks her head to see if Bailey is teasing.

"It's not the only place," she says, "but dolphin in specific areas of the Carolina Lowcountry herd fish into the shallows of the marsh flats, up onto the mud banks, and then come entirely out of the water to eat them. Wallow around on terra firma, more or less, while they're at it. It was amazing as a kid to watch. Still is. Cousteau himself brought a team to observe the behavior."

"Stranding," Isabella says. "Sure, I know something about the studies. That's your home?"

"My home." Bailey beams. "I was in high school. Got to meet Cousteau and that hunk of a son Jean-Michel—even got to help with the film crew. To say it made a big impact doesn't really begin to say it. Scientists snub their noses at Cousteau the engineer, but he sure rocked my world with secrets of the sea."

"Little wonder about the marine biology."

"Little wonder," Bailey grins back. "If it were all field work I'd have probably never left it."

"The dolphins will be there when you're ready."

They keep an eye on the distant squall line and when lightning joins the thunder they call it quits and ride to shore satisfied, each musing on what she's seen and sipping an icy Red Stripe. At the marina they have one more and pronounce the day well done while the afternoon shower passes over on its way to the Gulf Stream.

The fish market is next door and after so-long hugs with Isabella, Bailey chooses fat snapper filets, stops for salad makings and the perfect bottle of wine, and is busy thinking how she'll beg off the neighbors when she gets to the cottage and finds a note on the door saying they've decided to try the Italian place, inviting her to join them if she can. They'll be listening to some pirate play guitar at Shorty's afterwards.

Beautiful. She sets a white table on the beach and feasts beneath a sky filled with colors of eventide. Before bed she bathes Miss Ruby in the lingering midsummer light, and before daybreak they're on the way to Key West, rolling slowly across the Seven Mile Bridge.

From this vantage, highest point in the Keys at a whopping 65 feet, she watches the sun slip topside of the horizon. It's a languorous drive and Bailey envisions a day of piddling in Key West, capped off with the obligatory ritual of sunset at Malory Square.

Making her way down Duval Street she wonders what in the world she'd been thinking. Yes it's off-season, but it's also Saturday and tourists herd through the shops and bars. At the Southernmost Point sign she waits her turn to stand on the spot and mark the occasion. Top of Maine to tip of Florida. Stem to stern.

Stem to stern, yet still tight in the chest. She's done a hell of a job shaking the blues these last days. Vagabond blues—the can't-quite-put-your-finger-on-them blues—the ones you barely keep ahead of, the dare-not-look-around-to-see-how-close-they-are blues. She's ready for the big breath but the big breath hasn't come. Now here she is at the end of the line.

Almost. There are the Dry Tortugas.

Yes. The highway ends, but there's more to it than that. Alright then.

At the seaplane paddock she checks on flights and finds there's enough time to make hasty provision—a soft cooler with a small block of ice, cheese, juice, grapes, a twelve pack of snickers, and her Swiss army knife. In her canvas haversack a gallon of water, a jar of peanut butter, a slab of smoked salmon, four granola bars, two sleeves of Ritz crackers, and two bottles of wine she uncorks and pours into plastic water bottles.

Then the tent bag with mini hammock, sleeping bag, pillow, toothbrush and paste, sunscreen, lip balm, baby powder, beach towel, swimsuit, pair of shorts, t-shirt, wash cloth, shampoo, razor, flashlight, journal, fins, mask, snorkel, and the copy of *A Confederacy of Dunces* someone left at the cottage in Marathon. Done. Well within the 40 pound limit. Miss Ruby, snugged into her car cover against the shadeless parking lot, can take a rest.

~ ~ ~

# The Edge of Heaven

The plane flies seventy miles to the Dry Tortugas at such low altitude she can see sharks and dolphins, schools of fish, and several of the hundreds of wrecked ships that have fared unwell on the shoals surrounding these turtle islands, named by Ponce de Leon in 1513. In little more than forty minutes they circle Fort Jefferson, the massive 19th century edifice with its fifty feet tall brick walls—complete with moat—the largest brick structure in the Western hemisphere.

The gods have smiled on her, for with the exception of Ranger Jim and visitor's center workers she's the only person on the island. Mid-morning a group arrives on the ferryboat but by mid-afternoon they're gone. The ranger is kind enough to radio the seaplane folks that she'll definitely be staying the night and again the gods are with her—no inbound passengers, no other campers.

Though she's never visited, she's known of this place—and now it's hers. The sand couldn't be any whiter. The palms couldn't be any more elegant. The water couldn't be any more blue or clear. And there's not even enough land mass to heat the sky and make rain—hence the Dry Tortugas. Splendid.

An auspicious post for a fresh start—only there's no fresh water. Okay, a salty start—good omen for the path ahead—wherever that might take her. Wherever the hell that might take her. She dances about and sings a giddy nonsense song. Yes, my name is Mudd, she circles and shouts. Oh yes, just call me Mudd.

Up and down she dances and runs, rolls in the beach and wings sand angels around the campsite. Swims and rollicks and runs some more. My name is Mudd and I volunteer to remain. I appreciate the pardon but I'm staying put. I'll help with the Yellow Fever. I know you think I'm nuts, Bailey calls to the frigate birds that soar overhead on seven foot wingspans. It's true. I am.

~

Hours pass in tireless revelry and in the midst of it day fades from this spit of island far removed from everyone and everything, including lights. The night

sky is immense and crystalline, the ocean vast as the sky. Sovereign half mo
reigning over all.

This is it.
   The world eases.
   The breath has come.
   The waxing moon watches.

How many thousand times she has stood beside rivers and oceans and even lakes and created brief perfection by cupping her hand into a scope and looking through her loose fist at the place where sky meets sea on a starry night. Rarely this removed from the light, though. Water and sky so intensely woven, and the stars shining brightly in both. Never has she found Delphinus this quickly, the dolphin shimmering on bones of her kite-shaped constellation. The dolphin that roams sea and sky and walks dry land on occasion.

"Hey Mom," she calls out to stars in the ocean.

"Hey Mom," she calls up to the stars in the sky.

In joy she splashes the stars akimbo then watches them find their places once more as the sea stills.

When weariness eventually softens her vision she unfolds the sleeping bag and drifts for a while at the edge of heaven. Tired girl. Good tired and ready for rest. In the days of driving since she left the city questions have perched there on the hood of Blue Ruby. Questions insistent and always in sight. Answers evasive and never in reach. About Merissa's death. The chasm since then between her and Cecil. About her nomadic mind, her unsettled heart. Her work—what it is and what it isn't. About what's left behind and what lies ahead.

Now though, the solution to all of it comes. There it is, painted across the cosmos. She swells into full sounded laughter at the wisdom of her mother expressed in the vernacular of her father and calls out what now seems so very simple:

YOU CAN'T MAKE CHICKEN SALAD OUT OF CHICKEN SHIT.

Following this profound revelation she sleeps. And wakes. Sleeps and wakes to an exquisite sunrise. And each time she fades in and falls back asleep she blazes at her fine fortune, certain that she can fly. Through the sky and through the water, she is quite certain that she can untie the moon and fly.

~ ~

It's hot already for her first morning swim and when she comes ashore she takes a long pull from the sweet cold papaya juice and grabs her mask and fins. In the blue shallows off the fort she relishes solitude before the seaplane lands with day trippers and the box of reinforcements she's been able to request. The light is perfect for the rich miscellany of undersea life and she tags along with a school of blue tangs and studies a pair of scrawled tilefish as they tell and retell their story with each change of their body markings.

Two hours later the ferry arrives with group campers who'd missed the boat yesterday. They swarm the campsites to pick their spots and buzz about the island in pairs and foursomes and sextets.

And it's fine. It's all okay. She knows well what a fluke last night had been and surely can't complain about two dozen or so others who have sought what lies beyond the end of the road. Mostly college students mixed with a few families and couples. She swims with the kids and teaches them the reef, shows them how to bring fish closer.

That evening she washes with fresh icy water from the bottom of the cooler and skirts the edges of sleep before her neck and the backs of her knees get sticky again. The singing has diminished, but someone strums soft Spanish guitar and she wraps herself in the cool notes and rests in the shelter of the swelling moon.

~ ~

Next day some of them go, others come. Rules allow only three nights camping but that's fine, she's ready to roll. It's the day of summer solstice, longest of the year. Tomorrow celestial bodies will gradually tighten the reins on daylight until the time comes for them to slowly ease up again six months down the road. A good signal of change, she decides—the bending of heaven toward a different path.

Many campers are here to mark the solstice. Some have brought telescopes. Someone pipes the flute and others sing. They gather around a small driftwood fire fueled with dried reeds and palm fronds. Some dance while others look to sea in speculation. Joints are passed and someone shares slices of cool melon, the scene wrapped in flushing colors of a particularly brilliant sunset.

They make merry into the night and Bailey eventually takes her leave and walks to the tip of the island. Wind carries the voices off toward Cuba and she can listen again to the shallow sea. Once more she floats in the stars, a world away from earthly encumbrances in the light of the lowering moon.

~ ~

She straps in beside the pilot, a wild man who buzzes a huge shark and lands briefly to watch a pod of spotted dolphin play in the endless blue currents of the Gulf Stream. No doubt she could have convinced him to drop her there to follow her fortune, but not this day. See you later she calls as the seaplane revs and the exquisite animals continue the path of their certain destinies.

In Key West she dallies in the hot shower of the courtesy locker room, lunches at Captain Tony's, and finds an off-the-beaten-path phone booth before steering Miss Ruby out and upward, officially beginning the drive north to known waters.

"Hey Boss."

"Hey Boo."

She hears him ask his assistant to shut the door.

"I'm leaving Key West."

"Hot?"

"Damned hot. Beautiful though. I've been in the Dry Tortugas."

"Don't know it."

"Off Key West. I'll tell you about it."

"You sound a hell of a lot better."

"Helluva lot."

"Are you still coming?"

"I told you I was." She knows he hears the smile in her voice.

"Yeah well, sometimes that means later than sooner," he says, but she hears him smile back.

"I'm on the way. I want to gather us a feast, but I'll be there before long."

~

One thought is to cruise up A1A like she'd come, but her face and arms sting in sunburn and she's tired of sweating. Or she and Miss Ruby could drive the interior toward Orlando and catch the car train at Sanford—out of the heat and off the road, but still in motion. Alright then. Now the question is whether they can make Sanford in time for the train.

One way or the other she will pass by home before midnight so she calls Bert and says she's just checking to make sure he works tonight, that Cecil's probably out on the boat, so she's about to call Mister George and Retta to see what there is in the way of seafood. If Mister George could maybe pack a cooler and bring it to Yemassee.

She asks about the home folks and if Bert thinks his brother would even feel like messing with it. She wouldn't want to put him to any trouble and she knows Mister George would get up from his death bed to put shrimp on ice and drive them to the train station for her. Bert, as always, takes the cue and volunteers to call George. Says not a word about how she ought to call her father. Just the same as he says not a word to Cecil about how he ought to call his girl.

What this means is that when the auto train makes an unscheduled rolling stop in Yemassee there will be a duct taped cooler with crabs and shrimp and no telling what else and a note from Retta inside a zip lock bag on top of the ice that will say, We all miss you. Come home soon. Tell Ben.

~ ~ ~

# Pass by Home

After she makes the call she and Miss Ruby shoot up the highway following signs for Orlando. Four and a half hours later they're ahead of schedule and Bailey stops for picnic supplies and to gather a few things for the overnight ride. They're only half an hour from the station and she has no intention of getting there much before 3 o'clock. The good folks at Amtrak encourage auto train passengers to arrive around noon, but she's learned that lesson. First on the train means last off the train and she has no patience to stand around Lorton, Virginia, watching people claim their cars. It's way too hot for that.

At five 'til three she eases Miss Ruby toward the loading area and makes fast friends with the guys in charge, never a problem for Blue Ruby. One of them remembers her from the last trip and protests only mildly when Bailey slips him a twenty and a wink and asks if he can please be on the lookout for a package if they happen to slow down in Yemassee.

Rules of the auto train are that once your car is loaded you don't see it again until you arrive the next morning so, satisfied that Miss Ruby is in good hands, Bailey boards the passenger cars to explore the possibility of a sleeper. As chance would have it there's been a cancellation and there she is, bird in hand, no need to go tracking down people on a waiting list. It never hurts to mention Bert.

She locates the compartment, drops off her bag, joins the already lively bunch pounding beer and Bloody Mary's in the bar car as they toast conclusion of the eternal boarding rigmarole, then rides for a while in the lounge car where she sits in on a Monopoly game while a twelve year old takes time out to explore the train. Buy everything, he tells her, but make sure you've got $275 all the time. Sounds like good strategy but her buying everything has frustrated both of the boy's sisters before he returns.

She stays a while longer watching the flat lands of Florida disappear then jostles through train cars of variously nested passengers on the way to her sleeper. The same guy with the suntan and yellow hair who crashed upon boarding still sleeps that honeyed sleep of the unguarded. What a release that must be.

In her cabin she reads a chapter, eats an apple, sips a glass of wine, then takes her book to the car where he lies resting and watches the slow fade of day stretch through Georgia backwoods. Streaks of sunset catch in his hair and she desires to nudge him. With full dark travelers click their reading lights or curl into covers and yawn. She returns to her nook and strokes herself in the slow cadence of tracks, imagining his cornsilk hair brushing the length of her bare back.

The train tarries when they come to patches of streetlamps then picks up speed as they enter dark bands of countryside once more. Soon after Savannah they cross into Carolina, past Ridgeland and the countryside closest home, and decelerate on the approach to Yemassee.

There stands Bert in the clear light of the empty station. One arm raised, a brown bag in the other. Coolers on either side. As the train pauses the porter joins Bailey in the coupling alcove.

Door opens, and one man hands up the coolers while the other slides them aboard. Then Bert outstretches the paper sack she's smelled from the passageway—Retta's deviled crab. As she takes it he enfolds her slender fingers in his big hand and squeezes them safe.

"Thank you for this," she says, as he walks along with the train.

"I got my commission," he smiles. "Six there instead of eight."

"See you, Bert," she calls, but already he has become a lone figure on the platform as the train rolls north. She stands there with the silent porter behind her and waves as if she were on the platform of a fine caboose, waves until her friend disappears in the distance.

Once they tuck the coolers under the luggage rack nearest Blue Ruby, Bailey makes her way to the Pullman with heightened appetite. Her cornstalk is awake and looking at the window as she nears.

"Hello," he says to her reflection when she unthinkingly slows in the aisle.

She smiles hi and he says, "They stopped the train for you."

Ah, green eyes, not blue as she'd expected. "Only slowed for a handoff," she says, holding up the paper sack.

"Something seafood."

"Deviled crabs," she says. "Secret recipe."

The conversation and the piquant spice of crabs cause those nearby to move about and harrumph.

"Could you use a midnight snack?" she whispers.

"You bet. Have a seat."

"Nah, come with me."

Nothing more is said as they move through the hushed train. Nothing more as she opens the compartment and sees the steward has made the tiny bed. They sit cross legged on either end of it and eat two crabs each, then split another. When the wine empties she packs the rest away and watches him watching her. He thanks her for the treat and when he leans in to touch her face she smells cloves on his fingertips. The lights of Charleston grow brighter when he outs the lamp and they slowly take turns with buttons and zippers.

Through the night they move together with the rhythm of rails and doze when the train pulls into switch offs. When light chances across the cabin she sweeps a strand of his yellow hair and says the color of cornsilk will remind me of you.

In the foredawn they prop pillows to watch forms emerge from the Virginia woodlands. Passengers in nearby sleepers stir and the announcement of breakfast begins an intermittent unfolding of accordion doors. He slips out and is gone to the heartland, and when they reach Lorton she's first in line, contented and hungry and ready to hit the road. At a mom-and-pop near the station she breakfasts, and while grits are on her mind stops by a grocery store to stock Ben's cupboard before she gets any farther north. Good grits.

~

Traffic around D.C. isn't the worst, and she and Blue Ruby are in Philadelphia long before Ben gets home from work. His note on the kitchen counter says he'll be out with his office staff. Marcia, his assistant, is taking maternity leave and he's treating them all to dinner.

The note is the last of many he's left in a flip pad next to the tide clock, just in case. Notes saying I thought you might show up today—I'll be working late—call me at the office. Saying I'm at the gym—be back at 3. Saying I'm with friends at South Street—here's the number. Saying you've been on my mind so much I knew you must be coming—I'll be home by eight. Oh Ben.

She opens the big bank of curtains to a sweep of cityscape and steps onto the balcony to see what movement there might be on the Delaware River below—a few scattered vessels, one of them a tour boat with laughing gulls circling its stern, dipping into the churning wake. Ben Franklin Bridge off to one side, Walt Whitman off to the other. Betsy Ross down the way. She likes bridges.

Paper rattles behind her, blown from Ben's Best Thing Lately shelf, a letter from Mister George. She sets it beside a jar of Retta's prize Roma tomatoes shining ruby in spikes of sunlight. The small oil painting of two tangerines bobbing atop a layered kaleidoscope of seascape hangs over the table. Ben chose it from Bailey's work when he came to visit in April. There's a photograph from the last time he was in Kirk's Bluff of *Miss Merissa* and *Sonny Girl* at the dock, May Isle in the background. Cecil is on the back deck mending nets.

A glass trophy from Ben's last marathon is beside the tomatoes. He'll replace it when he competes again, marathon or triathlon, with the next trophy or ribbon or certificate and send this one to the home folks where Retta will display it with others of Ben's triumphs that line their long hallway.

Marathon man. Mister Longhaul.

Bailey telephones the office and Ben returns the call before he sees his next patient.

"Honey, I'm home," she says.

"Can you meet us for Marcia's dinner?"

"Sure," she says, "since I'm cooking it."

"There are ten of them. Twelve with us."

"Perfect. I brought more fish than we can eat. And I've got crabs and shrimp enough for days."

"You sure?"

"Does the fish allergy guy still work there?"

"Nope, he's gone."

"Better stop off for beer and wine. I need to get going with food."

"I'm glad you're here, Boo."

"I'm glad I'm here too, Boss. Bring the gang and come on."

~

The Reading Terminal is a perpetual extravaganza. Robust aisles upon aisles of vegetables and herbs and meats and seafood. Cakes and pies and strudel baked by the Amish ladies from Lancaster. Knockwurst and brats hawked by brawny mustached men. Hearty sausages that drape over the countertops. That she can use. Fish laid out in scaly rows with quartered lemons and parsley garnishes. That she doesn't need. Fresh bunches of twine-tied marjoram and basil, oregano and thyme, rose geranium and tarragon. She can do something with all these. Smell them if nothing else. The same little white haired man sells her a braid of garlic and three bulbed handfuls of scallions, unshaken earth still clumped in their roots. When he counts out her change he wavers a shy smile and gives her a tiny ribboned bag tucked with lavender.

From the cheese lady comes wedges of this one and that one and a two pound portion of hand churned butter. On to the bread and over to the fruit and across to the vegetables. When she can barely carry what she's collected she forces herself to head home but is caught by toffee and caramel. And the honey. This too from Lancaster, where bees have supped on sweet blossoms across miles of verdant farmland. Couldn't be as good as Murphy's though. She treats herself to a mammoth warm pretzel with spicy mustard and a beer, then balances the bags, and steps into the sunshine thoroughly pleased with the world and everyone in it.

~

Cooking in Ben's kitchen means cooking with childhood—pots and pans and ladles and crockery from both their houses, including his mother Henrietta's worn tin measuring spoons and her mother Merissa's perfectly seasoned frying pan that she's never thought of taking elsewhere.

Bailey's house and Ben's house were also home for each other as kids, and Ben has managed to blend the two and still have a swank Philadelphia bachelor's pad to entertain his sophisticated lady friends. She begins peeling and chopping and mixing with *La Bohème*, then turns to *Man of La Mancha* for sautéing and sauce making and frying.

~

When Ben and his friends walk through the door it is to a savory assemblage of shrimp and crabs steaming with sausage and corn, fish and shrimp frying in separate skillets, hushpuppies and potato salad mounded in deep platters, and a huge tray of thick sliced tomatoes with crisp hunks of cucumber. After the flurry of hugs and introductions, everyone situated with drinks, the two of them face one another holding hands.

They cut a fine figure, Retta likes to say. Ben Simmons is 6'2" of broad square shoulders that taper into a narrow waistline. His spiraled black hair is close cropped, his skin smooth and brown, and his hazel eyes range from brown to green. Bailey's are crystalline blue, her skin deep olive, her hair long and tawny brown, and her build streamlined so that when they dance their bodies sway in unison like tall strong marsh reeds.

"Hey Boss," she says quietly.

"Hey Boo."

"Hey Boss," she says again.

"Hey Boo. Are you okay?" he whispers and draws her near.

"Now I am," she says as they stand rocking. "I don't know what it is with me."

"You're alright, Booney."

He runs his hand down her long pony tail and brings it around the front of her shoulder. They bend into one another, foreheads touching.

"Come on," he says, "we've got fish to fry."

~

After the eating and exits are done, Ben and Bailey each raise a bottle of Miller High Life and clink in unison to The Champagne of Bottled Beer, as they have since high school, then set about cleaning the kitchen. Amid familiar clatter she tells him of her two week adventure—of Old Sow's churning waters and the drive along the ridge of the Blue Ridge, of fishing and skin diving and all the creatures she's seen. Of the Dry Tortugas and skimming the sharks.

"There was the lonesomest man, Boss." She dries the plate in her hand and places it in the cupboard but doesn't reach for another.

"I picked him up somewhere in Pennsylvania and he slept in the back seat for a while and got out when he woke."

Ben hands her a dripping plate and she stands there holding it.

"He asked if I had 'Stardust Memory' and cried while it played."

She dries the plate, then keeps rubbing it.

"I wonder sometimes if that's not me," she says.

He tenderly takes the plate from her, stacks it atop the others, and places his hands on her shoulders.

"It's *not* you Bailey. That will never be you. Do you know one of the things I love about you most?"

"No."

"You pack more living into two weeks than many people scrape together in a lifetime."

"What would be the point otherwise?"

"You say that because you're Bailey Martin."

When the pots are dried and hung they sit on the deck overlooking the city and pluck succulent white clumps from the mostly uneaten half bushel of crabs.

"Don't ever teach these people how to eat crabs, Boss." She fingers the growing mound of meat. "There's plenty here to make soup or devil them—your pick."

As they work their way through the pile she tells him of the old cronies from the pier at Sebastian, of their fishing buggies. And she tells him of her visit with his Uncle Bert. Their way of words, Bailey and Ben's, is a well-traveled path. All their lives each has shared with the other all that only one has gotten to see or do. As kids, if one got to go on the trawler or a class trip or into Savannah for supplies, the other went along too with the telling.

It's after one A.M. when they finish the crabs and settle into the living room. Ben pours two shots of bourbon and they sit on the floor, lean against the sofa, and watch a rerun of *The Andy Griffith Show*.

"That's good," she says when Andy's done whistling the credits. "Let's save *Bonanza* for another night."

"Well," he says. "Are you ready to tell it?"

"Well, are you ready to hear it?"

"Sure, but I already know it."

"Alright then, you tell it."

"Okay I will, Sonny Boy. Once upon a time there was a beautiful woman who sang like an angel and swam like a fish, and all she really wanted to do was swim about and sing. From time to time something, usually a man, would come along and she would try to be still and quiet but she couldn't, so she escaped again and again. The end."

"Cute."

"So, what was the last straw? No, back up, what was it about that guy anyway?"

She shrugs, stretches her head into the sofa cushion.

"Get the cards," she says. "You deal."

Seven card gin is their game and the match has been ongoing since they learned it.

"Seemed like he had his act together," she says. "And the art stuff. You came to that first opening he arranged in SoHo, saw how they ate it up."

She passes on the top card and he takes it.

"Crazy," she says, "but it was fun—the late nights, the city buzz . . . the dinner parties . . . you know . . . the scene."

"That bad, huh?"

"It wasn't really. Well, it was, but I was into it at first . . . talking art and politics and philosophy with bright people."

She flicks her thumbnails against one another and discards a jack of diamonds.

"But . . . ?"

"It's all recycled. Same clever quips, same superior sarcasm. I rarely bothered to bring another topic into the same stale conversations. And brother when I did they all looked like they smelled farts on the end of their forks."

She fans the cards and draws.

"Or worse,"—she brings her hand to her chest in mock drama—"like I'd worn the wrong black t-shirt, missed the memo that DK was out of vogue that week." She shrugs again. "They turned into cartoons."

"Not quite what you were telling me." He draws and discards evenly, without pause.

"I know," she says. "But then one day the light came on—there was a Blue Moon in May you know."

She stares at her cards, pulls one part way, pushes it back and slides a four of clubs onto the pile.

"Anyway, I stepped back from it, the whole contrived pile of chickenshit, and there was Kerret right in the middle. It dawned on dumbass me that I was some exotic showpiece for him, but only to a point. Otherwise I was expected to . . . well, conform to his supposedly nonconformist world."

"You?" he looks at her sideways as he arranges his cards.

She takes the top card, flicks it across the others in her hand, and discards it.

"We spoke about travel when we met, so I talked up trips to Thailand and Peru and Costa Rica. Remember, we took that trip to Costa Rica? But, Boss, I'm telling you that with the exception of being driven from the airport to the resort, the son of a bitch never left the gringo compound. I'm not kidding."

She rolls onto her elbow, lays the cards beside her, reaches over and holds Ben's forearm.

"For one solid week we sat on the resort beachfront and swam in the resort pool and got treatments at the resort spa and had cocktails at the resort bar and ate at the resort restaurants. It was beautiful, don't get me wrong, but we could have been in Palm Beach."

He lays his cards down too, looks at her and laughs.

"You think it's funny?"

"I think it's hilarious," he says.

"Well it is, dammit—but it wasn't then." They pick up the cards and play.

"All the rainforest hiking and horseback riding and surfing—arranged by the concierge. None of it interested him. This is paradise, he said to me, as he floated in the bean shaped pool with a Piña Colada and adjusted his tan lines. Why would I leave this for poverty and filth?"

"How many cherries?"

"The Piña Colada?" she says. "Lots."

"And . . . ?"

"And as long as I was back for dinner he was mildly interested in where I went and what I did. Any good finds, he'd ask, but he meant shopping."

Ben faces a card down on the discard pile and knocks on the coffee table. "Gin," he says, and lays out his hand.

"Nice," she says.

He sweeps the cards, shuffles, offers her the cut, and deals.

"Okay, Sonny Boy," Ben says, "so the obvious question here is why. You were with the guy for almost a year."

"Well . . . he seemed . . . stable. Hasn't that been part of the problem—my growing attraction to the wrong type? Never mind, don't answer that."

She lays down a two of clubs.

"You know what Daddy would call him? A sickening puke. But do you decide somebody is a sickening puke and just pull the plug?"

"Yes," he says. "You do."

"Well I didn't. I tried to go with it, be the spunky little Southern gal that had charmed him and his superficial circle."

"Knock," he says, and spreads another winning hand.

"That was quick."

"Luck of the draw," Ben says. "Here, you deal."

He gets up to pour them another shot and she stretches with a couch pillow across the thick Persian rug they'd bought for Retta, who had promptly returned it to Ben in the same package saying it was too heavy to drag onto the porch and beat.

"This is when I knew it was bad," Bailey says. She giggles and snorts and cannot stop. "I knew it was bad when I started fantasizing about knitting."

"Do I want to hear this?"

"I'm talking sex. The non-thrill of it. One morning after he'd slept over I was no doubt thinking about breakfast, looked down at him between my legs and it occurred to me that I could take up knitting, that if I only knew how to knit I could prop back on the pillows and accomplish something productive."

"Good god, Sonny Boy." He steadily discards and draws.

"I can't help it Boss, I'm drunk. And besides, that's what was going through my head. From then on I amused myself with sweaters I could knit, baby blankets for all the godchildren I'll have when you settle down and get married."

"Would you hush."

Her next card is gin and she pulls the pile over and shuffles.

"The sushi thing pushed it over the edge though," she says.

"Are we out of the bedroom?" He deals and she takes the spade queen on top.

"Yes," she says. "We're out of the bedroom and back at the unfunny dinner table, same worn out conversation, and I make some comment about how delicious the meat is and that maybe we'll do seafood sometime. Do seafood *now* he says to me. Right you are I say and reach into the aquarium I gave him and pull out one of the fish I gave him and hold it up by its squiggly little tail. I haven't really thought about eating it until I see the look of dread on his face. Shoot, I twang in my down South finest, I know ya'll call it sushi, but back home we just call it bait. Whereupon I swallow the little fellow whole and wash him down with a polite sip of Pouilly Fumé."

"Beautiful—don't tell me there's more?"

"No. The rest of them looked to Kerret for their cue and so were appalled."

"You sure they weren't appalled by your cornball sushi joke?"

"Smart ass. I'm not convinced they even caught it. But I do know how many miles they'll get retelling the tale. Anyhow, that was the night before I left. The rest you know."

"Well no, I don't."

"Remember the doorman? Raymond."

"Yep."

"He changed the locks when I left and will mail the new key here. I told him he could move in for the rest of the lease if he packs my stuff and ships it to storage. Is there room?"

"Sure. Is he sending furniture?"

"Just my desk. He knows how to handle the paintings, and other than that, it's mostly art supplies. Books and records. Clothes."

They listen to the dishwasher and she thumps her glass.

"I'm a mess, Boss."

"You're amazing, Boo."

"What am I doing? What in the hell am I doing?"

"You'll figure it out."

"I can't figure it out now, though. I'm going to bed. Night Boss."

"Night Boo. I'm glad you survived the Big Apple."

She stops halfway down the hall to her bedroom

"Gin," she says. "I forgot to knock. And I'm done talking about the Big Apple for a while."

~ ~ ~ ~ ~ ~ ~ ~ ~ ~ ~ ~ ~ ~ ~

## BEN
### (1962)

*When the bus dropped him at the head of the road six year old Ben walked the pine shadowed path towards the refrigerator but forgot the orange popsicle when he spotted the enormous gold car pulled right up to the front steps, road dusty but the shiniest thing he'd ever seen. He knew what that meant. A lot.*

*He tossed the Superman lunch box on the counter when no one answered his yells, ran out the screen door in full knowledge that the slam behind him would go unscolded, and was through the woods to the Martin place, up the porch steps, and into his mother's arms before taking a breath that mattered.*

*"How are you, son?"*

*"Good, Retta. Three gold stars since you've been gone."*

*"That's wonderful, honey. Has your daddy been feedin' you right?"*

*"Yes, ma'am. I love fried baloney. When can we go for a ride?"*

*"Soon, boy."*

*"Yes, ma'am."*

*He knew what that meant. Nothing. He slid from his mother's chair, stood before Merissa and said Hey Miss Merissa are you okay? I'm fine Ben, she told him, but he could tell she wasn't. This time he shut the screen door easy then lit out for the tree fort and scrambled up the sapling ladder, unaware that Bailey hadn't spoken a word to anyone in nearly three weeks.*

*When he stuck his head through the entry hole, feet on two different rungs, he looked in with sun-blinded eyes and said Boo, like they always did, and she said Boo back, like they always did. He could see her shape in the cutout window and then could tell she was wearing a blue dress for some reason and her hair was fancy in the back with a long horse braid.*

*"Are you going to church?"*

*"No, I'm coming home."*

*"I'll row you in the dingy."*

*"I'm already four."*

*"Yeah but you just got back."*

*"Alright then."*

~ ~ ~ ~ ~ ~ ~ ~ ~ ~ ~ ~ ~ ~ ~

The sound of it, sculling, suggests nothing of the comeliness, the synchronous reaches and pulls, reaches and pulls. Bailey is struck by the order, the discipline and decorum of the endeavor. Stone walls and boathouses perched at river's edge, glasses tinkling within. The camaraderie of fellows who ought to be jolly good even if they're not.

A curious river the Schuylkill, watery spine of this City of Brotherly Love. Formal—like Boston—picturesque but not real, not allowed to go as it will. It does of course, ultimately, for no amount of brick tons will hold a river back when it does not wish to be contained.

It's difficult to imagine the Schuylkill Expressway as a meandering river road where people slowed to watch the rowers practice, before it became the Surekill Distressway where crashed cars litter the side of the highway as reminders. Surely there's a way to get past this bedlam and down to the water she says to Blue Ruby, and there is.

Skipping stones on the bank of the Schuylkill she can block traffic enough to hear the Jericho, their river. The dolphins' unhurried blows, the long stroke of heron wings. She closes her eyes and is there in the warm salt water, drifting with the tide, into childhood.

These are gifts from the gods, Merissa would say to her and Ben as they raised the bright sails of their sunfish. Our waters are rich and clean. When you grow up you must care for the treasures of the river, not the wealth of people on her banks. If too many come, too many that don't pay attention, the gods will withdraw their favors. The dolphin will still be there, everywhere in the river, but most will only glimpse them. Take the time, Merissa was forever cautioning them. Listen to the river and take the time.

~ ~ ~

The place is dim when Ben enters the foyer and sets his keys and brief case on the driftwood table. Bailey never closes curtains.

"Boo," he calls tentatively to a stir in the corner.

"Boo," she says back, but not like she means it.

"Can I turn on a light?"

"Sure."

The canvas she's been working is darker than the room and she sits on the floor at the base of it looking to the wall.

He sits beside her, hugs her to him. "What is it, Booney?"

"I'm such a son of a bitch, Boss."

"Who says?"

"I say."

"What happened?"

"I was at the pool today and finally gave those lazy ass kids some grief—the ones that hang around acting cool."

"And?"

"They can't swim, Boss. They don't even know how to swim. I've never felt like such a fucking jerk."

"So do something about it."

"Oh, I volunteered right then—and they just stared at me like the shitbird I am and said nothing. Then I dared them. Nothing but the attitude." She laughs. "But then I called them a bunch of pansy ass cocksuckers and seven of them signed up for Tuesday."

"Get up from here, Sonny Boy. I need to get you to some real water."

She stands when he holds out his hand. "Where?"

"What about dinner on that four master at Penn's Landing?"

"*Moshulu*? I do love that boat, but it's stuck." She opens the curtains and sliding glass doors. "Let's go where we can see the stars. You up for a beach run?"

"Atlantic City?"

"Hilarious, aren't you? Cape May's alright, but Jersey's backing up. Let's go to Delaware, find someplace to camp. Get your stuff and I'll load Miss Ruby."

~ ~ ~

Ben schedules an open morning and drives to the Boys and Girls Club to watch her with the would-be-swimmers. In this hard knock neighborhood it's about the closest you'll come to Norman Rockwell—kids frolicking at the pool—the biggest kid of all slap dab in the middle. They recognize something in Bailey and are attracted to it. When she asks them they're compelled to try.

Children and teenagers of varying shapes and sizes drape the edge of the pool with their left arms and legs dangling in the water, heads turned right and resting in the crooks of their arms. Their bathing suits are florid but towels hanging on the backs of pool chairs are dingy washouts.

Okay, splash, she says, and they do—kick and splash as much as they can with two dangling limbs. Good, good, she says. Now look across at the opposite side of the pool from where you are. Got it? Okay, walk on your heels over there and get ready to lie back down, this time with your right arm and leg in the pool. Wait 'til I tell you.

Up they get, giggling and bumping into one another, pointing to ask which side is the right one. When they're satisfied they've found the proper place, Bailey tells them okay, go ahead and lie down, and like a dozen brightly clad dominoes they fold onto the concrete coping and wiggle their torsos toward the side of the pool. Okay, splash, she says. And they're at it again, churning the chlorine seeped water.

The idea, she explains, is to get them comfortable everywhere in the pool. Her methods are her own, fun being the cornerstone of instruction. Next she has them pile into the shallow end and jump. Jump and circle their arms like windmills. After that they hold on to the side and work their way around the pool to the steps again. It's like an aquarium in frenzy as they cluster to her, bouncing tiptoed, clinging to the safe zone wherever she is.

She was a fish growing up—they all were—but Bailey could dive the best and stay under the longest and float the farthest. Always the swim captain. Always the champ. The girl that grew into the woman who maintains a silent insistence they dance rings around the fire and never come close enough to feel the flame. A burn he would happily risk but never demand. Forget marathons. Forget emergency rooms. Nothing else in his life requires the fortitude it takes to steer clear of that abiding fire.

Funny, Ben thinks as he watches the would-be swimmers, the salt and pepper ratio is the exact opposite from his and Bailey's school in those early years of integration. They were fortunate in Kirk's Bluff where blacks and whites lived side by side and the focus was outward, toward the river, but it wasn't entirely a cakewalk. And invariably it was the same few bigots. You can always walk away from words, Retta counseled him, and she made a game for it—Duck's Back. Let it roll off, she said, like water off a duck's back.

It worked pretty well in elementary school, but when he got to middle school teenage Ben, tall and strapping and tired of even the occasional taunting, was done with the game. That's alright, George told him, but don't you go looking for trouble. If it's coming at you and there's no way around it then strike it down and be prepared to strike again if need be. But son, he said, don't ever let me hear that the trouble was you. That's not who we are.

The more able-bodied he grew, the more Ben found he was strong enough to walk away after all. It only took a few strikes, and it only happened at school, never on the river. All bets were off if it had to do with Bailey, though. Messing with him was one thing, but mess with Bailey and watch out.

~ ~ ~

*God bless a honky tonk. Swimmy slow dancing to some country and western crooner, rolling in some sweet baby's arms. Preferably a big ol' sweetheart of a guy. One who sends his momma flowers and would worry if he knew you were on the road alone. Concerned even that you're on your own in the world, nice girl like you, girl a fella like him could sure enough care for. Sure enough.*

*The ease that comes after say six or eight slow dances, a little whisky, the comfort of two bodies that stir into and away from one another in complete abeyance and nobody has to talk. All there is to do is hold on and let go. Let go and be held. Sway and turn in the blood rise as your body comes alive to itself and tiny pricks of electric lust surface on your skin. The truth of appetite right there on the dance floor. Everything pared to the simplest elements—solace and arousal. Moving in a bubble, a blip apart from everyone else, apart from yourself.*

*Even if it means playing three slow songs in a row, a good honky tonk band will pay homage to dancers enveloped in the music and become part of the moment with their guitars and microphones and drums and you. And when that third song ends, as it begins to wind down, that is the time to take this creature now synchronized to your body, take him by the hand and lead him outside, whispering shhh, hoping he won't break the spell before you can reach for the belt. The jangle and ever-so-slight slap of leather, button undone and then zipper, as each tiny track peels apart, slipping your dress up and leaning onto the warm hood, absorbing the tremor of motion and release. Sweet pleasure skimmed off the top of desire at its unfaded best.*

*And zippety-do-da-day, you're out of there. On the road to where the adrenaline wears off and you can coast in a trance of satisfaction until there's a place to pull over and rest. Maybe take a swim in some hotel pool and keep driving. You've thought nothing of journeying for hours sometimes, out of bounds, to someplace near the big highway, corridor of anonymity, nowhere near home.*

*Sometimes you think maybe you should have taken him up on his offer, could have gone on back to his place and continued to play. Maybe even dance again tomorrow night. But this doesn't happen. If you stay and he takes the day off or calls in sick, he won't take you dancing. The intensity of the night before cannot be reenacted. It's like those Civil War buffs who dress up and try to replay history, but you can't recreate either one—love, lust in this case, or war—without losing the immediacy of its truth.*

*You can get a rush pretending but you may as well go light another fire and leave that one to smolder.*

~ ~ ~

A rainy Saturday and they've each finished a second cup of black coffee and raisin toast.

"Can we look at the bank statements?" Ben folds the newspaper to the sports section he'll read before bed.

"Now, Boss? Hell, I just got here."

"You've been here three weeks and we haven't done this for months."

"Is there plenty or not?" She loads the saucers and knives, lids the butter dish.

"There's plenty," he says.

"Then what do we need to talk about?"

"What we always need to talk about. Are the statements right? Should I pay these bills? Did you really order a collection of hand carved boomerangs?"

"They're gorgeous," she says. "Each one's a different constellation."

"Right," he says.

She stands before the refrigerator with the door open.

"More coffee?" she says.

"No thanks."

"Toast?"

"Come on, Boo, quit assing around."

"You think this cantaloupe's good?"

"Probably—you bought it Wednesday. Alright, just listen to this. The big piece that sold last month and the one this week at the east-side gallery put another twenty thousand and change into the kitty. But should you pull work from that place in Tribeca?"

She stands at the sink scraping seeds down the disposal.

"I think it's fine. He's Kerret's connection, but the guy's getting his cut."

She moves to the sink and scoops out slices of fruit into a blue stoneware bowl that was the favorite of Cecil's mother.

"How many paintings are still in New York?" he says.

"I don't know—a dozen maybe—mostly at the SoHo place. And the ones I left at the apartment. You took that load when you came in April."

"Of course."

"Why do you say it like that?"

"Because you inevitably do just that—start bailing before you realize there's a hole in the boat. What about the aquariums?"

"Ah yes, we haven't talked about the aquariums. It's a good story. Well, it could have been a good story. I'll tell you when we don't have such serious bidness to tend to."

He leans back in one of the metal lawn chairs—Bailey's solution to the overstressing of so many kitchen chair legs—red, yellow, blue, and green. The yellow one is cheerful, but Ben sits in the green one and she goes back and forth between red and blue.

"Okay, Sonny Boy," he says. "How's this? You make it. You spend it. I'll keep tending to the paperwork and tell you when the till is low."

"Thanks, Bossman. You're a prince among thieves. How about I take you to the fair next week?"

Now it's he that stands with the refrigerator door open.

"Are we playing COP tonight?"

"Not tonight," she says. "I might go fishing."

"Not much fishing when there's nothing to show for it."

"Now Boss, you know I'm a catch and release kind of girl."

~ ~ ~

When the Ferris wheel pauses before spilling forward she asks Ben to point out the direction of the apartment where he lived that first year in Philadelphia—a row house off Haverford, one of those meccas of marginalization where Jewish blocks and black blocks bleed into one another and each enjoys the other's soul food.

"I liked it there," she says. "You kept that little victory garden."

"But you couldn't see the water."

"Or was it that you got above your raising and didn't want to get your hands dirty."

"Screw you, Sonny Boy."

"Oooh—a nerve. Is it your prestigious practice and ever-so-affluent patients?

They've come to a complete stop at the pinnacle of the Ferris wheel. Lights of the amusement park dazzle in neon pulse below them and the night bright city fans beyond.

"What the hell's going on with this thing?" Ben says. "And what the hell's going on with you?"

She hangs her head and looks at him sideways.

"Should I feel guilty that I make plenty of money and don't even have a job?"

"For godsakes, Boo. Did you feel guilty the years you busted your butt—mostly doing a grown man's work on your daddy's boat?"

"No—it's what I needed to do."

"How about the year before grad school when you farmed yourself out on Toomer boats to pay hospital bills?"

"It's what I needed to do."

"That's the point I'm trying to make, Booney. Just because it's fun, just because your muscles don't ache and you're not using your degree doesn't mean it's not for real."

The basket swings as if the mechanism is about to begin but then it stops again.

"I don't know, Boss"

"It's what you need to do now. And the paintings are good, really good, whether you care to believe that or not. The critics say so—and the work sells. Lighten up on yourself."

"I slipped the guy a twenty to stop us up here," she says. People do it to propose."

"What?"

"I thought if I could get a little higher and see a little farther I might be able to figure some things out. The twenty was the only way I could think of to have them stop the thing."

Ben shakes his head and looks up at the sky.

"Besides," he says, "the work you do with those kids—and the work I do at the clinic, thank you very much—counts. We don't get paid, but it's work that matters."

"You're right, Boss. My bust."

She leans back and they watch the moon, shoulder to shoulder. Sounds from the midway expand in the quiet.

"Don't you ever want to go home?" she says.

"Sure, don't you?"

"So why don't you?"

"Listen to me, Bailey. Hear me when I tell you I don't want to play humble hero dedicating myself to my people—educated black man who could turn the world around."

"I'm only saying—"

"—Can't I just be some guy who's a cardiologist, leave work behind if I'm not on call, do some volunteer hours on the side, train for a marathon every now and then, buy my momma a new jeep?"

"What are you talking about—new jeep?"

"Flannery O'Connor bought her momma a new jeep, talked about it anyway."

"That would be a fine sight, I'll grant you that. Retta toolin' around Kirk's Bluff in a zippy little jeep. Actually, she might just love it."

"That's what I'm saying to you. I want to have that option, to phone Smoaks Honda and Jeep, fork out the cash, and tell them to deliver it on her birthday. Or better yet, fly down myself and take her to pick it out. Make a road trip to visit Aunt Beulah. I can't do that if I'm busy being Doctor-Do-Good."

The gears of the Ferris wheel grind once more and they reach for the rubbered bar as the cage swings backwards on the way down.

She turns to him, places a hand on his grip.

"You're absolutely right," she says. "I can see you so clearly back home I forget—about you. Go right ahead and do it, Boss. Rake in those Yankee dollars and we'll get us a fleet of jeeps one day, and Boston Whalers, and seaplanes. Hell you could just pay some other doctor to run a clinic right there on the bluff."

"Smart ass."

The carnival attendant unbolts the door to release them but doesn't say congratulations like usual.

"Come on," Bailey says, "let's take another turn on the merry-go-round."

~ ~ ~

*It's not that you're totally opposed to talking. Sometimes it's lovely when there's someone who can do both. Maybe one of those boys in the band. In this case, you can't get too cozy with Big Strong Arms since he'll put up a fuss when you tell him to run along without you.*

*No, in this case you dance with them all. Raunchy blues songs. Maybe you even sing one or two. You know how. The stage has been yours before. Down and dirty and everybody's part of the fun—the democratic spirit of the honky tonk dance floor as you feel their eyes swallowing your body, filling their fantasies. But when any of them comes on too strong you laugh and keep moving. It's all a show anyway, foreplay for the bass player you've chosen.*

*And after last call and last dance you help break down microphones and wrap miles of chords while they hand truck big black amplifiers to the band truck, wipe down guitars, disassemble drums. Everything in its place. When you've done what you can to help you sit with the bartender as he closes shop as well, and all of you echo with a tinge of ear-ringing melancholy, for it's like packing the circus tent away after the floodlights fade.*

*There is little talk among people who have spent their voices, who know the routine so well they simply put themselves in gear and go. Light jokes, often only gestured, punctuate their labor—all of them with amp static filling their heads, drifting down from the stage rush, the saturation of speakers and lights, Marlboro and sour mix.*

*It's another antechamber undreamt by the solid citizenry, this world of the stage, the road. Comfort to those who know it. And when the work is done you take a walk, drink a cup of coffee, converse in bits about places you've seen and want to see. You've made the unspoken promise of tonight and that, along with all else in this booth at this hour is settled. Everything's within reach.*

~ ~ ~

She stands at the walk-in closet staring at winter clothes and summer clothes. Coats and skis and microscopes. Hat boxes and camera bags and fishing rods and spools of canvas. Boots and bottles and blankets and bows and bedrolls. A saddle. The room behind her, her bedroom at Ben's, is filled with books and shells and paintings and pennants and photographs, remembrances of childhood, of travels, of generations past. All of it dear. Much of it subject to the Salvation Army if Boss weren't such a sentimental pack rat.

The first time she'd vacated an apartment he'd pestered her into returning for the important things she'd left behind. A notable lesson, him bossing like when they were kids. From then on, one way or another, valued possessions make their way back to Ben's or Kirk's Bluff. She's looking from one thing to another when she hears him in the hallway.

"Boo," he says.

"Boo," she says, the signal it's okay to enter.

It's Sunday and they didn't see the *Rusalka* matinee because he was called in for an emergency. She wasn't there the night before.

"Me COP or you COP?"

"Your turn," she says. "Cook or pick?"

"Too late to cook but I'm starving. I pick that Italian place where the waiters sing—make up for the opera bust."

"Suits me," she says.

"Closet shopping?" He reaches for the light string.

"It's okay," she says. "It's all in there somewhere."

"Boo?"

"I'm thinking to give D.C. a try, well Alexandria. I found a big loft near the Torpedo Factory."

"Why not go home for a while?"

"Not now." She shuts the closet door.

"Why not stay here then?"

"It's time Boss. I can see you starting to worry."

"It's not that I worry."

"Oh?" She sits on the edge of the bed.

"Okay, it is that I worry," he says. "Mostly it's that I'm never sure if you're coming home."

"I get that," she says. "The thing is, I'm never sure either. And it's not right. It's never right when you don't know whether to listen for me or not."

He sits on the bed beside her. They talk to one another in the mirror.

"It's okay, Boo. Really. I listen for you anyway. No matter what."

"I know," she says. "But I'm tired of making you crazy. I've already taken the place."

He stands.

"What is it?" she says.

"Nothing," he says. Bites his tongue and swallows metallic tasting spit.

She knows that if he insisted she lie back on the bed, look into his eyes and say what's real between them, there would be no move to Washington. The willpower not to do that. The willpower both ways.

He reaches a hand to her.

"Is this a load up the car or a rent the U-Haul?" he says.

"Let's just load up the car for now."

~ ~ ~

Driving into Washington she watches childlike for a glimpse of the monuments—Washington's towering obelisk, Lincoln's stately Parthenon, mostly Jefferson's poised rotunda. Everyone's favorite, right? As far as cities go, she likes D.C. The breadth of it.

The loft is on the top floor of an old warehouse that overlooks the Potomac. One huge room, walls of hundred year old brick, ceiling high and open. Long arched windows take up much of the wall space, all uncurtained but with folds of sheer cloth hanging to the side and big semicircles of whisper-white light that fan the floor in front of each opening. Oversized aquariums separate the cooking and eating area from the sleeping space from the work section from the storage—an animated cross section of undersea life. The largest is an inshore saltwater tank, and jutting off from this eight foot rectangle are two smaller tanks of festive tropical species.

She's placed paintings on each of the brick exposures, none of them hers, but as she looks around in the last days of unpacking she changes her mind and hangs a sizeable 3x7 canvas that feels like the Jericho River. Coaching from Boss. She's cut this deal with him to pay more attention both to her work and everybody else's.

Boss. She's also made a bet with him that she can go seven weeks—he said a month but she said make it seven—without bunny hopping. Bailey calls it catch and release, but Retta likes to call it bunny hopping and counseled her years ago that bunny hopping is as natural as breath, never to be ashamed of fun if it's fun for everybody involved. Retta also told her that hopping with just one bunny can make life a lot simpler, but so far their paths remain un-crossed—star-crossed, maybe.

# PART II

# Somebody Else's Song
# (1988)

# Chances Are

Trajectories collide in the September countryside. Padgett Turner has taken a day off to look at property, in the market for a place where he might spend time with his boys on weekends. Nothing fancy, as long as it's off the beaten path. This place, less than two hours away but in the outback hills that skirt Shenandoah, qualifies. The ad describes a twenty acre tract, some of it suitable for farming, with a sturdy house built in the late 1920s, a post and beam barn, several outbuildings, a spring fed pond, and a stand of mature hardwoods. There's mention the homestead has been unoccupied for some time and house and grounds are in need of attention.

He drives past the for sale sign, notes fresh tracks in the driveway, doubles back, and parks in a thick patch of pines and brush on the far edge of the property where his truck can't be seen. The tracks lead to a big blue convertible parked in the backyard near the cloistered pond. He circles the empty house, peers into dirt daubered windows, retraces his steps, and detects movement inside the trellised scuppernong vines.

A woman steps forward with a basket, sucking the sweet from of a handful of grapes and flipping the hulls away. Her long brown hair is braided down her back and she's wearing a dress that makes her look like some peasant woman from a little village somewhere.

She's spread a picnic beside the spring, apparently waiting for someone. Harmless. He approaches, but before he speaks she invites him to sit, saying she's brought lunch. He asks if she isn't waiting for someone and she says no. He asks how she knew anyone would be out that way at all and she says she didn't know. Then he asks why she thinks he will join her for a picnic and she says she has no idea whether he will or not, so he shuts up and sits.

There's smoked salmon and cornichons, a baguette and butter, pears and nectarines and wine, and they eat and drink and speak very little. When they do it's of spring fed ponds and what lives in them and what can't. Light flutters on the fresh water and shadows are consumed around them.

Padgett tells her she's surely picked the nicest spot around to have a picnic and she says no, the nicest spot is hidden. There. She leads him into the grapevine, spreads her cotton shawl, lies on the leafy ground, and motions to him with apparent assurance. He lies beside her in the scent of ripe scuppernongs and they look up at the grapes, some gold and ready to harvest, others green and solid, and there's nothing else in the world but to lie beside her and gaze into the tangles. The scent intoxicates.

Nothing is said and there is no expectation of words. She moves over him and touches a finger to his lips like the whisper of silk. The sun rains through her backlit hair and he can't tell if she's happy or sad or why he'd even wonder and then she stands and walks out of the arbor and he is struck from a place beyond memory. Unequipped.

He watches the dream of her move through the clearing but has no capacity to follow, hears the old car fire and drive away, yearns to tell her everything but not have to say it.

~ ~ ~ ~ ~ ~ ~ ~ ~ ~ ~ ~ ~ ~

*The shot ripped past the wind, into the rabbit. Dead.*

*Fine shot Padgett, the grandfather said as the boy ran toward it. Fine shot.*

*That made three. The one the grandfather hit to remind the boy how to do it. The one the man, the grandfather, backed up when the boy wasn't quite quick enough. And this one. Dead on. Fine boy. Fine shot. And the dogs were running some fine rabbits. One more would be enough for supper. Another couple and they could feed Liza and Tick too.*

*The ground gave beneath them, several seasons soft, leaving the smell of wet dirt and wet leaves, too tender for men to know, trailing behind them.*

*They continued through the woods, slowly, as quiet as the rabbits, the grandfather making note of the dogwoods with fading red ribbons around them. He and the boy had tied them half a year ago when the trees fanned in sprays of white lace against the crazy green of young spring.*

*They had marked the trees for Violet, the boy's mother, the man's daughter, and would return for them soon, now that it was winter and the trees stood bare, as if lifeless. They would dig the roots up and move the trees to where the boy and his mother lived, so that when the lace fanned again it would be through the strength of dirt some miles distant.*

*This was the third winter of the boy's gun. A four-ten. Gift from this man, his grandfather. Many rabbits and squirrels. Many stews and roasts. Carrots and potatoes simmering in big cast iron pots on his mother's stove or Liza's. At home with his mother he wasn't yet allowed to use the gun.*

*The boy thought he saw the rabbit first. They hadn't heard the dogs for a while. A fat one. But the grandfather, knowing the wind, knowing they would be able to walk right up to the rabbit, was already looking for the proper stick. Long enough, but not too long for the boy. Heavy enough mainly, and solid. So much of this wood rotten with all the rain. Fifteen feet and the rabbit was yet turned away, white tail to them, nibbling fresh shoots of fern.*

*When he spotted the right club the man ever so gently picked it up and reached forward for the boy's gun. When he felt his grandfather's hand on the stock the boy froze, as motionless as the rabbit, his own fingers locking onto the steel. He wouldn't turn to look at his grandfather, hadn't known until that moment his grandfather had been finding a club, that it was now in his grandfather's hand, waiting to come into his.*

*In the unflinching stillness the three of them heard a mockingbird tell somebody else's song atop the myrtle bush off beyond the fern patch.*

*The boy thought the rabbit might scatter as his grandfather pulled harder than the boy's grasp on the gun and replaced it with the grave stick, but it didn't. It never moved at all, except to chew and reach back down for more, while the grandfather pushed the boy onward to what made sense.*

*Never waste shot on a rabbit when you can get close enough to wallop him. It was one of the first things his grandfather had told him about rabbit hunting. But until now it had never happened. Until now a rabbit had been a little patch of fur on up ahead that would mean stew for supper. Until now it had nothing to do with tiny whiskers twitching and the pink insides of ears.*

*This wouldn't be like with the gun, when the grandfather would shoot rather than have the rabbit get away. It had to do with other things and the boy knew it.*

*At the last possible second the boy jumped before his grandfather could push him and came down hard with the club. Not hard enough. The rabbit sprang and the boy sprang with him, crying, the man yelling hit him again. He did and the rabbit stopped, but not altogether, not yet perished. The boy stared as the rabbit jerked, but he could not move, the grandfather steadily yelling hit him again.*

*When the jerks turned to nothing more than nerves twitching, the blood of the rabbit swelled inside the boy and he came down again, harder, harder, pounding the bloody rabbit, unable to stop, flesh coming through, fur sticking to the club. The man was yelling something else now, but the boy could not hear because he was screaming himself, nothing with words, screams to drown out the thuds, to drown out the soft smell of the new blood, the limpness lying in the dirt.*

*The man was on the boy now, pulling him away, into his down jacket, his flannel shirt, holding his arms around him until the boy ceased flailing, until the club dropped from his hand, until the boy went limp in his grandfather's embrace and stopped screaming, pendent but finally able to take in air.*

~ ~ ~ ~ ~ ~ ~ ~ ~ ~ ~ ~ ~ ~ ~

Padgett Turner takes the left hand of his excited son Daniel and the right hand of his not-so-excited son Michael and leads them into the East Building of the National Gallery of Art, knowing the design of the place itself will be enough to amuse them. They wander past Calder's mobiles and pause at pieces by Rothko and Pollock, Lichtenstein and Klee, the boys comparing their own efforts and pronouncing they could be famous some day.

They're most taken by the House of Mirrors exhibit where shoes are removed and feet shod in footies before they can enter. Inside is nothing but mirrors—on the floor, on the ceiling, on the walls. There's a bed, a dresser, a table, four chairs, even a toilet, all constructed entirely of mirrors. Everywhere they look the boys can see only themselves, an infinity of their curly blonde hair, the blues of Danny's shirt, the reds of Michael's. Picture perfect boys in something like a picture perfect world. Pretending.

They wave and jump and spin in the myriad and whirling reflections of themselves, and as soon as they exit they're ready to go again.

"Come on, Dad," Michael says.

"Maybe another time," Padgett says, but his ruddy face flushes darker.

"It's really not scary," his younger son patiently clarifies.

"You're chicken," the older one says. "It just feels weird because there's only you, everywhere you look. You never stop seeing yourself."

"Next time," Padgett says as his boys lace their sneakers. Christ Almighty —one mirror is more than he wants staring back at him. He turns from them to forestall the rising demons. "Come on," he says, "let's check out the other building."

They ride the people mover to the West Building and the boys are wide-eyed when told the Rembrandts are well over three hundred years old, incredulous that anything could last that long. As Padgett leans into *Philemon and Baucus* to discern each brush stroke it's incredible to him as well. That's it, he tells himself. Steady, Turner. The youngsters' rowdiness is subdued as they move through the hushed halls of the Old Masters, but when they get to the Impressionist galleries their father is spending too much time at too many paintings so they venture ahead.

Padgett seeks an empty corner in one of the smaller gallery nooks and stares into the serene, imperturbable brown eyes of a Renoir, pretends they mirror his own, as he talks himself out of the red zone, reminds himself there is no danger in this labyrinth of rooms, cautions himself that his children await him. Insists to himself they will never wait long.

He finds them standing behind a woman with an easel who sits before a painting of children by the sea. She's painting the exact scene and they're mesmerized. She tells them she has special permission to copy these works, and when Michael asks if that's cheating she laughs and says yes, but the idea is to look closely at masterpieces and learn from the greats.

And then Padgett sees. It's her. The grape arbor. It is she.

"Excuse my sons," he tries to say, but she turns with a smile and though there's no sunlight through her hair, there she is. In the swirl of senses he hears Michael ask her name.

"Bailey," she says. "And you?"

"I'm Michael," he tells her, "and this is my little brother Danny. He's six and this is my dad."

Brush in hand, she smiles at each of them.

"Nice to meet you." She turns back to the canvas.

Silence as the boys watch and Padgett tempers his pulse enough to compliment her work and ask if she does portraits.

"Of a sort," she says.

He looks to his sons and asks with upturned palms.

"Sure," Daniel pipes.

"Okay," Michael shrugs.

They promise they'll be able to sit still while she paints so she gives Padgett her number and says to call later in the week.

~ ~ ~

"Hey Boss."

"Hey Boo."

"I saw him again."

"Who?"

"The one in the arbor."

"I thought you didn't." Ben is doing pushups when the phone rings but switches to sit-ups so he can hold the phone with his neck.

"I didn't. I'm not. I bet you seven weeks and it's been almost a month. But listen."

"Okay."

"I told you the eyes, but it's not just the eyes. There's something else. Something in the gut."

"Hmm," he says, as if listening to a patient.

"A pull that makes me want to come close—but run away at the same time."

"Hmm." He closes his eyes, pushes his powerful shoulders up and down, and holds his well bitten tongue.

"I saw him at the National Gallery with his two little boys."

"Great."

"He asked me to do their portrait."

"Since when have you painted portraits?"

"Why not?"

"Watch out, Boo."

"Okay, I gotta go."

~ ~ ~

A week later she ushers them, Padgett and his sons, into the loft dressed in jeans and a billowy white blouse, deep brown hair tied loosely with a silken scarf. She's made jasmine tea and pours for the four of them. The boys bewilder their father by taking the cups and saucers in hand as if they'd done so every afternoon of their lives, but as they drink and nibble ginger snaps they look around the room wide-eyed. It's like the House of Mirrors might be if somebody wonderful actually made a home there.

"Have you always lived in Washington?" she says.

"Yes ma'am, well really Bethesda." Danny answers but his eyes never leave the aquariums.

"He has," Michael says with big brother swagger, "but I lived in Camden until I was seven."

"South Carolina?"

"Yes ma'am. But then we got rich and moved here and got two new houses." Big brother reaches for another cookie.

Padgett has listened to one or the other of them blurting this kind of synopsis since they were old enough to understand something of the inheritance, but it's especially awkward for him now.

"*Reader's Digest* version," he says, redfaced.

The afternoon is spent sketching the boys in different poses as Bailey opens herself to whatever it is she thinks she's doing, and when they come for the next sitting dressed in yellow and blue sweaters and khakis and saddle oxfords she places them back to back on a low pillowed platform while Padgett settles into an armchair with a strained sense of pride and protectiveness. When the music clicks off she absently asks him to reload the stereo.

"What would you like to hear?"

"Another flute piece maybe, or a piano sonata. Something airy."

Two tapes later they call it a day and make a time for the weekend while the boys take a last look at the aquariums, still deciding which fish are their favorites.

"Who's that guy?" Danny stands before a white marble miniature of the Oceanus sculpture at Trevi Fountain.

"Oceanus," Bailey says. "The Greeks say Okeanos—the Titan god of the sea. He's the same one in that mosaic with his wife Tethys."

"A merman?"

"Well, he's a god, but yep, he's of the ocean so he's got that fish tail and crab claws for horns."

"And a star on his forehead."

"Yep," Bailey says. "Part of his deal is he controls when the stars and planets and moons rise and set into the water."

"Stars in the water?" Michael is unconvinced.

"Ancient Greeks believed everything in the sky comes out of and goes back into the sea."

"They knew a lot of stuff," Danny says.

"You've got it, buddy."

~ ~ ~

In the next days, hours between time at work and with his sons, Padgett sits in the small space he's sealed off in the basement. It's entered through a sheet of plywood in the electrical closet behind the laundry room, never when the boys are there. He replays all the "airy" classical music the guy at Olson's record store could recommend—Mozart, Vivaldi, Chopin, Debussy, Berlioz, even some Bach and Beethoven. Fauré and Poulenc. A switch from his usual Metallica, Led Zeppelin, Black Sabbath, Def Leppard, and Dio. Not so far from Pink Floyd. Nothing's far from Pink Floyd.

Even there in the shadows of his cave he can see light as it bounces around her room from cobalt pitcher to small crystal hurricane lamp to vase of white flowers to silver picture frame. Each time she lifts a brush the light catches her bracelet and creates a circlet of waves on the ceiling. He is not qualified for this, wishes he were.

~ ~ ~

Next week before they leave for Alexandria, Michael and Danny are tugged the entire two blocks between their mom house and their dad house by Maynard, their Boykin Spaniel. In the backyard Maynard fetches the ball until his tongue drags the ground. If the boys wear him out he can come in the house and curl into his bed for a nap, otherwise he is an uncontrollable maniac that whips around like a hairball tornado. When they suggest Bailey would like to meet him and maybe he could be in the portrait their dad says no, but when they ask Bailey she says why not, there's a fenced playground downstairs, and then their dad says okay.

When they get to her apartment Maynard is still drowsy so Bailey works him into the composition and begins sketching right away, saying she's pleased with the more comfortable expressions of the boys. But then the spaniel wakes with fully charged batteries—time for more fetching.

Bailey stands at the kitchen sink rinsing grapes and watches them play.

"You're quite the devoted father," she says without turning.

"Didn't have one. Mine always will." The snarl is immediate and intense.

"Sounds like a threat," she says. Puzzled.

"Not at all," he says, damning himself, calming his voice. "More a promise I made myself when they came along."

There's been an early cold snap and drafts run heavy through the old warehouse building. A kerosene heater is lit near the easel and Padgett could move closer to share the warmth but he likes the distance to look at Bailey with her back to him and the boys in a time lock of innocence, a scene he can engage as he pleases, or seal away for a while with *The Killer Angels*, the book he's brought along. Bailey stands and sits, pivots and leans, but she works quietly, and the boys have become accustomed to their routine of poses and breaks. They all know their parts, are easy with them, and music wraps the room in sweet reprieve.

Padgett ranges between what was just said and where he might take the boys for dinner and how she spends her time. And how sometimes she looks exactly like she did that first day in the arbor and sometimes she looks completely different. He wonders if it's possible that she doesn't remember. Everything about her is beyond his training. When he hears her asking him to choose more music he realizes she's repeating herself and begins a tape of Liszt's second piano concerto.

He settles once more into the frayed chair that's become his accustomed spot and considers the edge she heard in his voice. Thoughts turn to his mother and Beaton, that son-of-a-bitch, and Nam, a place he'd hoped to avoid but instead is with him every day of his life.

Mr. Beaton will help you someday his mother had said to him as a child, many times over. Because Beaton was such a big shot Padgett had assumed. Because Padgett's grandfather was the caretaker of Beaton's Carolina hunting plantation, Beaton might put in a good word for him somewhere, sometime. Or Padgett could drop Beaton's name and impress somebody.

But not until Padgett was a high school senior and his mother's heart-strings ripped at the undeniable nightmare of Vietnam did she tell him. College or no college she feared her son might be called up, a fear that spawned confession because Beaton, she was certain, could ensure Padgett the same protection afforded those of privilege. Maybe he could, but Padgett never gave him the chance. Violet Turner tried to explain to her son that she had been young and in love, that she had believed Beaton loved her as well, that she remained of that belief. When she found herself with child she was sent to live with her aunt until the baby came. Him. Padgett. How about that. He had a father after all, except that he didn't. Fucking A.

He had hunted with the son-of-a-bitch. Well, he had saddled the horses and ridden with the Yankee bastards and released the birds for them to shoot. So full of "yessirs" and "nosirs" it put a rock in his stomach to remember. As a young man Padgett had spent part of every summer with his grandparents at the caretaker's cottage, and he knew Mister Beaton very well. His father.

His mother told him this as he came of age in the belief that they could reach out to Beaton for help. Instead Padgett bottled the rage, went straight to the recruiting office, and signed on for special services. Hello Phoenix. Goodbye. In the end nobody but the ghoulies rose from Phoenix. And they rise to meet him both daylight and dark.

"I'm starving, Dad."

"Me too. Can we send for pizza?"

Padgett looks to Bailey for the part he missed, but she shakes her head and smiles.

"Fine by me," she says. "I was thinking about Thai, though. Anybody interested?"

"Tie?" Danny squinches his freckled nose Dennis the Menace style.

"Maybe we should stick to pizza," Padgett says.

"It's a kind of food," she says, "and it's really more fun at the restaurant."

"What about Maynard?" Michael says.

"Can't he stay in the bathroom?" Bailey says.

"Sure," Padgett says. "If you're good with that."

"Then let's roll," she says.

Bailey brings quilts and bundles the boys into Blue Ruby. The ride is just far enough to make soup sound even better and they hurry down the stairs past the neon signs and potted plants that flank the door of the dimly lit restaurant.

The table is prepared with red and gold cloth of the same pattern that covers the walls and ceilings, and on it they eat lamb and chicken with their fingers and laugh with red curry sauce on their faces, the boys devouring strange dishes as if they're cheeseburgers. Padgett leans into the black leather booth and drinks the plum wine Bailey has ordered, aware that he would never have ordered it himself, knowing exactly how the boys feel.

~ ~ ~

It's a night his sons are with their mother, a night when none of it holds. Booze. Demons. Floodgates of fatherhood. Voids to fill, voids that gape forever. Beaton. The son-of-a-bitch that died and left him five million dollars. Five million goddamned dollars out of the clear blue sky and he hadn't so much as laid eyes on him in fifteen years. The Boston millionaire with darling grandchildren and yachts and a cottage at Cape Cod and another in the Hamptons and a "little place" down in Carolina where he hunts. How do people have five fucking million dollars for bastard sons?

Padgett was supposed to have been given the money anonymously, with only the law firm and accountants aware of the transaction. The certified letter informed him a man had recently deceased, that the man was his biological father, that the man had never forgotten him, even though circumstances prevented acknowledgment, and that since Padgett had never known him, it would be better for everyone concerned if his identity continued to be withheld, but that he hoped the gift would prove to Padgett that he had never been a fatherless child.

He could withdraw any or all of the funds at his discretion. They had been deposited in an interest bearing escrow account at Chase Manhattan Bank but could be transferred to any bank Padgett saw fit to designate.

Of course Padgett knew the money was from Beaton. Beaton who went to his grave unaware that lovely Violet Turner had broken her vow of silence trying to protect her son from the useless war that robbed his soul outright. Violet had gone to her premature grave while that son, Padgett, was in Southeast Asia learning to become invisible.

His mother never married. When Padgett was shipped back to the states he drove to Missouri where Rose, his mother's sister, told him that his mother understood how angry he was and why he wouldn't answer her letters. That Violet was proud of him for serving his country. That she loved him beyond measure and always would. Some of it truth.

Rose said her sister died loving two men who had turned their backs on her. But she could never stop hoping that one day Beaton would do right by her, do right by his own heart. That one day the stack of delayed letters would come from Padgett. She had forgiven both of them but the day came when Violet Turner simply could no longer saddle up her broken heart and ride on.

The sonofabitch, Padgett thought. Maybe Beaton did love his mother. And look what she had to show for it. Him. Padgett. He wasn't so sure he'd been worth it.

Fuck Beaton. Padgett didn't touch the money or so much as acknowledge receipt of it. When Beaton died Padgett was already working his way through college, married to Liz. Michael was born and they'd moved into family housing at the university, bought a set of bunk beds at a garage sale because it was the only thing that would fit with the crib and all the baby's things. Padgett slept on the top bunk and fell out one night trying to get to his mother. Thought he heard her calling, but of course it was only the baby. His mother had been dead for years.

While he was in country training to pick off Charlie's informants. Identify and neutralize. Capture and kill. There were few interrogation details for Turner. He was too good with a rifle.

Yes, fuck Beaton. Years passed but Padgett's attitude about the money didn't change. He'd come back some way other than a body bag, gotten through college, knocked up a girl, made a beautiful baby, smashed a lot of furniture, limped along in a mistake of a marriage, found an under-the-radar job, made another beautiful baby but didn't want to limp anymore. Wanted to stand upright and walk. Wanted to make peace with the demons that besiege him daily.

So joke of jokes, Beaton and PTSD had helped him after all. Liz found the letter and flipped her lid but then calmed herself and negotiated a deal. The Catholic dictum she'd clung to in the years she'd refused divorce could be gotten around if he signed a paper acknowledging he wasn't of sound mind when they married. As trade she would withhold details of his agitation and violence, of the terror he'd brought into the household. In the eyes of the Catholic Church the marriage would be annulled and Liz could have her slate cleaned and ready to receive most of the fortune from Beaton's will. Oh the indulgences—alms and spa treatments.

Negotiations stalled when Padgett refused the annulment, but once she knew of the money she couldn't resist it. Threatened prosecution. There was no way for him to win. They moved to Bethesda where she could be near her family and bought two houses with the same floor plan in a neighborhood where most of the houses had the same floor plan and he got his divorce.

She would have full custody of the boys but would allow him to see them as often as he liked—unless she changed her mind. Trust funds were created for Michael and Danny, and of the remaining nearly three million dollars she would keep two and Padgett could have one.

If he had any problems with the settlement she would gladly sit on a witness stand and tell of dark words and deeds that would land him supervised visitation every other Sunday, maybe. She could tick off a list of flashbacks that ended with guns in the baby's room. Broken glass and battered bathroom doors. Padlocks on the bedroom. Tape recorded rantings and threats and indiscernible drunken babble. A logbook of every outburst since the year they were married. Well documented danger.

Well cataloged anguish.

Later Liz was pleased to tell him the annulment was approved anyway since he didn't fill out and return the paperwork to formally protest her request within the allotted time.

And now there is Bailey.

Bailey, who uncorked a bottle of plum wine and somehow made Southeast Asia palatable. He looks around him at the holes he's punched in the sheetrock, the patches that never hide anything.

~ ~ ~

When the portrait is complete Padgett arranges to come for it alone. Bailey has chilled a bottle of Perrier Jouët for the occasion and pours each of them a flute.

"Ready?" she says.

"Let's do it."

When she undrapes the cloth he can't believe the difference since the boys' last sitting. The "finishing up" as she called it, has taken the work from quite good to outstanding and joy washes from the canvas. She has created motion around the figures so that they're alive in the kind of multi-layered current of colors that he's seen in her other work.

"To the boys," she says, and they touch glasses and drink. Then she bends slowly to him with the tenderest kiss he has ever known and walks into the kitchen for strawberries and chocolate.

"You've nailed them, Bailey," he says. "It really is wonderful."

She steps back and looks at the canvas as if it were someone else's.

"I'm pleased with it myself. Thank you."

The strawberries are plump and sweet and smell like warm springtime.

She takes a bite from one, holds the green stem of it and feeds the rest to him. Then another. A third.

When he can no longer look into the blue pools of her eyes she takes a step back and unbuttons the clasps of her brocade jacket, lays it on the arm of the sofa, slips out of her faded jeans, and raises the black camisole over her head. These fall silently to the floor and as she stands before him he watches the briskness rise into her skin.

With relief and caution he pulls her into the blue striped chair where he's spent so many hours these past weeks and gratefully wraps his arms around the proof that she is not a dream. It's hard to trust such peace, but there it is before him.

~ ~ ~

"Hey Boss."

"Hey Boo."

"Have you been reading about the whales?"

"Not much. I was hoping you hadn't seen it."

"They can't breathe, Boss. They're trapped in that shallow ice and can't even breathe, much less feed."

"It's sad, Booney."

"They're banging their heads on the ice. The little one has terrible cuts."

"It's sad, Boney, but is it nature?"

"They shouldn't be there. It's a glitch in the system. A fuck up. They're so scared, Boss. I can't take my mind off the little one, how terrified she must be. And there's something else."

"Yes?"

"I can hear my mother calling to them."

"Boo."

"I can hear her, Boss. She's singing."

"Oh lord. You're going there."

"That's what I'm calling to tell you."

"Alaska, but where?"

"Barrow—it's the tip of the top—then a forty-five minute snowmobile ride to the site."

"And you can just waltz right up—never mind, forget I said it."

"There are swarms of people. Journalists from everywhere. Too many people, I know. Too complicated. But I've got some training and I can use a chainsaw."

81

"And if—"

"—And if nothing else I can listen," she says. "Two days ago the scientists couldn't get the whales to go to the next air hole. It was too shallow. They kept going back to the one that was already refreezing. Then two Inupiaq elders advised quietly to start thinking like a whale and open the holes in deeper water. They did and the whales followed. Do you see what I'm saying? Most people there aren't even listening to the whales."

"You've got your tickets?"

"As far as Fairbanks. I'll figure it out from there."

"Just you?"

"Just me, but you're right. There is Padgett—he's real. The catch and release queen has finally gotten herself hooked."

"Take care of yourself, Boo. I'll be here when you get back."

He traces the lean shape in the enlarged photograph of her slalom skiing on the Jericho River. Merissa took the picture and he's driving the boat. Bailey's waving to them and at the edge of the photo are the tips of his fingers waving back. She's just crossed a wake and is entirely out of the water. Flying.

"I know you will, Bossman. I might visit Grand Mère and Papa while I'm out that way. Maybe even drive myself home in a solid gold Cadillac."

"I won't tell Miss Ruby."

Bailey had learned that if she skied slowly enough the dolphins on the back river would occasionally rise along with her, especially the pale one crabbers called Haint. It never happened if the boat was too fast, and it took them a while for Ben to find exactly the right balance of speed that would keep her upright, but just barely. Even in the photograph he can feel her in motion. He knows she has to be in motion, but he longs to hold her still. Bailey girl, ever confident but sometimes uncertain. This, though, was a glory moment, golden.

~ ~ ~

# Barrow

On the morning of October 28 a meager sunrise allows for a certain adjustment of light meters on thousands of cameras carried by hundreds of journalists from dozens of countries come to witness the peril or salvation of three, now two, gray whales off Point Barrow, Alaska. The Inupiat names of these whales are Putu, Siku, and Kanik, translated to English as Ice, Ice Hole, and Snowflake. Others have called them Bonnet, Crossbeak, and Bone.

They were discovered three weeks before by an Inupiaq hunter, and since that time have become the focus of international attention as many people with many motives join to free them from the ice trap where they slowly suffocate and allow their free passage to open water and presumably on to their winter feeding grounds in Mexico, thousands of miles southward.

Kanik, the nine month old baby has ceased to surface by the time Bailey makes her way to Barrow. Snowflake. Bailey believes there's more to the story.

Barrow is the most northerly town in the United States, more than three hundred miles north of the Arctic Circle. On this day the temperature reaches eighteen degrees below zero, but it gets much colder, five months of subzero weather. When the sun sets in mid November the polar night lasts until late January. And when the sun rises in May, it is daylight for a solid three months—zero hours of dark. Lives are different. Some creatures live and die in the space of a single sun, but that is not how life was meant for whales.

In the course of the three weeks there have been multiple malfunctions, botched efforts, lapsed communications, and plain old lack of common sense. But more so there has been diligence and determination, elbow grease and compassion. Native crews and others, including Bailey Martin, have worked around the clock with chainsaws to open a series of small air holes, life lines leading the whales toward deeper water. For the past few days a Soviet icebreaker has bulldogged its way through the frozen water toward the shallows that trap the whales, and this is finally the day of success. A channel has been opened.

When Ben calls Retta and George in Kirk's Bluff he's heard nothing from Bailey but reads to them from the *New York Times* about how the Soviet ship, flying both the Stars and Stripes and the Hammer and Sickle, finally cleared a path to open water. About how the last 400 yards the whales swam under the ice after the final chain-sawed air hole and how they pushed their way through the slush. About the crowd cheering as the whales began to swim the two-and-a-half mile channel toward the freedom of the North Pacific in the wake of the icebreaking vessel.

Retta holds the earpiece away from where she and George have listened with their heads together.

"Halleluiah!" she says.

"Tell Cecil," Ben says. He hangs up the phone and high steps around the kitchen until he can settle back down with his coffee and open the Philadelphia paper to see if more news is there.

"No need to call Cecil," George says to Retta. He jingles his change and grins. "I'll walk over to the dock."

~

Padgett too has been watching and waiting.

~

Bailey, jubilant and exhausted, is among those who witness the whales as they swim the last few hundred yards of newly carved channel and roll once they reach the open sea. Halleluiah indeed.

~ ~

The next day in Tatitlek where her grandparents were relocated after the earthquake, Bailey sits by the woodstove rubbing calendula ointment into her wind cracked skin and looks around the small cabin at shelves brimming with souvenirs—rocks and bones, feathers and shells, masks and beadwork. Their other house has gone to sea, but it takes so little to amass so many treasures.

"It's good to be warm," she says to her grandparents. "Grand Mère, please tell me what troubles you so."

"You're right, Asherah. My heart is full."

After all these decades in Alaska Adèle Selanoff, Bailey's grandmother, Merissa's mother, retains the resonance of her native French speech.

Asherah is Bailey's middle name, as it is her mother's middle name, and the middle name of the grandmother who stands before her now, and her mother before her. Since longer than anyone knows, the tradition has been to pass along the legacy of Asherah to each firstborn daughter. Asherah, the queen of heaven—she who walks on the sea.

Adèle Asherah pulls a chair closer to the fire. She is slight of stature, but when she speaks it is always with authority and calm assurance.

"Great Mother is sad about the disrespect being shown our earth," she tells her granddaughter. "Humans are the only creatures who disregard the rhythms of nature. We blast holes in the ocean floor and scrape out the hearts of mountains. We halt the flow of rivers and blow poison into the air. What do we think will happen?"

She rests her chin in her hand and leans into it. This is a home where silence is welcomed.

"Mostly the earth does not complain," she continues. "But sometimes her anguish cannot be stifled. Before the great earthquake we wouldn't listen to the whispers; we paid no mind to the gentle pleas or even the louder cries. Then came the mighty roar of Alignak. Everyone heard that. But who will take heed? Who will learn balance from these messages?"

The old woman stands and looks northward through the plaid curtained window. Her stance, like that of her daughter and granddaughter, is that of a dancer, shoulders back, feet planted firmly but nevertheless with the appearance of someone about to take flight.

"So many gathered around those whales," she says "because try as we might to deny or ignore it, most of us know we are all gasping for breath. Life is fragile. Those whales, if they really survived the trauma, could be harvested again by a boat just like the one that cleared their path to freedom. Not for sustenance. Not with respect."

She pulls a stool in front of Bailey, sits, and takes her granddaughter's hands into her own, continuing to massage ointment into the needy fingers.

"The lesson of the whales, she says, is that we are capable of acting beyond our greed. It is possible that we can work together, all people. The capacity for selflessness remains within us if we will only acknowledge it. It's good, Asherah, that you have come to witness. We must do what we can to ease the pain of all who suffer—two leggeds, four leggeds, fins, and feathers alike. When we can learn to care for all, the spirits will smile on us."

She kisses the palms of Bailey's hands.

"Be heartened by the little one," she continues. "I too heard the voice of your mother. I heard the voice of mine as well. It's a big place, Alaska. It takes the breath of a leviathan to call attention to struggle, just as it took an earthquake that shook the world. Yet in six months few will think twice about those whales. Of all who joined to help, did you pay attention to those who didn't? Many were too busy running the race for our resources."

Adèle encloses Bailey's now tender hands within her own and looks into the same crystal eyes she sees in the mirror.

"Know this, child. You must always choose life. Even when the burden of heartache seems too heavy a load you must seek the forward path."

They rise and as Bailey holds her grandmother tight she breathes the reassuring scent of elderflower perfume that is made for Adèle each year in Honfleur.

"Thank you, Grand-Mère."

"Take beauty from the story of the whales. What I've learned in my own journey is that you must seek the truth that is yours and respect the truth of others. And open yourself to love and beauty. That's about the best any of us can manage."

The old woman, dressed for an excursion—as she is unfailingly dressed for an excursion, in high leather boots and a green woolen waistcoat—turns to her husband who has been nodding before the fire in the cot where Bailey slept the night before.

Isaac Selanoff, known to everyone as Bear, is a big man, too tall and broad for the foldaway cot, but when Bailey is in the house Merissa is there also, and he has lain quietly in the pleasure of both generations of daughters and the talk of his wife.

"Would you agree with these words, my husband?"

"Every one of them, ma chérie," he nods. "You have said it well."

~ ~ ~

# Winter Songs

"There really aren't any rules," Bailey says as she hangs the Neptune ornament near the top of the tree. "Usually I place the larger ones towards the bottom and the smaller ones higher, but it's all good."

"What do you say, Dad?" Danny takes tissue from a crystal dolphin and twirls it over his head.

"I say hang the heavy ones on a sturdy limb and make sure the fragile ones don't get walloped by Maynard's tail."

The loft smells of cinnamon and ginger and Bing Crosby sings the same holiday songs, then Nat King Cole sings them again. Bailey has already wound the lights, including four strands of antique candy cane bubble lights, on the stocky blue spruce, twelve feet tall.

Why not, Bailey had said when the four of them combed the Lion's Club tree lot earlier that week. The ceiling is huge—why not a grand tree? Besides, I've got tons of decorations in Philadelphia and I owe Boss a visit.

Boxes large and small, new and battered are spread around the room. The boys scavenge for treasures but are careful with each of their finds.

"What about these?" Michael has opened a set of little wooden boats, simply carved of various woods.

"My father made those for me when I was a kid. One each year. I'd find them in my stocking, but I knew they were Cecil's gift."

As Bailey and the boys decorate Padgett sits on the floor with newspaper spread before him, gluing red ribbons on a basket of seashells. The four of them have spent every other Saturday or Sunday on a ramble, usually to the beach, mostly to see the ponies at Assateague. Sometimes they bring Maynard, who is a great fan of Blue Ruby. He stands with his hind legs on the edge of the back seat and his forepaws on the fold down console in front, redbrown ears sailing in the wind. Now Maynard lies beside Padgett and entertains himself with a new rawhide bone.

"What's this, anyway?" Daniel holds a small figure with mangled bits of felt and fur.

"Ah," Bailey says. "All these ornaments have stories, but that one . . . that one has special magic. It's a tiny doll my grandma sent from Alaska when I was a little girl. Her parka was shiny red with white fur around the hood and sleeves and her mukluks were soft caribou hide. She knew lots of things and I kept her by my bedside, but then she disappeared and I was incredibly sad. I didn't want a new doll. I wanted her—and one day there she was again. My dad told me our puppy had chewed her, but I knew she had been off on some fantastic adventure and barely got away with her life. When I got too old for dolls she became a Christmas ornament."

"What a mess."

"You're right, Michael," she laughs. "But I love her just the same."

"Here you go." He hands Bailey the doll by its matted arm.

"I like the ulus you brought us from Alaska—wait 'til you see what I carved," Danny says. "Do you always go there?"

"Nope, but I've been lots of times, mostly to visit family. That's where my mom grew up. My grandpa is half Chugach."

"What's a Chugach?" Danny looks up from the miniature train set he's unpacking.

"A kind of people. You've heard of Eskimos. That's what some people say. And my grandma is from France. She went to Alaska to study anthropology a long time ago."

Padgett holds one of the shells by its ribbon, supporting it with this other hand. "I'm not sure how long it'll take the glue to set," he says.

"We could save them for Christmas," Bailey says. "Some people don't even decorate their trees until then."

Bailey hands Michael a dinosaur she knows he'll like.

"Christmas?" He reaches for the ornament. "Won't we be at the lake house? It's a Brontosaurus."

"All this time I thought it was Brachiosaurus," Bailey says. "Lake house?"

Padgett props the shell against the cardboard box with the others lined as if awaiting a firing squad. He eases Maynard's bone from him and hides it under the couch.

"Of course we'll be at the lake house," he says. "Hey boys, Maynard's getting restless. How about taking him for a break."

They stand at the window to keep an eye on the boys. Bailey washes cups and saucers and waits.

Padgett steps to the side and reaches with the drying rag, but she sets them in the drain board.

"It's Liz's family's summer house," he says. "It's a huge place, and they all gather there for the holidays—every year, everybody—so it's the only way I can be with the boys at Christmas. It's that simple."

"Really?" She turns to where he stands pulling the dish rag between his two fists. "That simple? You're divorced, Padgett."

"I'm not divorced from them. And there's no such thing as taking turns. You know that."

He flashes rage and she steps away from him.

"I'm sorry, Bailey. I don't mean to be an asshole. Please understand what this means. When Liz heard what a great time Danny and Michael had here Thanksgiving night she threatened to keep me away. I can't take that risk."

"You might have told me, Padgett."

"I didn't know how. And it's not like you talk much about your plans."

The tension surges again, but he rides it out, makes himself walk to the window and look at his sons.

"This has all been a whirlwind," she says, "and god knows I'm not trying to fence anybody in. But—"

"—But what?"

"But the way I don't talk about things and the way you don't talk about things are two different ways, and you're starting to make me rethink my entire attitude about words."

~ ~ ~

Bailey stands beside the Wrecking Tree Restaurant and Bakery on Red Rooster Cay in the Bahamas Out Islands and inserts coins with her right hand from the cache of change she holds in her left. The sticky phone is cradled with her bent neck.

"Hey Boss."

"Hey Boo. Let me guess—you can't get a flight out."

"You think I'm kidding. Call and see for yourself, Sonny Boy."

"It's still two days before Christmas," he says.

"Not happening, Boss. There's a cluster 'til Tuesday. Come for New Year's."

"Where are you?"

"Red Rooster Cay. The Pilot House. It's the same deal—same back of the truck transport, same dog, same bicycles. I've already staked out the front bedroom but you can have the bike with straight handlebars."

"Now that's what I call incentive. . . . If I left on the 29th that would only give me five days in Kirk's Bluff."

"You'll be ready by then. Tell the home folks Merry Christmas. I'm at a phone booth and the lines might be long."

"I'm not telling anybody anything."

"Thanks, Boss."

"I'm sure Cecil will be at our house for Christmas dinner if you want to call then and leave him a message."

"Thanks, Boss," she says again.

"You and your daddy are a pair of stubborn asses."

"Thanks, Boss."

"Call him," Ben says. "For fuck's sake, Bailey, it's Christmas."

~ ~ ~

The low brick wall is patched with masonry cement, leaning in places, crumbling in others. Same with the headstones. The moss dripping canopy from two massive live oaks nearly shades the entire little Belfair Baptist Church cemetery, burial grounds for many Simmons forbears, including George's mother and father. Each grave is now marked with a bright red poinsettia, flamboyant in the clear winter light.

George and Ben sit side by side on a wrought iron bench and admire their work. It is how they've spent the afternoon of Christmas Eve, rain or shine, every year of Ben's life, including those for which he holds no recollection. In warm enough winters they load the truck with thirty-seven poinsettias carefully tucked under a light canvas tarp, and when the forecast is cold they forego the tropical blooms and furbish the graves in boughs of pine and cedar tied with shining sprigs of bright-berried holly.

They, father and son, watch cardinals and chickadees take turns at the bird feeder they've filled, content in quiet company.

"Do you still recite poetry when you run?"

"Yessir, to steady my pace on the long hauls," Ben says.

"What's the one about the jar?" George says. "The one where the fella doesn't quite get the girl but is supposed to be content that at least she won't do him dirt?"

Ben recites the passage from "Ode on a Grecian Urn" and then George has him quote the part about "unheard melodies" being "sweeter."

"Son," George says, "it may well be that a Mozart or a Miles Davis can conjure music sweeter than others can actually hear, but for the rest of us no imagination is sweeter than being in the room when Miles Davis blows 'Sketches of Spain.'"

Ben laughs. Says, "I suppose you're right about that."

"I believe I am," George says. "And I believe I'm right when I tell you it's nice that the girl in that poem will always be 'fair,' but such consolation won't keep a man warm at night."

Ben sees he's been got, shakes his head. "Listen, Pop," he says. "It's not like some novel, some movie scene where I say how I feel and we run off down the beach happily ever after."

George cocks his head Ben's way but holds his tongue.

"A best friend means a whole lot more to her than a man," Ben says. "She's got all the men she could ever want, but she's only got one of me."

"Couldn't the man be the best friend too?"

"Seems so to me, but she'll never believe it."

"Must chafe an awful lot."

"You have no idea."

George cuts his twinkling eyes to his son, reaches over and grabs his leg how-the-horse-eats-corn. "I just don't want to see you cold of a night up there in Philly," he says.

"Well, sir." Ben grabs his father's leg back and they squeeze to see who can take it the longest. "I wouldn't worry about that if I were you. Philadelphia may be the city of Brotherly Love, but the sisters can be a downright pleasure too."

"Well anyhow," George says as they release in a tie, "what I want is a grandbaby—and chivalry won't get me that."

~ ~ ~

On Christmas morning Bailey combs the beach gathering junk and gems. From the heaping collection she adorns the fledgling Abaco pine in front of the cottage with frays of coral, broken shells, scraps of aluminum cans that have shredded in the surf. From her suitcase she unpacks the tattered Eskimo doll she's brought as an angel for the tree top. When she unwraps the tissue there's also a small box in silver foil with a twice folded note that says, "They remind me of your eyes. Please know that I love you." In the box is a pair of simply set aquamarine earrings. That afternoon she swims and walks the beach again. "I love you too, Padgett," she writes in the sand, hopeful the message will somehow reach him.

~ ~ ~

"God, that was fun."

Bailey reaches for the light switch, shoes in one hand, big straw bag in the other. She sets these things in a pile by the back door and rinses her dusty feet with the water hose at the steps.

"Yes ma'am it was," Ben says as he gives her a small towel.

"I forget how gorgeous you are, my dark skinned Adonis." She hands the towel back when she's done. "Those island girls were ready to jump some Benjamin bones."

"Hush, Boo." He springs toward her and snaps the towel at her tanned ankles.

"You hush, you fool nigra."

"You hush, you crazy Eskimo."

"That would be Eskimo octoroon to you, mister."

She laughs and unloads tin foiled takeouts and a handful of cassette tapes from the island bag.

"How many tapes did you buy?"

"How many places did we go?"

"It was a long night."

"It *was* a long night? Does that mean we can't play this new music and dance in the sand?"

"We do have neighbors, dear."

"Those people? Hell, they're from Carolina too. They'll be over here shagging before we can crank the music."

"Bailey Martin, are you buzzed?"

"Sho 'nuff, Ben Simmons. Pick a tape and let's dance."

"How about Barefoot Man," he says, and balances the boom box in a lounge chair.

There is enough moon to make the sea shimmer and they kick up sand for the boogie side of the tape, but one song into the slow dance side the stars swirl a bit too quickly and they agree to call it a night. They've skirted this fire dance since adolescence and soon they will lie in beds separated by a paneled wall, each feeling the slow beat of the music and the pulse of the other's swaying body. Slow dance and alcohol is a combination they've avoided all these years, and now they shift from the ever unspoken subject.

"We're set to fish with Lincoln on the 2nd," she says, "so that leaves tomorrow and New Year's Eve and the First—and I call New Year's Eve."

She steps into the water and watches him fasten one of the hammocks.

"Okay," he says. "I pick tomorrow and we'll split the difference on New Year's Day."

"Deal. How shall we spend tomorrow?"

Flecks of bright green phosphorous sputter as she swirls her feet in the shallows.

"Boat's lined up?"

"It'll be at the dock in the morning. I've been tagging along with the Sawyers."

"Okay," he says. "Then let's have breakfast, walk the beach, park our asses in these hammocks and read. Take the boat to Cap'n Jacks for grouper roti and fried plantains, skin dive at No Name Reef, come back to shower, and then park our asses in these hammocks for a nap. Eat cracked conch and drink beer and pick up where we left off on the gin rummy tournament. You?"

"Alright. I say let's get up on New Year's Eve and take a morning swim. Bicycle into town for some of that coconut bread. Gather a few mangos, pick up some of Miss Mary's conch fritters, pack the boat, and find a reef we don't know. Then find another we don't know. And then another. Watch sunset, come back for lobster and conch salad—on the beach—and swim to the mooring buoy at Sea Gardens Reef before midnight to watch fireworks from the water."

~ ~ ~

And that is exactly what they do.

After the fireworks and champagne, Ben fills a pot for the peas to soak, and on New Year's morning they stand in the surf at sunrise, clasp each other's hand high over their heads like champs and think about the year ahead and what they want that year to bring. A miscellany of dreams with myriad possibilities to unravel.

Bailey cleans the collards and warms the Johnny Cakes—a gift from the bakery ladies. Ben steams rice for the Hoppin' John and, what the hell, why not more lobster. 'Tis the season, and they bought plenty when they provisioned.

They dress as if they'll be dining out, crisp linens in the tropical sun, and eat at the picnic table in the shade of coconut palms. Bailey has decorated with a bright floral cloth and clusters of bougainvillea. With the white sand and blue water background no one would call it anything but paradise.

Dessert is mango sorbet and guava duff—and chocolate.

"That was a mighty fine New Year's feast," Bailey says. "How'd you like to have Christmas?"

"Let's do it," he says.

Ben clears the plates, and Bailey brings a single red ball from the tree she's trimmed and loops it on a seagrape bush beside the picnic table. She's made him a huge set of windchimes from prize shells and driftseeds collected as she's combed the beach these past days. The nickernuts and baybeans are native, but the horse eyes and sea hearts have floated on trade winds far from their jungle homes.

They put Bailey in mind of childhood tangerines and she wonders how far she and Ben could have floated if they'd been allowed out-of-bounds—or at least whether the tangerines and sea hearts might have come upon one another somewhere out in the Gulf Stream. In honor of their adventures past, present, and future, she's attached a Satsuma at the bottom of each of the seven strands of the chimes.

The shells and driftseeds are connected with fishing line and descend from a smooth curve of driftwood. Ben runs his fingers across the wood and touches each of the shells and pods, then picks the perfect limb to catch the sea breeze and carefully hangs the gift.

"Thank you," he says, and kisses her forehead.

For her there is a hand bound book he has made from photographs of her artwork.

"Oh my god, Boss. This is beautiful. How did you do this?"

She strokes the cover and beams.

"It was your idea really. When you sent me the photo of the portrait I thought how great it would be to have images of all your work. We've never done that. So I tracked down as many paintings as I could from the receipts and had some kid from the art school photograph the ones I could find around New York and Philly. People were totally helpful. Some sent me photographs themselves—and they were all satisfied collectors, by the way."

"What a wonderful gift."

She flips slowly through the pages, reminded of efforts long forgotten.

"Not all of it's there," he says. "But I made it so we can fill in pages. Happy Christmas, Booney."

"Happy Christmas, Bossman," she says with a long hug.

He props the book upright on the table.

"It's impressive work," he says. "You know that don't you?"

"I'm feeling that way more and more. It's been good to take the classes. At least I understand the rules I'm breaking."

A long swim later, Ben stretches into a hammock and Bailey lies nearby on a straw mat in the warm sun.

"I wish you hadn't spent Christmas by yourself, Boo."

"Christmas, schistmas. I've been working on my tropical tan."

"Bullshit," he says. "I know you've been lonesome. What happened to loverboy anyway?"

The cross-patterned ropes pry into his shoulders and he adjusts to a new position.

"Nothing happened. He spent Christmas with his sons, just like he should have. And I've never been scared of lonesome."

She leans on her elbow and squints to where he's blocked in the sun.

"What's happening with Padgett is big," she says.

"You thought it was big with Murphy."

"It was big with Murphy. But it wasn't for the long haul. He knows that."

"And this is bigger?"

In the corner of his eye he sees her watching him.

"Yes," she says. "It's bigger. Way bigger."

Now he turns to her.

"Be careful, Boo."

"You always say that."

"Then how about this? Don't get in over your head before you know where you're swimming."

She laughs, rolls the mat, and wallops the bottom of the hammock.

"I'm already there," she says. "But I can swim over my head, remember? Now come with me. I've got something to show you."

They swim a hundred yards or so through the lush eel grass, watch a pair of eagle rays unsettle themselves from the white sand and fly away on elegant wingbeats. Bailey follows them, trance-like, repeating the rhythm of their slow motion flaps with the elongated gestures of her arms. Her body channels into the flow of each wingbeat and she follows until they're clouded in deep water.

As she swims back to Ben he can see her smile even with the snorkel in her mouth. He smiles himself and makes an O with his thumb and index finger. Okay, she gestures back, and points to a patch of reef where blue tangs move in unison through purple and yellow sea fans, past vibrant parrot fish scraping coral for lunch.

Farther out there's a ledge where the deeper, swifter current cools the water around them and Bailey points again, this time toward a fair sized nurse shark barely moving and completely visible. She continues in that direction, but Ben grabs the tip of her fin and tugs hard. Come on, she gestures, but he shakes his head with an insistent no and won't let go of her fin. The shark, apparently unconcerned, slowly swishes its tail as a remora settles onto its sandpaper skin.

"What the hell are you doing," Ben says when he splashes to the surface. "The idea is to swim *away* from sharks—have you lost your mind?"

He breathes hard and shakes water from his ears.

"The Sawyers showed me where it hangs out," she says. "I got close enough to touch it Wednesday." She treads water and laughs.

"Yes, you've lost it," he says.

"I'm scared of it. That's why I want to come close."

She reaches for her long braid and readjusts the elastic hair tie that's loosened in the water.

"It's a nurse shark, Boss. It's not gonna mess with us."

"So now you're good with sharks?"

"No, but I like it at the edge. Come on," she says, "they showed me where a turtle lives too."

~

An afternoon squall brings them in from the beach and they sit at one end of the dining table assembling a puzzle of vintage airplanes in flight and drinking rum drinks with pineapple and lime. Bailey finds pink swizzle sticks and flowery paper parasols in the pantry and adds them to their cocktails. They toast the New Year, and when the umbrellas become impossible, Ben wipes the wooden toothpicks and pushes them into crossover sections of Bailey's braid. He's already picked hibiscus for her hair.

"Very festive," he says.

"Thanks, Boss. Remember when I wanted to be a NOAA storm pilot?"

"Sure," he says. "I also remember when you wanted to be Jacques Cousteau."

"Still do. What I really want is to be Jacques Cousteau *and* a hurricane hunter."

"Cousteau I get, but I never understood the NOAA thing."

"Are you kidding me? Chasing hurricanes? Riding the eye of the storm?"

She finds the piece of cloud that closes the outer frame of the puzzle and wraps her knuckles twice on the table as she sets it in place.

"Fun like a shark, huh?"

"Exactly," she says. "Think of all the things pilots and deep divers see—cloud heads and underwater mountain ranges."

"You do remember we were terrified of sharks?"

"We were kids," she says.

"We were smart," he says.

The skies clear briefly, but before they gather towels and sunglasses more rain comes, harder now, driven with stinging sheets of wind. The ceiling fans slow and the light over the stove flickers and outs. Island living. The cottage is paneled with deep finished Abaco pine—walls, ceilings, cabinets, and floors—and when they light the paraffin lanterns the den glows with honeyed comfort.

Bailey gathers stray cards from the deck they left on the porch, packs them into the box, and leans into the open French doors. When she closes her eyes she feels the lightning dilate her pupils.

"God, Boss, those summer storms. Big rolls of thunder and lightning slaps. Mom and Retta would hug us close and make it a lullaby. Nothing in my world has ever made it okay like hard rain on the tin roof when we were kids."

He stands beside her and waits. She's talked more about the restlessness this past couple of days than she has in years.

"They say that uneasy feeling you get in a bad thunderstorm has to do with magnetic fields in your body and barometric pressure, but I go around with that feeling so much of the time. It's not about happy. It's a nag, that's all, but it makes the world unsettled. Maybe it's part of what there is with Padgett . . . he's not comfortable in his skin either, but somehow together . . . I don't know, it helps."

Stands beside her, waits.

"Anyway, I loved looking out at the gray and listening to Mom and rain on the roof, having a reason for being out of sorts. Don't you see? The rest of the time there's no excuse for feeling like a storm."

Stands beside her.

"When it would finally start to calm, like this, the in-between time when the storm's over but the world hasn't quite gone back to normal—that's the part I love best—when you've gotten so used to hearing the rain you don't notice it's only falling off the trees. You look out and the water's flat calm and the birds start to sing."

Waits.

"But I think I'm the only one who wishes for more thunder. As much as I love the birds, I find myself hoping they'll be quiet and let the storm sing."

"Do you hear the birds now, Booney?"

"Yes."

"Do you wish they'd stop?"

"No, Boss. I don't. It's always good with you. But I can't live my whole life in the kiddy pool."

"Maybe not, but you can't go off the deep end either."

"Oh, that's cute. That's a good one." She claps, stomps, laughs while she's stomping. "There's nobody in this whole wide world that quietly gives me shit like you do."

"There's more time on the meter if you need it."

She rises on tiptoes, pulls the long strand of her braid straight over her head and twirls herself with it.

"Will you tell me something, Boss?"

"Sure," he says.

"What the hell are we doing moping around on the first day of the new year?"

"I think that's what the mockingbirds are asking."

"Alright," she says. "I've had enough sharks and whining. You pick."

"Bluff House horseshoe tournament or dance contest at the Blue Bee," he says.

"Why not both?"

"Let's get going then," he says. "We're burning daylight."

~ ~ ~

Some mornings before work Padgett comes to the loft early, not even sunup, and slips into bed with her. He brings something warm from the bakery and makes coffee while she fluffs the pillows and they eat side by side and talk about the day—her project for art class, if she's volunteering at the pool later, whether he's in the field or at Langley, if he'll be with her or the boys for dinner or if the four of them can spend time. He draws her bath and shakes crumbs from the bed while she makes his lunch then soaks in the claw foot tub nestled into the back pocket of the aquarium cross hatch.

They spend week nights watching Bergman and Huston movies or listening to each other's music. Sometimes they face one another on opposite ends of the couch with bare feet touching and read. When he makes dinner it's a rotation of grilled steak, country fried steak, and ribs. A lot of potatoes. Camp food.

"All that bird hunting and you can't cook quail?"

"Sure," he says, "but I lost the taste for it."

With the boys they go to ball games and explore museums. At Air and Space Danny's favorite is the climb-aboard rocket ship and Michael's is the Enola Gay. At the Natural History Museum, it's all about dinosaurs. Wherever they are, Danny runs ahead to make sure he sees everything first, and Michael does the best he can to be the grown up older brother.

One Sunday afternoon at the National Gallery, Danny gives Bailey the best compliment she's ever had about her artwork when he gravitates to Kandinsky's *Sea Battle* and says this is like your stuff—only I like yours better.

They've formed an Around-the-World Club that tries different ethnic food, but unless it's the four of them Padgett usually votes to spend evenings at the loft. Yet no matter how late he stays, even into the night, he without exception returns to his house in case the boys need him.

# Bearing Straight

When Michael and Danny are at Disney World for spring break with their mother and cousins, Bailey takes Padgett home to Kirk's Bluff for the first time. Well, home but not all of home. They'll stay on May Isle, the small hammock where Merissa and Cecil built a cabin early in their marriage with the intention, especially Merissa's intention, to make it their home place.

But when time came for Bailey to be born Cecil was offshore and Merissa couldn't start the skiff motor. Instead she rowed to the mainland dock and would go no farther. Merissa called for Retta, who was too far to hear but came anyway and the baby—she, Bailey—was born in the rowboat afloat on the Jericho River. It's a point of pride for her that she was both conceived and birthed on the water.

Henrietta had been midwife to plenty of babies and Merissa never had any intention of delivering in a hospital, so everyone was happy about the situation but Cecil. Merissa was willing to take the risks of island living but Cecil was not. He went through the war with the sustaining belief that his service was to make life safe for his family, and he couldn't abide the worrying about his wife and child while he was at sea. He wouldn't have it.

They compromised. Moved into Cecil's family home on the bluff across the river but kept the place on May Isle. Since the cabin and dock were on the remote back side of the island—a site chosen by Merissa for its beauty and seclusion both—there would now be a dock and boathouse built on the front side as well. Much closer to the mainland, much easier to get to shore if need be.

Merissa would load Bailey and Ben and whatever friends might be around and boat over for day trips. When they talk about the "glory of god," Merissa told them as they watched osprey dive into the water and dolphins dive out of it, this is what they mean.

May Isle was alive with heron and egret rookeries, deer and raccoons, and creeks of Jericho were filled with fish and dolphin, the occasional shark and turtle, alligator and stingray. Shrimp and crabs galore, oysters and clams. Sometimes Cecil came too and it felt like camp. They'd spend the night and encircle long blazing fires to roast weenies and marshmallows and listen to Merissa weave stories or strum her mandolin and sing. Sometimes Retta came and they all danced and at least tried to sing. Even Mister George bent his rule about boats when it came to May Isle, saying across the river is hardly the same as out to sea.

Now Bailey gets to show it all to Padgett—a son of Carolina but in no way a river rat. It's early March, with one of those bigger than imagination blue skies, still enough nip in the air for early morning sweatshirts. Bailey had phoned MoJo two weeks before asking that he take Merissa's skiff out of storage and over to the marina to have the motor tuned, saying she might be down that way some time in the next month. To just leave it at the marina unless Cecil had a problem with that. I'll ask him if I need to, MoJo had said.

Now Ray at the boatyard tells them as long as they're riding past Bull Island and not through the cut, they ought to fish the hole under old man Pinckney's dock, that you could bet on the trout being there once the tide gets a good ebb to it.

She's raw energy, excited to be in home waters, anxious to show him the Jericho and May Isle—all of it. There's plenty of daylight and fresh trout would be perfect for dinner so they idle into a creek, cast for bait, and drop anchor just down from the Pinckney dock. They adjust lines, she finding comedy in his freshwater tactics, bait hooks, and zing along the edge of the bank. Padgett fishes the bottom with buckshot and Bailey fishes the top with a cork. Once they're still enough for the sun to find them they pull off sweatshirts and settle into the river sounds.

"Want to bet?"

"On what?" She plops an easy cast between the pilings.

"First, biggest, and most," he says.

"Depends on what we're betting."

"Whoever catches the first won't have to clean any of them."

"Alright," she says. "What else?"

"Whoever gets the biggest cruises while the other one cooks."

"Fair enough. What about for most?"

"You call it."

"I'll have to show you," she says, and makes the same face she used on Nicky Woods when she sweet talked him out of his cinnamon roll each Friday of the third grade.

"Deal," he says. "How about whoever loses the first bait buys us a round?"

"Okay."

She loses her shrimp on the fourth cast, reels in, unscrews the thermos cap, and pours a cup of steaming coffee for them to share.

"What about the rum?"

"You want rum?"

"You got a problem with that?" He slams the rod across the gunwale and rocks the boat.

Ugly edge, but he catches it. She tries to.

"No, Padg, I don't have a problem with that. I was just thinking coffee."

The waters settle and before long old man Pinckney's drop pays off. Bailey catches the first one, a nice speckled trout, well over the fourteen inch minimum. Padgett reels in the biggest, a redfish close to three pounds, and Bailey lands another half dozen before the gnats get bad and they pull up anchor.

She weaves past sandbars, keeping to the big channel with the ease of instinct. There isn't a bend of the Jericho she doesn't know happily and well. When dolphins come out of the water behind them she pulls back on the motor and grins.

"They'll come closer with the motor idling, she says. "Listen for the blow."

No sooner said than a full-sized dolphin curves slowly from the water and exhales a gentle whoosh of breath, and as she arcs a smaller, darker version rises beside her and exhales as well. Twice more they surface as Bailey makes their breath her own.

"A mother and newborn," she says. "Likely there's an auntie nearby."

"Beautiful."

"Oh yes. This time of year they're in these shallow creeks with the babies. Let's see if they follow us."

But the dolphins continue on their watery way and Bailey steers to the back side of May Isle.

Unloading the boat she yelps and whoops and makes twice as many trips to the cabin, goosing Padgett when she passes him on the way for more. They had tried not to over pack, but the more they talked and planned, the bigger the mound had gotten.

"Somebody's been here," Padgett says at the head of the dock when they walk up with the first load.

"It's okay," Padg. "Kids maybe—probably Mister George checking on the cabin."

"Recently. There are footprints and wheel tracks."

"Don't worry," she says. "I'm the only Goldilocks you'll find in your bed."

The cabin is small, built mostly of cypress. The boards are even, the lines true, but it nevertheless has the ramshackle look of a kid's tree house. The planks are weathered and the roof is tin, and Bailey has always thought it the most wonderful house in the world.

Once it's primed the well works like a charm. There's a cistern on the roof for rain water, a propane stove. It's one big room with the kitchen area to the right as you walk in the door, the sleeping area off to the left. Between is a red plaid sofa with pine end tables, two fat easy chairs and a hatch cover coffee table. The bathroom juts from the bedroom side. Thick braided rugs cover the heart pine floor and there's a stone hearth fireplace that doubles onto the porch. The inside walls are the outside walls, and there are huge timber beams across the ceiling.

Six paned windows alternate with sections of cypress walls on three sides of the cabin, and the roomy screened porch runs all the way across the front. On it are six rocking chairs, two cots, a porch swing, a card table and chairs, some driftwood, knickknacks, and a stack of split oak in one corner with fat lighter in a bucket beside it. Perfect. Henrietta has definitely sent Mister George.

The air has cooled by the time they organize the coolers, not quite nippy enough for a fire but Bailey starts one anyway. She makes the bed and mixes hush puppies while Padgett cleans the fish. She's peeled onions for the red rice, grated carrots, and is chopping cabbage for coleslaw when he comes in the kitchen door to nuzzle her with his chilled red nose and they walk out to watch sunset. More dolphins, five of them now, take turns scalloping the river's edge on the incoming tide.

"You can pretty well count on seeing them along this stretch of the river no matter what," Bailey says. "Certain places seem to draw them. That's one reason Mom picked this spot for the cabin."

The temperature dips once the sky purples so Padgett goes for a bottle of red wine and brings sleeping bags. She settles onto his chest and they lie in the quiet chill listening to the long river beneath them as the sky opens wide with shimmering stars and a scythe of silver moon.

An hour later Padgett wakes stiff-limbed and goes up to check the fire where the rice cooks. Coals are barely glowing but the rice has scalded and stuck to the bottom of the cast iron pot. His urge is to hurl all of it—rice and pot—into the wall, but he remembers something his mother told him, so instead he settles an upside down cup into the rice, wraps the handle with a dish towel and moves it to the counter, then stokes the embers and puts on the water kettle. Bailey feels him missing and comes in to fry the fish, best ever. They stuff themselves, leave the dishes, take pillows to the dock and fade into solid sleep as the slow moon lowers into love. In the first stir of dawn she wakes before shapes take hold and smiles, knowing exactly where she is.

~ ~ ~

A pack of hunting dogs bay as they walk to the house and in the clearing Bailey sees the practiced woman grooming her dirt yard.

"Retta," she calls when they're in earshot.

Henrietta Simmons stills her rake and squints.

"Oh Lord," she says, "looky here what the tide washed up."

The two laugh in kinship and embrace in the swell of stories bygone and beyond, pulled together in a long rocking embrace by love on the other side of words.

"Looky here. Looky here," she keeps saying as Bailey sways in the great arms of that tall walker, woman of roots.

Retta turns to Padgett and says, "This girl sure looks fine. You got anything to do with that?"

"Not sure I can take any credit, Mrs. Simmons."

"Henrietta, son. And you?"

"Turner," he says. "Padgett Turner."

Henrietta takes his hand in both of hers, turns to Bailey and says, "I know it's your stomach brought you to see me, child. You two go sit and I'll see what I can find."

"George is at the house," she calls after them as she strides toward an outbuilding at the edge of the clearing.

"Mister George," Bailey says into the screen door as they climb the front steps. A voice rather like that of John Wayne drifts from the windows and doors. A more direct one says, "What can I do for you?"

"It's Bailey, Mister George, Retta sent us up."

"Well I'll be," he says when he opens the screen door dressed for work but in his bedroom slippers. "Damned if it ain't. Retta said."

He is a spry, wiry little Bantam rooster of a man, bespectacled, a perpetual spring in his step. He opens his arms to Bailey as would a dance partner and the two of them make three twirls before they hug.

"My-oh-my," he says. "My-oh-my."

Bailey introduces the men and George gestures to the hide covered rocking chairs. He slides Retta's seed trays out of the way—almost ready for Good Friday planting.

"Hold on a minute," George says before lighting onto his seat. "I've got something you'll like." Bailey listens to him jingle the change in his pocket as he walks to the kitchen, an ever and always sound of childhood, just like Retta's raking.

George reappears holding a pint bottle with a partially peeled Seagram's Seven label.

"Elderberry," he says and hands the bottle to Padgett. "Fresh batch."

Padgett opens and smells it and George says hold on another minute, I do have some manners. This time he returns with three jelly jars that he sets on the porch rail. He pours a ration in each and the three of them nod to each other, raise their glasses, and drink.

"That's what I'm talking about," George says.

The mild sweet taste of the elderberry wine is a surprise of old for Padgett, a taste he knew as a young man from pulls allowed at hunt camps from time to time if the weather was raw or the blood running. He sips and thinks of his grandfather as Bailey and George speak of their own people. Retta leans and pulls in the garden as goats and dogs and cats skitter and doze.

The porch looks like a museum exhibit featuring the development of television. Seven of them are stacked against the wall, dating back to the Fifties. There's also a satellite dish beside the house and the voice in the background is confirmed as John Wayne when they hear Rooster Cogburn say that life ain't an easy game, sister.

"Should we help Miss Henrietta?"

Before Bailey can answer George says, "She'll let you know when she needs you. Sit tight and enjoy that elderberry."

"Will do," Padgett says. "Hits the spot."

George turns to Bailey. "Everything tight on the island?"

"Yes sir, thank you."

"Well, your daddy's at camp."

"Yes sir. Thank you for the wood too."

"Welcome," he says. "Retta said."

When Henrietta draws near the house her arms are filled with big waxy emerald collard greens.

"Would you wash these while I get a chicken," she says to the newcomer.

Minutes later Padgett hears the cackled scrambling and looks out the kitchen window to see Henrietta's strong arms ring the neck of a chicken with a single motion, then bang it onto the chopping stump and ax off its head. His stomach gnarls and when he looks again she's already plucking. He watches this woman and loathes the way his weakness works.

When Henrietta comes in to finish cleaning the chicken he isn't done with the collards. She sets the bird to the side, turns on the oven and stands beside Padgett, tearing greens into little pieces as she rinses them.

"I always pull out the big stem in the middle. Some folks don't," she says with a sly smile. "But then again some folks' greens don't melt in your mouth either. You've never cooked collards before, son?"

"No ma'am. I've eaten plenty though—maybe not this many."

"This mess of greens will cook down to one bowlful. Believe me, they won't go to waste."

She simmers chunks of bacon in a large cast iron pot and when she lifts the lid to stuff the greens Padgett's appetite soars. She has him rub oil into eight sweet potatoes and place them in the oven while she rinses the fat chicken, seasons it, puts celery and onions into its cavity, wraps it in tin foil and places it one shelf up from the potatoes.

When she's done she turns to Padgett and says, "I couldn't help noticing there's no ring on your hand. A free man in shackles. There a reason for that?"

He stumbles unspoken words, red faced, and finally says, "Yes ma'am, there are all kinds of reasons."

Henrietta wipes her firm hands on her apron and places them on Padgett's shoulders. She looks long into his brown eyes and says, "You don't have to tell me what they are. I can see." Then she whoops a big laugh at herself and says, "Not that you'd be obliged to tell an old woman your business anyway."

They unclutter the counters and join Bailey and George. As the kitchen smells grow richer and mingle, the elders weave story into story of Bailey as a child, of the mischief that managed to follow Bailey and Ben, of her reign as state swim champ, of the Olympic trials.

"Olympic trials? Had no idea," Padgett says.

"Not as impressive as it could have been," Retta says. "Tell him what stopped you."

Padgett looks to Bailey, then Henrietta. George chuckles. Bailey shrugs her shoulders and smirks.

"Chlorine," she says.

"Chlorine?"

"Chlorine," Bailey says. "I could swim all day, faster than most, farther than many, but they don't let you train in the river."

You'd think Bailey was their own begotten daughter if it weren't for the shade of her skin and the mementos touting Benjamin Simmons in every nook and cranny. His own glory moments from elementary school track meets to last spring's triathlon.

"Come help me," Henrietta says to Padgett. "Let them catch up. By the time we set the table everything will be ready."

She pulls the chicken from the oven and replaces it with the deviled crabs she took from the deep freeze on the back porch earlier then leads Padgett down the trophy lined hall. The home they walk through is a curious mixture of old and new, fancy and modest. The structure itself is hardly more than a shack but in it are modern appliances and beautiful furnishings.

In the dining room a highboy is filled with Limoges china and Waterford crystal, sterling candlesticks in several pairs. He takes plates and flatware from shelves and drawers and Henrietta plunders a chest for linens. She hands him the ones they'll be using but continues to dig.

"Here we go," she says, and unwraps tissue from an exquisite set of embroidered handkerchiefs. In the center of each is a little bouquet of violets. There are four of them and she feathers one with her fingertips, hands him the other three.

"I did these for my hope chest. Seems like a hundred years ago," she says. "I want you to have them."

As he opens his mouth to protest he catches the kindness in her eyes and says thank you instead. Awkwardly he holds the delicate work and says quietly, "My mother's name was Violet."

"I know that," she says. She clasps her big knotted fingers part way around his forearm and continues her solemn whisper.

"When it's time to move on you have to go, son. Remember that." She squeezes the arm with certainty then steps away from him to call Bailey and George to supper.

Bailey eats until she moans with pleasure and when Henrietta slips into the pantry and comes back with the chocolate cake she's made ahead for Sunday dinner Bailey moans even more but eats it just the same, teasing Retta about holding back on her.

"I know you and chocolate, girl. If you'd seen this before supper the rest of us would've had crumbs."

To Padgett she says, "I'd tell you she's always been a bad one to spoil her appetite, but the truth is the appetite's always there."

On the porch afterwards Bailey and Padgett sit in the wooden swing, the other pair in rockers. They listen to the chairs creak in the calm of early dark, enough light to witness each other's faces if they'd tried, and in the long drawn minutes Bailey says, "It's good to be home."

No one feels the need to say anything in reply.

"Oystering still good?" she says.

"You know it girl."

"Crabs?"

"Startin' to come in—peelers in a few weeks."

Quiet again as a chuck-will's-widow continues her plaintive call.

"Whatever happened to old Buster? Is he still crabbing?"

"Buster's dead, child. Drowned. Made a dolphin patch."

"Good Lord. I thought Buster could swim."

"Better than most of 'em," George says. "Whole lot better than most. Not with them boots sucking him down though. Them boots fill, you gone."

"How'd it happen, Mister George?"

"Out pulling traps by himself. Lost his balance, we reckon."

"I sure hate hearing that. I thought the world of old Buster."

"Like us all, girl. But Buster was gettin' on up there." George says. "All there is to know for sure is it's gonna be one thing before it's something else."

Bailey listens to his gentle voice, the warmth of Retta wrapped around her, and is certain that this place, this exact place where the river edges the sea is where the roots of the world are held fast.

When the time comes Henrietta packs them plates full of leftovers and George sends along an Old Gran Dad fifth of wine. Padgett tucks the tissue wrapped linens inside his jacket and beams the flashlight. The dogs bay again as soon as they step out of the clearing, and the last thing they hear is Henrietta calling them aggravating durn curs.

Hush comes and the home folks rock for a while longer.

"How's that sittin' with you?"

"There's a darkness to him," Retta says.

"Well, you sure seemed . . ."

"Seemed means nothing," Retta says. "She brought him here and it's way beyond seems. But every grin teeth don't mean laugh."

"He surely must stand Ben's bristles on end."

They listen to the boat start, the farthering quiet of it.

"Storm's brewing," Henrietta says. "All she can do is ride it out—'til she's ready to untie the moon and get past it."

~ ~ ~ ~ ~ ~ ~ ~ ~ ~ ~ ~ ~ ~ ~

## RETTA
### (1962)

*Something wasn't right. There should have been word they'd arrived safely. She'd rather take a beating than ride a jet airplane, but Henrietta knew something was not right. Just in case, she went through the rigmarole of telephoning Merissa's family who had heard nothing but were unworried, that being the mindset of outback Alaska.*

*Cecil was shrimping offshore in Georgia waters and Henrietta left George to get a message to him, not distress him, but tell him she thought Merissa and Bailey should have been there by now. That she'd gone on ahead and would telephone later to get word or give it.*

*She filled a small suitcase, packed food that would not spoil, and gathered the yellow trimmed Morning Star quilt, knowing for sure she'd get cold and more than likely she'd have to sleep on a floor somewhere along the Jim Crow way.*

*There were buses and airplanes, large and small. Ferry boats. Henrietta swore to herself she would never be contained in such spaces again and prayed to God she was right. Mistreated by more people in more places than even she would have believed, she set her mind and sat in back—or wherever the hell they wanted her to, as long as they got her there.*

*Forty-six hours later she was exhausted in Anchorage where she tried to find news, but her questions were paid little heed and her story even less. Then she thought to tell them that Merissa was her wealthy Missus and that she herself had been de-layed traveling in the colored section. Oh status—that opened some ears. She was taken to the hospital where Merissa slipped in and out of consciousness and was left to care for her mistress, the nurses relieved to have a maid cover their watch.*

*Carefully Retta placed the quilt across the bed and steeped the herbs she'd brought from her garden with hot water from the tap. She drew Merissa close, channeling the love of home into her frail body, rocking her through the delirium and easing sips of the brew into her parched lips. Soothingly, lovingly, Henrietta cradled her and spoke to her about Bailey and Cecil and the river and about herself and George and Ben, about fish fries and honeysuckle and the Carolina wren nesting in the fern basket.*

*And when the moment came that she saw the first flicker in Merissa's eyes, Hen-rietta left her to sleep and set out to find Bailey. The confusion of outrageous mis-communication was multifold, but by late afternoon a door was opened and Bailey ran into Retta's strong brown arms and cried in frightened disbelief, then cried with steadfast reassurance. Retta held her and hugged her and checked her head to toe, then carried her to the payphone to make the collect calls home.*

*Merissa was still sleeping when they got to the hospital but Bailey ran to her mother's bed and climbed onto it, burrowed into the quilt and wouldn't let go. Merissa felt the cling of her child and pulled her closer, disoriented and weary and grateful.*

*Retta dragged a chair to the foot of the hospital bed and unlaced Bailey's new traveling shoes, then she leaned onto the mattress where Bailey's little legs left a space and held one of her tiny sock feet and one of Merissa's slender feet and whispered love prayers until exhaustion took her. The door was cracked twice in the night but no one dared disturb them.*

~ ~ ~

*In Chenega, Adèle and Bear were overjoyed to see not only their daughter, who hadn't visited since before the baby was born, but also their cherished granddaughter. In private Henrietta told them what she knew and they listened patiently but held no space for tragedy in their overwhelming thankfulness. Bailey didn't leave her mother's side, nor did she utter a single syllable, but everyone flourished when she smiled.*

*Slowly Merissa came back to herself. She spoke with Cecil every other day and went for walks with Bailey each morning after breakfast. Henrietta spent time learning Chugach ways in the kitchen and in the forest. In the evenings, known only by the clock, as there was precious little in the way of nightfall, they gathered for food and music and dance, often circled with family and friends, and when the unshadowed moon grew full Merissa said it's time to go home.*

~ ~ ~

*The three of them rode the ferry to Bellingham and the train to Seattle and a cab to the automobile dealership where Henrietta brought forth the wad of money sewn into the waistband of her slip and counted out the down payment on what came to be known as the Solid Gold Cadillac. A 1962 Eldorado Biarritz convertible, fins and all. They went for ice cream and toured the brand new Space Needle at the World's Fair while George wired the rest of the money and then they loaded the space ship of a car and headed East, mother and daughter in the backseat, Henrietta at the wheel.*

*This was Henretta's first and last automobile trip across the continent. From then on she journeyed no farther west than New Orleans. But what a road trip it was. She took her sweet time chauffeuring while Bailey and Merissa nested and napped and healed in the sunshine. When night came they healed beneath the stars, and when it showered they rolled the top up and healed in the rain. Bailey wouldn't know her voice again until she heard Ben's but healing happened all the way home.*

*She listened to Merissa sing and read and tell magic stories and stories of family they'd been with in Alaska and family where they were going in Carolina and family that had gone ahead to the spirit world. Henrietta told stories of her own. They filled the child, and the places they saw imprinted such that when Bailey traveled those roads again she knew them as story roads. Words themselves prod and confuse and may not have truth in them, but in stories truth can always be found.*

*They took the high road and toured whatever sites Retta picked, loosely backtracking the path where Sacagawea led Lewis and Clark, across Washington and the tip of Idaho, into Montana—the most beautiful state—and on to Dakota where they veered this way and that. Sometimes the train ran alongside the road and sometimes it was horses, long mane and tails flying.*

*They had their pictures made at Glacier and Rushmore, Crazy Horse and Bear's Lodge, and they stopped at most every marker and roadside attraction between there and home, for even then Retta was fairly certain she'd not pass these ways again. As they had in Alaska, they witnessed marvels and majesty and much that would never be understood.*

*When they wheeled into Kirk's Bluff Retta handed George the keys to the Cadillac and said Happy Birthday. What could he do but grin and love it? He washed the road dust and peeled the sticker and drove it everywhere he went, still drives it this quarter century later. George Simmons, the old goat with the jingle in his pocket and a Solid Gold Cadillac. "You can call me Mister," he said when he cranked it for the first spin around Kirk's Bluff. Bailey took him at his word.*

~ ~ ~ ~ ~ ~ ~ ~ ~ ~ ~ ~ ~ ~

Now Henrietta reaches for George's hand without turning and says, "I'll leave you to your thoughts. I need to lock the hen house anyway."

He squeezes her fingers. "I'll be in after while," he says.

~ ~ ~ ~ ~ ~ ~ ~ ~ ~ ~ ~ ~ ~

## GEORGE
### (1962)

*She said wait here, I'll be back. Tell Cecil I see no reason for alarm but Merissa and Bailey have been delayed somewhere and I'm going to see.*

*Retta never sees reason for alarm but when George radioed, Cecil pulled in his nets and started back to shore. After dark though, Cecil radioed back to say the prop was slipping and they were limping on in. Was there any word? Nothing yet. Retta had phoned from Seattle and said no news is good news but she would keep on until there was something to tell. At daybreak Cecil used Saxon's ship-to-shore to say the prop finally fell off "Miss Merissa" so he was riding in with Jimbo on "Dixie" while his crew waited for another boat to fetch the part. That if there were a boat that ran on shrimp heads and sea water he'd buy it tomorrow.*

*As he had for most of his life, George watched for and listened to both of them, Cecil and Henrietta. She's the tough one. She knows what she's doing—and everybody else—and if it doesn't suit, she makes it so it does. You don't mess with Retta. You just move out of the way for that proud walker.*

*He'd be there waiting when they got back. Somebody's got to feed the dogs.*

~ ~ ~ ~ ~ ~ ~ ~ ~ ~ ~ ~ ~ ~

Bailey and Padgett finish leftovers for lunch on the far side of May Isle over-looking a wide spread of open marshlands.

"Ice is about gone," she says. "And we forgot the oreos."

"Lead the way."

They bait four crab traps with fish scraps and drop them along the mouth of the creek on the way to the marina. It's a warmer day but still cold enough for oysters, a treat they can harvest at low tide. An older dolphin with a long slit in its dorsal fin swims in the waters ahead.

"Sometimes they can't submerge fast enough to miss the props," she says. "People don't give a damn—some people. Nobody's ever made me under-stand the need to rush on the river."

"To each his own," Padgett says.

"Sure," she says, "as long as it's not you getting run over."

"People like speed," he says.

"Then let 'em take some—or go to the race tracks."

When they get to the marina Bailey walks ahead while Padgett ties the boat. He starts up the ramp, then stops and watches her. Her hair's in a long braid down her back and tawny wisps of it are windblown around her head. He smiles at the sureness in her step, at the way the dock hands turn to watch her, at her not having a care in the world just then except whether the marina stocks oreos or not.

~

That night they sleep with sunburned faces and salt behind their ears, their bodies cupped and uncovered. When the sun spreads through the tree line she wakes Padgett. There are no curtains across the front of the cabin and only sheers on the side windows, so the room is washed in amber as they make love in the tender first light and fall back to sleep until midmorning.

After bacon and coffee and very strange pancakes, Bailey decides they should have a vegetable garden. Her mother's daffodils, long ago bulbs wait-ing for the right season, have popped in these first warm days of the year and Merissa's perennial garden is overflowing with herbs. There are enough tools in the storage shed, so Bailey digs and hoes and thinks about what they might plant while Padgett climbs onto the roof to patch the stove vent. He'd looked up from inside and seen daylight peeping through where it shouldn't have and they bought pitch at the marina.

He sits on the roof crest when he's done and watches Bailey fight a big root that's holding fast. Wishes they'd be there often enough to tend a garden but knows that what she's doing will come to nothing.

"Come see what I can see," he calls down to her. "Bring the beer."

They sit on the peak of the roof looking out over May Isle and the Jericho River, Kirk's Bluff on the other side.

"Our kingdom," she says, and wipes dirt from her forehead. "Can we work in the garden tomorrow?"

"Sorry, kid," he says. "We really need to get going fairly early."

"Tomorrow's Friday. Don't the boys get back Sunday?"

"Yes," he says. "But I need to make sure I'm there when they do. You okay with that?" Machete in his tongue.

"No worries, Padg," she says. "We need to pull the crab traps, though." Attempt to deflect.

"There are worries, Bailey—and a trap is exactly what they feel like." No way around it.

"Don't get twisted up" she says. "We can go whenever you like—it's not a problem."

"It is a problem. And I hear the sarcasm—don't think that I don't."

He crushes the beer can and sticks it in his back pocket.

"You get so worked up," she says. "Tell me what it is."

"*It* is you. *It* is them. *It* is that I'm trapped in the middle."

"There's no trap, Padgett. You love me and you love your children and—"

"—and I can't have it all."

"Why not?"

"Because the pull to you is one way, and the pull to them is another. I can't go both directions."

"Why can't it all be the same direction?" She reaches for his shoulder but he turns aside.

"Because they have a mother that won't let that happen—"

"—But—"

"—But nothing, Bailey. I know you think it can be fixed, that everything can be fixed, but it can't. You'll never understand how it is with her—or why. She asked for emergency numbers here, your numbers, before they left for Florida—but that's as far as it's ever gonna go with her."

"It's something," Bailey says. "It's a start."

"It's about the boys—not about me, and certainly not about you." He gathers the tar bucket and tools. "I'm done talking about it."

"Please don't get so angry, Padg. It'll work out. Why don't you pack up the gear and I'll go pull the traps. We can at least take the crabs by Retta's. She'll appreciate them."

~ ~ ~

"Hey Boss."

"Hey Boo."

"Just lettin' you know I'm going steady."

"Oh?"

"Padgett's given her my phone numbers."

"Who?"

"The ex—Liz—the boys' mom. It's crazy she hasn't had them, but anyway, now she does. Here in Alexandria and at home in Kirk's Bluff."

"Seriously, Boo? I've got a waiting room full of patients."

"Aw hell, Boss. I'm excited about this."

"Yes, I've heard. You're hooked."

"Not just hooked—line and sinker too."

"And all the other fish in the sea?"

"Don't need it done. Seriously."

"And you're feeling good in your skin?"

"I thought you had to go."

"Are you? Tell me, Bailey. I want to hear."

"Alright. I smooth and tug but the fit's never quite right. It's like leopard skin on a seal."

"So he hasn't cured that?"

"No, he hasn't cured that. But I've told you before it's something we both understand."

"Listen, Boo . . . . . . . . . . . . . . Can you hear me?"

"You're not saying anything."

"Do I need to?"

~ ~ ~

Jake's Gym is about as far as Ben can get from a sterilized office, the disinfected hospital, his unsullied life. Once upon a time the picture windows must have allowed passersby and wide-eyed boys quite the spectacle of sparring boxers, prime men pummeling speed balls and pounding punch bags. Shiny stainless weight machines and freshly mopped linoleum floors. Smokin' Joe Frazier, another son of the Carolina Lowcountry, is said to have trained there for a time.

These days a skanky mop bucket leans in the corner it hasn't left for years. Windows are smudged and smeared with decades of hot dog fingers taping up prize fight posters and flyers for in-house boxing matches, lost pet pictures and want ads. A miscellany of broken down equipment and broken down men are scattered about the darkened space, spotlit here and there by the occasional fresh light bulb. Clanking doors open into dank sweat and stale beer, cigarettes and onions, and the whole place reeks of second rate frustration.

But it also smells of prowess—the persistence of men out to prove something. Ben loves it—the heckling old timers, the stink, the power and pain. He comes here instead of taking lunch some days. Other days after work.

Physician heal thyself.

When he's outside, running, it's different. Then it's about freedom and willpower and stamina. It's holding your head high and succeeding. Competition is irrelevant. It's the doing of it, the mastery of purpose. The relentless insistence to run pure. Pure. When the dark side is driven back he can run with wings that start out light and get heavy but turn light again before the run is over.

Jake's place is the purgatory that makes way for the wings.

Ben comes to lift weights and jab speedballs, but mostly to hammer the heavy bag. Would like it if medical evidence didn't keep him from the ring, but you can't help what you know.

Two of the could-have-been-but-never-weres have pulled up rusty kitchen chairs and straddle them backwards. They watch Ben and share a cigarette and a bag of soggy french fries.

"Doctor Man's got it going today." The one called Vern dips his fry in a catsup packet.

"Yessiree, that mister gentleman could knock out a mule's eye this fine morning." Dink, the scrawny one, grins through a snaggled eye tooth.

"Afternoon, Dink. This fine afternoon. Yeah, he's got it going all right. Knock 'em dead, Doctor Man."

Ben opens himself to the wrath, lets it run the ropes of his body. All the pent up ire. Infuriated punch after punch after punch after punch. Bastard, he bellows aloud after every third swing.

"Louder, boy," Dink hoots. "That's right, son, keep your feet grounded and frail hell out of it—whoever it is."

Ben craves the contact of skin, wants leather on leather to be leather on flesh. Sweat channels down his face and his primal gut calls slash every other punch now. He is a man on fire.

"Sure you don't want to get in that ring, Doctor Man?"

It's not the ring he wants. It's up in the face of that mother fucker jerking Bailey's chain. Mother fucker with no clue of the prize she's offering.

"Watch him." Vern crumples the french fry wrapper and drops it on the floor. "That right there is serious business."

"Hot almighty, boy, burn it up," Dink says.

Ben throws the punches harder and quicker, now with one long roar that drains every outraged pulse of his being. Mind and body. Spent.

"He'd have nailed that round, my friend."

"Right you are," Dink says. "I'd lay gravy on that."

Ben doesn't even hear them. He used to hang around and listen to their stories, eat a fat cheeseburger from next door. Not these days, though. These days he's still got to run. Take up wings before he forgets how to wear them.

# Delicate Bones

*Listen:*

Two weeks later, shortly after midnight on March 24, 1989, an oil tanker runs aground on Bligh Reef near Bailey's grandparents, homeland of the Chugach, homeland of many others. *Valdez*. The Exxon ship dumps 10.8 million gallons of crude oil into Prince William Sound. Quarts of oil? Forty-three million quarts of oil. Consider that. Casualties? These are conservative estimates. Not conservative as in to conserve something. As in underestimates.

Sea Otters: 2,800 oil saturated carcasses.

Harbor Seals: 300 oil saturated carcasses.

Seabirds: 250,000 oil saturated carcasses.

Bald Eagles: 900 oil saturated carcasses.

Harlequin Ducks: 1,000 oil saturated carcasses.

Drowned in thick black oil. Consider that.

Salmon? Herring? Uncountable.

And humans? At least four dead. Another 32,000 directly harmed by loss of livelihood. Loss of heart? Imagine.

When Ben calls Kirk's Bluff this time, there's no need for him to read from the *New York Times*. News of the disaster is everywhere.

Bailey travels to Alaska as quickly as stand-by flights can transport her. Now she sits at the feet of her grandparents, oil soaked and bone tired after three days of shore cleanup. Never mind the dead ones. The dying are the ones Bailey cannot reconcile. They won't stop washing ashore.

"Not even half a year ago I told you to watch where there is greed," Adèle says to Bailey. "This is what happens when avarice overflows. Alignak revisits. Now watch to see who cleans the mess." Adèle reaches for the hand of her husband, usually a man of very few words.

"We who make a life among all creatures are left to clean up the mess," Bear says. "And who will feed hungry mouths when the food lies in a slick of oil? We again."

He grows quiet but the words still come.

"There will be no wisdom gained for these people," he says. "Ten years from now Exxon will continue to turn profits, shameful billions of dollars, and life here will suffer many years beyond that. The cleanup will be abandoned but the damage will not stop."

~ ~ ~

A week later Bailey returns from the disaster scene to her grandparents' modest home, just as oil soaked, even more weary, and sits on the braided rug before the wood stove at the feet of her elders. Adèle once again brings the smoked fish and bread and insists that Bailey eat before she bathes. Bailey pleads with her grandparents to come away from this place of sorrow.

"In another life I would have flown from here," Adèle says. "But we cannot go—and you cannot stay forever."

Adèle takes the empty plate and hands Bailey two doubled garbage bags, one for the clothes that might be washed and one for the clothes that can't be salvaged. The latter is considerably larger. She places them near the mudroom door where food she's prepared for the front is stacked in cardboard boxes on top the washing machine. The tools Bear has repaired are in a crate atop the dryer.

The following week Bailey sits on the rug yet again and wipes a strand of her long hair. Her fingers come away slimy and dark and she softly rubs her thumb across the tips of them and stares. Adèle stoops to her granddaughter and draws her close. The tears of both women bead on Bailey's vest.

"You must choose to live," Adèle says. "I have told you this."

~ ~ ~

When Bailey leaves Alaska it is to Carolina she returns. It's been long enough. The pain of her mother's death stirred up with *Valdez* is more than she can abide. It is clear to her now that she's hoarded the pain, but it's not hers to hoard. It's theirs to share. Hers and Cecil's. She calls from Hartsfield and as the plane lands in Savannah she spots the solid gold Cadillac in the parking lot.

"Yessiree, bobtail. Your daddy will sure be happy about this," George says as he unloads Bailey's duffle bags from the trunk. She has asked him to take her home, to her house.

Cecil is offshore but when he returns that evening it's to kitchen smells that overflow onto the side porch where he stores his gear. Merissa's slow cooked shrimp Creole. He smells it from the roux up, every spice and flavor. Leaves his boots at the door and steps onto the kitchen tiles in sock feet.

Even so, he stands the full height of his 6'2" frame. He is a big box of a man, 220 pounds but not an ounce of fat save a slight roll in the middle. Handsome, squared features. His white blonde hair has grayed into a palomino silver that marks him even further. It was a fine figure he cut beside his petite wife Merissa in her smart linens and St. Tropez bikinis and even now he never walks into a room unnoticed. Around docks he is royalty. On boats he is a king.

"You alright?" he says to the daughter he hasn't seen in three years.

"Yes sir. You?"

"Been better, but I'll do."

Neither father nor daughter lingers when they embrace—never have.

"Let's eat on the dock, Daddy,"

"Is it as bad as they say in Alaska?"

"Worse."

"Adèle and Bear?"

"Holding up."

"Hell of a thing."

"Yes sir."

~ ~ ~ ~ ~ ~ ~ ~ ~ ~ ~ ~ ~ ~

## CECIL
### (1962)

*Cecil had been offshore with the crew for two days, having pretty good luck, when the call came from George. It was a long trek to Alaska in the early Sixties and they could have been side-tracked anywhere, but Henrietta always knows more than she says, so Cecil pulled up the nets to head home. Truth be told there was the nag that bedeviled him, that he should never have taken Merissa away from her family, that one day she might return to her homeland and never come back. A silly nag, he knew, that festered with the fear of what he'd do without her. He knew she loved him, knew they were happy together and building a solid life, but there was the unceasing mystery of her—since the very first night.*

*He'd signed on with the Merchant Marines after the war, knowing he'd settle in Carolina but not yet willing to haul home the extra baggage he'd picked up in the Pacific. He was stationed in Alaska and had plenty of shore leave, but he mostly lay in his bunk and read. That night though, that full moon night curiosity took him into the little town. A night off the boat, he thought, maybe decent grub.*

*The hall was already packed when he got there, thick with layers of smoke and sweat and hot breath mixed with the perpetual roll of drum and voice. Nerve wracking at first, relentless. He tried to open himself to it but couldn't—not until she stepped out with the other dancers.*

*Like everyone else in the room he gave himself over to her. All the line of him uncoiled as she danced and danced and rapture gathered around her, vitalizing the other dancers and drummers and spectators. The villagers at least had a frame of reference, but Cecil Martin had never witnessed or dreamed of such beauty in motion.*

*The song had begun with a dozen or more performers but in time the others drifted to the sides and melded with the watchers. Energy focused more and more on the swirling buckskin skirt under a blaze of red blouse. The flow of dark hair and glimpses of silver adornment. Small footpads of beaded moccasins were all that grounded her to the earth onto which this now otherworldly creature must eventually walk as an everyday woman.*

*He was embarrassed at first by her sensuality but realized the others too swallowed her with their eyes, without guile or guilt or shame. Later they would call it the night of Merissa's illumination. The more she danced the more everything stilled around her, not completely still, for the room swayed in her wake. Even the children were transfixed, and the old most certainly, for they recognized that this night, in these moments, she had not only transcended maidenhood and become a true woman, but she had gone beyond even that into a place where words would not reach.*

*On and on she danced, flew, transformed, in a space with the rest of them but not of that space, for they all felt her wheeling in starlight. It was the drummers, feeling the will of the elders, who brought her back into the moment, the physicality of the room and the people in it, with notes that gradually slowed and contained her once more.*

*For the villagers she represented the vastness, the greatness, the wonder of the universe funneled into the lithe vessel of this particular young woman. In her they witnessed a symbolic essence of the sublime. For Cecil it was the other way. For him she wasn't the symbol of beauty and grace—she was the actuality of it. And through her he glimpsed, albeit intermittently, not a distillation but a direct portal to the knowledge of outlying wonder, worlds beyond the commonplace, space out of time, the possibility of bliss.*

*She was the only poem he ever knew.*

*Because he had borne witness he became part of the story, part of the legend so that when he returned to lay before her family fish enough to take them through winter then began to fill the larders with meat, he could not be denied. He must be reckoned with. But he must wait—for her to finish college and satisfy her parents of her sound decision.*

*And now they, Cecil and Merissa, had a daughter and he yearned to run calling after both of them but fought to control his fears and know the telephone would soon ring. At long last the call did come, and he wanted to run to them even harder but he had learned through the years to trust Henrietta, so that when she assured him all would be well but that Merissa must be given time with Bailey he had to believe her.*

*He worked the boat and made their bed but kept the poetry in his heart, for none but Merissa would believe it anyway. The first week was hell, the second week twice so. Then Merissa said they were on the way and he got the house ready. He'd clumsily tended Merissa's garden for nearly a month and the day of their homecoming he vased flowers in every room and took an armful to George for Retta. George tied yellow ribbons on the driveway trees and they waited on the Simmons porch where they would hear the car sooner.*

*When the travelers finally pulled up, Cecil furled Merissa and Bailey into the breadth of his arms, held them together and separately, cupped Merissa's head into his chest and stroked her dark hair. Bailey swung from her daddy and squeezed his prickly neck as always, but when he leaned back to look at her and said, well, tell me all about it, she wiggled out of his arms and started to run but then caught herself and walked to the driftwood tree fort that hung over the river. When Cecil moved to follow her both women, one on each side, touched his arm to stop him. Then they told him a story that surpassed all his fears and he was outraged and humbled by his selfish longing and attempt to contain it.*

~ ~ ~ ~ ~ ~ ~ ~ ~ ~ ~ ~ ~ ~

Bailey has brought bags of her tainted clothes and gear with her from Alaska to Kirk's Bluff. Garbage bags filled with oiled belongings that will never be clean again. She has also brought armfuls of matted feathers and would have brought more but her grandfather looked at the pile and shook his head. From it she makes art. Homage.

She holes up in her mother's long sun room and smears oil on weighted white paper—a page for each creature's bad death. From chords of clothesline stretched from one end of the room to the other and back again twice she hangs the papers to dry. In the days that follow the pages crisp and rattle like delicate bones when Bailey opens the windows against the stink of oil and carnage. Though insignificant to many, these are the neighbors of her mother and grandparents, of all the Chugach people. Respect.

~ ~ ~

Early in May Bailey and Padgett ride into to the foothills of the Shenandoah where they first happened on one another. The dilapidated homestead is back on the market, the young couple that bought it having decided the project was bigger than their dreams. The grape vines are lush green this time but the pond looks the same. A dragonfly ruffles the surface with translucent wings, and in the ripples Bailey hears Retta's voice but can't quite catch what she's saying.

"You never eat the melon," she says.

"Don't care for melon."

"How can anybody not like a sweet juicy melon—must be a good story there."

"Bailey, listen to me. You love stories. You think stories need to be told."

"Don't they?"

"Not always."

He looks at her, goes to speak, quiets, takes off his sunglasses. Takes hers off too and speaks to her in an even, flat voice.

"That's how we were trained. Targets were far enough away you could convince yourself they weren't even people. See that melon across the field, they'd tell us. We've got what we need from that melon. Pop it and show the rest of them. It's nothing but a melon on shoulders. Pop it before it walks. That's it. Nothing but a splattered melon."

"I'm so sorry." She shuts her eyes and wilts. "I'm so sorry."

"That's exactly what it looked like too. A big ripe melon in a faraway field that had nothing to do with you or the weapon in your hands or the aim you just took."

"I'm so sorry."

"Don't be sorry for me, Bailey. I don't want your fucking sympathy."

He replaces his glasses, hands hers back, trembling.

"I want you to somehow understand everything," he says, "but I don't want to tell you. I want those stories locked away. There are way too many of them."

He lays his head in her lap and closes his eyes. She follows a great blue heron as it stalks the bank in silent precision. Heartbeats become steady once more and he says here's a story for you.

*Listen:*

*Once there was a maiden walking alone in the heart of the forest, daydreaming as she picked wildflowers one late afternoon. When she bent down for an especially pretty red one she nearly touched a long thick snake and recoiled in terror.*

*Why are you so afraid of me, the snake asked. I will not harm you.*

*Taken aback, the girl didn't flee, but she backed far away from the snake and watched very carefully where she stepped.*

*Another afternoon soon afterward she was again in the meadow picking flowers when a voice came from the nearby rocks. You see, said the snake, I will not harm you.*

*I have watched you and could have hidden myself from you, but I didn't. It's so lonesome to be despised. Please continue to gather your flowers and I will lie here in plain sight and will not move until you leave.*

*Again and again this happened. The maiden gathered wildflowers in the late afternoon sun and the snake lay still on the rocks. As the days passed her fear of the snake gradually lessened and as it did she allowed herself to come closer and closer without fear.*

*The snake told her of his plight, of how he only wished to be spoken to without malice; even more so how he longed to be touched. Simply touched by someone.*

*After weeks and months the snake grew less and less repulsive to her and one day she agreed to reach out with just one finger and touch the back of the snake. In time her touches became full strokes and in more time she actually held the snake in her arms and allowed him to circle her shoulders. And in time beyond that there was friendship and trust and even love that was shared between them.*

*One day after picking flowers the maiden lay on the very rocks where she had first touched the snake, drowsy in the afternoon sun, the snake coiled about her in contentment.*

*And at that moment she was blindsided by a horrible pain beyond any she had ever known or imagined, and the snake slithered off a short distance and paused before it slinked away entirely.*

*Wait, she cried in anguish and disbelief, the poison already making its way through her unguarded body. Why? Why? I trusted you. I held you and cared for you and let you drape about my shoulders, and now you have envenomed me. Why?*

*I was lonesome, the snake said. And I have loved you. I will always love you. But I am a snake. I have always been a snake. You cannot be surprised that I am a snake. This is my nature.*

"That's comforting," she says.

"Don't ask me for stories, Bailey. I'll tell you what I can."

~ ~ ~

# Crossing the Divide

They sit in the club car eating peanuts as the train pulls into Kingstree. Padgett reads the quartered sports section and Bailey stares at the deep black Carolina pine woods. It's Friday evening, Memorial Day weekend. Bailey thought it would be fun to take the train and avoid I-95 holiday traffic.

"It'll be alright," she says into the window.

"I know it means a lot to you, Bailey, but I should never have let you talk me into it."

"We can turn around."

"And what would he think then?"

"It wouldn't matter—he'd never have to lay eyes on you."

"I mean of you. What would he think of you?"

She watches for the moon to slip between cracks of trees and he smears newsprint between his fingers.

"I'm having a Bloody Mary," he says. "Want one?"

"No, thanks. Here, I'll get it for you. I need to stretch anyway."

~

Cecil Martin stands at the far end of the platform when the train rolls in, well apart from the straggling clumps of people making conversation and listening into the tracks while they wait. Yemassee is literally a whistle stop, so Bailey and Padgett and a few others stand at the rear of the car with their luggage in hand as the train coasts into the station.

She knows well where her father will be standing, the spot where he's stood every single time he has come to fetch her since she'd first gone into Charleston with her mother for a new Easter outfit. A fluffy white dress with a puffy white slip and lace panties and socks and shiny white patent leather shoes with a pocketbook to match. A lace hat too, with a long satin bow streaming down the back. A picture of her in that outfit has been on the mantelpiece for well over two decades. The dress is yellow in the frame now, but something about the way it looks makes you know the truth of it is white.

She presses her two hands against the glass as the great machine clacks to a stop, just as she had after that first Easter shopping trip and every time since then, home from college and occasionally job interviews, sometimes the hospital, but not in the three years since her mother's death. Her father peers into the train windows but doesn't move until it's proven she is there.

Bailey gets off first with her overnight case, sets it on the concrete when Cecil starts toward her. Padgett steps onto the platform behind her, manhandling the remainder of their luggage while she hugs her father tightly. Neither father nor daughter lingers or speaks as they embrace. When Padgett approaches Cecil takes Bailey's bags from him and walks ahead toward the truck without acknowledgment that Padgett is anything other than a porter.

"Bert's got the day off?" she says.

"Evidently," her father replies.

As they walk to the truck Bailey says, "Cecil Martin, Padgett Turner. Padgett Turner, Cecil Martin."

Cecil nods slightly as Padgett sets down the luggage to extend a hand but he extends nothing.

The ride to Kirk's Bluff is a great deal of silence mixed with straggling small talk between Bailey and her father. Henrietta's kitchen garden is full of vegetables. It hasn't rained for a week. Plenty of trout and bass. Padgett is asked nothing and says nothing.

When they pull into the yard Cecil takes his daughter's suitcases from the bed of the truck and carries them into the house and upstairs to her room. As Bailey and Padgett come into the foyer, Cecil ruffles the top of her dark brown hair, tells her goodnight, and is gone, into his own bedroom.

Padgett looks at her in disbelief, standing in the picture lined entrance with his bags in his hands.

"Pleasure to meet you too. Sir." He whispers with gritted anger.

Bailey laughs easily. "I didn't count on it being this bad."

"A man of few words, your father."

"Stop it." She pushes him toward the stairway. "He's probably got his ear cupped to the door."

"I don't think he gives a damn what we say."

"You'd be surprised," she says. "Just set the stuff here for now."

In the refrigerator Bailey finds the snack she's known would be there, wrapped in tin foil. One serving.

"We'll share," she says.

"It's okay. Knock yourself out."

"Come on, Padgett. He made sure to put it on one plate, but there's enough for at least two people here."

"Really," he says. "I'm not hungry. You go ahead."

She picks at the shrimp salad and opens a couple of beers as he looks around the kitchen, picturing her there as a little girl, but his mind clutters with thoughts of her father, and of his own children.

"Why don't we call it a night, kiddo," he says.

"Are you sure?"

"Yeah, I'm done."

"How'd you like me to slip in later and do you some more?"

"I wouldn't be able to get it up."

"He sleeps like a rock. Wait'll you hear him snoring."

"Doesn't matter. Sorry, Bailey. You said he's a hard ass, but this is more wacked than I imagined. What's the fucking point?"

"Tomorrow will be better," she says. "Wait and see. There's just no easy route when it comes to Cecil Martin. Easy's never been his way." She laughs and pokes his stomach. "Tough guy—like you."

~ ~

In the guest room Padgett lies in the stiff bed and listens to overlapping heart-songs of chucks-will's-widows. It seems only minutes later when he hears a man calling Bailey's name. Her father.

"Does he know how to fish?"

"Of course he knows how to fish," Bailey says in her too-early-in-the-morning voice.

"Well, is he getting up?"

"Why don't you ask him, Daddy? He can talk for himself."

"Aw hell, I'm going on then."

Aw hell is right, Padgett thinks, his feet on the hardwood floor, reaching for his pants. Padgett would lay money he'd spent more of his early years in the woods than anybody he knows, but fishing is something he's done very little of, off-shore fishing, never. He's going this morning, though, by god. Fifty fucking miles out there or not. He's pulled worse duty.

He slaps water across his face, yanks on a khaki shirt, grabs his sock stuffed boots and a bathing suit and is on the stairway landing when he hears a series of whistled notes no one would describe as cheerful and sees the bulk of Cecil Martin walking through the front door. There are no lights on in this part of the house except what leaks from the front porch.

"Get you some breakfast," Cecil says without breaking stride or looking Padgett's way. "Likely we'll be out a while."

In the kitchen he finds the bulb over the stove is lit, so dim it makes him almost tip-toe across the vinyl floor. There are four sausage links lined on one side of a doubled paper towel, the imprints of four others lined opposite them. On the clean white stove a stout pot of slow blurping grits is turned as low as the flame will allow. Two pieces of Roman Meal bread wait in the toaster, peach preserves and the butter dish on the counter nearby. Deep brewed coffee in an aluminum percolator and a carton of orange juice beside the refrigerator. A plate, cup and saucer, glass, utensils, and a paper napkin sit on the round oak table.

Padgett can't believe he slept through the breakfast smells. At least it's sausage, he thinks—nobody could sleep through bacon. And the bastard has acknowledged Padgett is real. There at the worn kitchen table, hours before sun-up, he eats his breakfast, a good breakfast, in the quiet dark. The kind of quiet dark that makes you somehow believe things are right with the world. At least they could be. He almost wakes Bailey again to say goodbye, then decides no, and follows Cecil to the boat.

*Sonny Girl.* A crazy looking wooden hulled jalopy, leftover or pieced together from what Padgett couldn't say. A forty-eight foot snapper boat that has helped earn Cecil a living for his family going on thirty-two years. They aren't out for snapper this morning, though. Cecil and Padgett and the two man crew are heading to the Gulf Stream for Marlin. Blue Marlin. Big Blue Marlin.

Padgett isn't intimidated. He saw the mounted fish in the den when Bailey showed him around the house last night. Two hundred pounds tops. A huge fish no doubt, but no real trophy when it comes to Blue Marlin. He knows that much.

When they board the boat, Cecil looks toward one of the crewmen, a gangly leather skinned man of forty or so, doubtless of Celtic derivation, and says, "That's Joe." Joe gives the slightest nod as he passes on his way to the wheel house. Cecil then points his cap in the direction of the other crewman, a young black man, skin only a few shades darker than Joe's leather, a horse of a man in red and pink flowered trunks who still somehow looks as if he ought to be on stage in a velvet curtained theatre acting out some ancient tragedy. "And that's MoJo," Cecil says, without cracking a smile.

On the way out, MoJo rigs bait lines, mostly mackerel and mullet, a few ladyfish and ballyhoo. Many of the bait fish are two or three pounders, all of them over a foot long. Going for the gusto, Padgett thinks. At least the bastard's going for the gusto. Cecil stands over MoJo like a school marm, watching every line he rigs, whistling his odd tune from time to time.

As the sun sends pale orange feelers along the horizon *Sonny Girl* crosses from the cool murky green into blue-green, into a clear swimming pool blue, then into the rich indigo of the Stream itself, a full ten degrees warmer, where whirls of the deeper color eddy into the lighter shades that flank it. From the air the different colored ocean appears to be divided as clearly as sections of Amish farm land.

Leather Joe, the boat's captain, has worked with Cecil for twenty-three years.

"You the one Miss Bailey brought home, eh?"

"I'm the one," Padgett says, dishing it out in the same tone.

"Scared?"

"Of what?"

"That this here little boat ride might be a one way trip. For some of us."

Padgett wants to laugh, really wants to laugh, but takes a long sideways look at Leather Joe, gauging the bluff. Some of it bluff. Not all of it, though.

"Miss Bailey's the only one Cecil's got now."

"I know that."

"Nothing means more to him."

"I'm sure that's true."

"Known her myself since she was a little thing."

Padgett quickly tires of this game. "No doubt she means a lot to us all. Show me where we are on the chart."

"I don't need no chart. What is it you wanting to see?"

"Just curious."

"Meow. Meow-meow-meow."

This fucker's insane, Padgett thinks with muted rage.

"Meow, meow, meow," Leather Joe continues, slapping the side of his stained work pants, hollow cackles sounding between his cat calls.

Padgett focuses on Bailey, the way she looks when she comes out of the water and smoothes her hair back. The way she wipes the salt sting from her eyes and smiles at him. Hold on, Turner, he says to himself. Keep it together.

"Are you in love with Bailey too?" Padgett asks him evenly. That shuts up the meowing.

"What are you talking about?" Leather Joe winces.

"Are you?"

"You gonna do right by Miss Bailey?"

"Are you?" Padgett pounds, relentless now, but holding on. Holding on.

Violence calls from the hard, tensed muscles beneath Leather Joe's skin and echoes in the scars of its surface. But it is not the only voice of violence and Padgett is ready to take the pain. Ready to give it.

"I think the world of Miss Bailey, that's all." Leather Joe backs off from them both. "You see what I got to think of you."

"We both see," Padgett says. "Let's just keep watching."

~

After all the waiting, all the settling down, all the noise and the quiet, it seems like a slap of dream when it happens. The big fish hits, the line snaps from the outrigger, MoJo grabs the other rig and reels in like a high-gear machine, Cecil makes a gesture to Leather Joe, and the boat throttles down to an idle. Without knowing what's happening, Padgett feels MoJo grip the rod with one hand, jerk Padgett's right arm into the fishing harness, then do the same thing with the left.

"Snatch it," MoJo says through everything. "Set the hook. Now, man. Snatch it. Set the hook."

Padgett yanks the rod with a surge of anger, feels the hook sink into something solid.

"Hold on, brother, and reel like hell. It's you and him now. Just you and him." MoJo jumps from side to side and hoots like he's at the soccer finals.

The big fish blasts out of the sea. Blue Marlin alright. And what a blue. Mounted fish never look like they do in the water but this one—Padgett never knew anything like this existed. It's cobalt blue, Bailey's blue, with diamonds of light flashing around it from the flailing. He wishes she were there to see him fight it.

"That's it, man. You're doing fine. Bring him in now," MoJo says. "Bring that bad boy right in. You're doing fine."

The sight of the marlin breaking the surface combined with the force on the end of the line gives Padgett a blazing adrenaline rush. Now he understands. He's set the hook in the fish alright, but one has been set in him too, and it pulls him outward to the life and death and sport of the thing just as hard as he is reeling the big monster inward.

"Use your body, man," MoJo says. "Take the weight of him with your body. That's right—free up your hands to work the reel."

The fish turns into the sun, and as MoJo helps swivel the chair toward it, Padgett catches a glimpse of Cecil. Standing there. Doing nothing while all the commotion is happening on the back deck. Whistling. Just standing there watching and whistling. That's fine, Padgett thinks, knowing the fish on his line outweighs the one in the den by at least a hundred pounds.

When the fish turns again Cecil signals Leather Joe in the tower. The boat doesn't change positions, though, and Cecil signals once more.

"Goddamn it, Joe," Cecil yells to the tower in the same instant that the boat churns forward, the rig snaps, and the fish is gone. The slack in the line is taken up by the wrench in Padgett's gut and he tastes the burn of sausage and coffee at the back of his throat. Just as quickly as it has come, the power pulling him, the power he is pulling against, has vanished. Everything goes limp.

"Damn, man. This is worse than I thought," MoJo says, careful in his lighthearted laughter, as much to himself as to Padgett.

Cecil has climbed into the tower with Leather Joe and the two yell at one another over the noise of the engine.

MoJo grins. "Mister Cecil seems to have no use for you, and Joe even less. How come?"

He looks at MoJo hard. Don't ask me questions is the look that glares from Padgett's sunglasses. He marvels at the ease with which he could with full authority take this boat and everyone on it, alive or not, to Cuba, or have it confiscated at the coast guard station at Charleston. But instead he allows this ball busting, so fierce is his desire to find ground with the father of the woman that he loves without end.

"Three men on this boat with the shut down blues," MoJo says. He throws his arms wide and does a little hot foot. "Open yourself to the sea, brother."

Padgett is still holding the rod, feather-light in his hands now. "What exactly just happened?"

MoJo looks to the wheel house where Cecil and Leather Joe continue to argue. "Joe didn't take the signal," he says. "That's what happened. Mister Cecil gave him the signal when the fish turned, but instead of following into the fish, Joe gunned it and popped the line. Adios."

"Why?"

"That's what I'm asking you, man." MoJo re-rigs the broken line. He had cast the other one the minute the fish was lost.

"Cecil's daughter brought me here."

"Our namesake." MoJo pats the side of the boat.

"Right."

"And?"

"And I guess I have a complicated past."

"Got it." MoJo grins. "Bad boy. Teach bad boy a lesson and pop his fish."

MoJo's outlook is irresistible and Padgett can do nothing but laugh with him.

"What's your island?" Padgett asks.

"Tortola, man. Where the love flows free."

"So how'd you end up with these two sweethearts?"

"Oh, I end up everywhere, sooner or later. That's why Mister Cecil took me on. That and the fact that I'm the best Marlin deckie this side of the Ribbon Reef."

They're trolling again now, both outriggers ready for a strike. Cecil and Leather Joe are quiet, but Cecil stays in the bridge. All of them settle in for more waiting.

"Did Cecil have anything to do with me losing that fish?"

"Not at all. He gave the right signal. He might not like you, but he's true blue with it comes to fishing."

"Hell of a big fish too."

"Not bad for these parts," MoJo says.

"Not bad? It was bigger than anything that old bastard ever caught."

MoJo bellows a huge belly laugh and wallops the deck rail. When he bends his dreads spill over in a dense matted coil. "Why would you think that, man?"

Padgett's gut rumbles with the grits and sausage. "Because I saw his big prize hanging in the den. It couldn't have been more than two hundred pounds."

MoJo laughs even broader. "That, my man, was the first marlin your little lady friend caught. Fourteen, I think, when she got him."

"Bailey?" Padgett looks to MoJo's hands to see if he's lying. "That's Bailey's fish?"

"I'm telling you, man, Cecil Martin is the real thing when it comes to fishing."

"Bailey's fish? No shit."

MoJo leaves Padgett on the back deck and unwraps the ham and cheese sandwiches he made earlier that morning, moist white bread not yet soggy from the cooler. He takes a couple, along with potato chips and iced tea up to Cecil and Leather Joe who eat in silence now that the yelling is done.

"Tell me about Cecil Martin," Padgett says when MoJo returns with their lunch.

They eat the sandwiches and drink the strong tea and MoJo speaks of Cecil fighting in the Pacific during the second World War, of how he lost hearing in his left ear when a mortar round exploded beside him, the same explosion that blasted his friend through the fronds of a palm tree twenty feet high. Navy men who never should have been ashore anyway. Cecil's friend George Simmons served on the same ship as a cook.

MoJo tells of Cecil marlin fishing off Australia after the war, when word of the big fish off Cairns was just beginning to spread. Of the Blacks over a thousand pounds he caught in those days. Of how Cecil had knocked about for nearly ten years, catching government supply ships in some port and working his way around to another.

First, though, he'd come home to Carolina, where his father had been the lighthouse keeper at Bloody Point and his brother had taken over when his father died. He bought a trawler while he could get the down payment with GI Bill money—two actually—the sleek newly built *Miss Merissa* and the project boat that came to be *Sonny Girl* thrown in with the deal. Cecil knew he'd eventually settle here and fish for a living and he cut a deal with the Toomers to work *Miss Merissa* while he was gone. *Sonny Girl* was another story, named for Bailey who turned out not to be the Sonny Boy he'd been calling her in the womb.

"Honest to god," Padgett says. "I knew there was something to him, but I didn't peg him for a drifter."

"Oh yes, my friend, he roamed the world. Africa, Europe, South America —not much in the South Pacific. Said he'd seen enough of that. Made his way to Australia quite a lot, though. Those big black marlin had given him the fever, and I know how it is. Two years ago I was working the same places he fished back then."

"Well I'll be damned," Padgett says. "I'll be damned."

"Found a bride in Alaska—part native, part French—one that grew up by the water and understood the sea. One that spoke proud and danced and sang and smiled a lot. A beauty they say—sure looks it from the pictures. You'd be surprised how much he speaks of her if he's of a mind. Merissa. Brought her back to Carolina. She bore him a girl child, the only one they'd have. But you probably know all this."

"Some," Padgett says. "Bailey's funny about memories."

Talk runs out for a while, so Padgett leans on the rail and tries to picture some of what MoJo has been telling him. It's early afternoon, and the late May sun is slowly scorching its way westward, sending its 94 degree heat in a breathless box that encloses the boat and everything around it. A dolphin jumps, snapping Padgett from his daydream. He steps into the head to change out of his jeans and into his bathing suit and picks a new spot to lean against.

"He's testing you." MoJo drapes his arms across the rail beside Padgett.

"How so?"

"That fighting chair."

"What about it?"

"It's not a fighting chair at all."

"I don't get you," Padgett says.

"It's a barber's chair."

"I still don't get you."

"When Mister Cecil got this boat years ago he had that contraption rigged from of an old barber's chair he'd bought at an auction. Cheap, you know. Not knowing yet if people would pay him money to come out and fish. They did, though."

"People pay him to fish on this old boat—tourists you mean?"

"Tourists. Locals if they ask. Most days *Sonny Girl* is a snapper boat. Snapper and whatever else Poseidon sees fit to share."

"You're telling me people really pay to fish with this rattletrap equipment?" Padgett sweeps an open hand around them.

"No. What I'm telling you is he's got a fine fighting chair, Fin Nor reels, all of it. I figure he wants to see how you measure up—against him when he was a younger man and had to use the rigs he's got you using now. And the old chair."

"From what I see, he couldn't give a damn one way or the other."

"Hard to know what's happening in that head of his," MoJo says. He's got his ways, friend. He's sure enough got his ways."

"And the other Joe? He's got some ways too."

"Piranha," MoJo says. "Bloody killer fish." He hisses and spits both ways then crosses the deck to check outrigger lines.

Padgett takes a better look at the chair and can see now, sure enough, it's exactly like the one in Mr. Chauncey's barber shop when he was a kid. His skin tingles cold as he feels again that first electric buzz on the back of his neck. He can see himself sitting inside Mr. Chauncey's mirror, lost under the big gray tarp fastened around his neck.

He sees the combs standing inside a clear jar that was the same kind you could get peanuts from at McCormack's store. This one has alcohol in it, though, black combs and alcohol, and some scissors. He smells the alcohol and hair tonic and even the soft powder Mr. Chauncey uses to whisk the back of your neck when he's done.

Padgett watches himself, the little boy that he was that first time, with two big tears perched on the rims of his eyes. The ones that roll onto his cheeks when Mr. Chauncey tells him to lean his head down so he can finish the back. His mother is in the mirror too, farther away, with tears of her own she's trying to keep to herself. She isn't watching anything Mr. Chauncey does with the scissors or buzz tool. Her focus is on the reactions of her four year old son's face in the mirror. When Mr. Chauncey brushes away the snips of Padgett's brown hair, then wheels him around in the chair and gives the child a hand mirror to look at the back of his head, Padgett can only see his mother in the mirror, smiling now.

Mr. Chauncey pumps the chair down, takes the money from his mother, and is sweeping away Padgett's snips of hair from the rubber mat when the two of them step into the street on the way to the ice cream shop. He and his mother. Like most everything in his childhood.

Padgett tries to remember the ice cream and what else he and his mother did in town that day when another dolphin jumps. This one is nearer the boat than the first, and before his mind has the second it would take to wonder if the dolphin is white or only looks that way in the sun, there is another jump, the real thing this time, marlin, thirty yards behind the boat. With it is the simultaneous snap of line zinging from the outrigger.

He's ready. It happens all in a motion—the fish strikes, the line yanks, he takes the rod into his hands, is strapped into the chair, snatches hard and deep, and the hook is set. The boat grinds from the five or six knot trolling speed, past the two knot speed of the fish, to a dead idle.

The sting of the hook sends the marlin shooting left to right across the boat's wake, trying to shake off what's pulling against her. Then she roars out of the water, like a full throttle Harley Davidson, and Padgett really sees the size of her. At least twice that of the first one. The marlin strips 300 yards of line on the first run and hurls herself into the air before she settles in for the deeper fight. MoJo whoops, reels in the other rod, straps Padgett more securely into the chair, and turns the chair into the fish—all with agility that blurs into a single moment.

"That's it, brother. You made the hookup. That's the big part. You've got her now. Bring her home. Bring her home, brother." MoJo dances the deck and echoes his own whooping.

Padgett hears MoJo, but from some other place. It's as if MoJo and Leather Joe and Cecil and all the rest of it exist elsewhere, and there is only Padgett and this monster fish and the tug-of-war line that connects them.

"Five hundred I'm guessing," MoJo says. "At least five hundred pounds of fighting blue devil. Fine fish. Make her yours now. Make her yours."

Over and over again the marlin hurls herself from the sea, completely out of the water, flailing from side to side, then crashing once more, sending spray into the air like a geyser. Her eyes are the size of the saucer Padgett had set his coffee cup on that morning, forever ago. They aren't looking at him, the eyes. They are searching wildly for what has gone wrong with the world, the world that had been hers until she felt the sting of a hook and the weight of horror behind it.

"It's me you're looking for, Harley," Padgett yells. "Yes, me. I'm the one that's got you. I'm the one that won't let go."

As the boat backs into the fish, he cranks line, inch by lifelong inch, fighting for every lap of the reel, hearing somewhere MoJo telling him to use the weight of his body, to free his hands for the reel. Noises come at Padgett from everywhere—MoJo's cheerleading, the grind of the boat backing down, the gears of the reel straining.

After nearly an hour the marlin sounds, her pale cobalt stripes gleaming, and MoJo is there with the gloves he tried to get Padgett to wear earlier, gloves he still refuses, and the iced tea that he doesn't refuse, that MoJo pours into his mouth and he swallows with sloshing gulps.

Cecil comes from the wheel house and stands behind him, off to the side, watching, just as he had with the first fish, saying nothing. He signals Leather Joe when the marlin sounds, and the boat backs harder towards the fish, giving Padgett line to reel. Then Cecil disappears.

"Where you going, Harley?" Padgett sings to the big blue Gulf Stream, to the thousand feet depth that lies between him and the fish.

"What are you calling that fish, man?"

"Harley," Padgett says. "My big girl, Harley."

"Like the motorcycle?"

"Yep."

"Got you," MoJo says. "Wrestling a motorcycle might be easier though."

MoJo paces and Padgett can feel each pound of his heart for the nearly forty minutes the marlin is under water. Then, out of nowhere, out of everywhere, up she surfaces again, greyhounding. Launching herself out of the ocean and diving back into it in straight powerful leaps. No flailing this time, only straight leaps, her taut sickle shaped tail holding her massive body in line, her long bill pointing forward and away.

"I wish Mister Cecil were down here," MoJo says. "You and this blue devil gonna wear me out."

"I thought you were the best deckie this side of Australia," Padgett teases.

"That I am, brother. But nobody works the deck by himself."

"You mean Cecil's usually back here too?"

"Sure," MoJo says. He's busy testing you—trouble is, I don't need testing. I'll need help when you get that devil to the boat though."

Fine, Padgett thinks. Let the bastard stand there and watch. No problem. Outdated rigs, barber chair, all of it's just fucking fine. A detail he'll secure.

An hour later MoJo brings more tea.

"Damn that's good. I could take a bath in it."

"Is that so?" MoJo says, and reaches for a deck hose. "Try this." He sprays Padgett's blistering back then douses him from top to bottom, except for his hands.

"You're a good man, MoJo."

"Not so bad yourself," MoJo answers, giving him one last squirt to the back of the head.

In another hour Padgett's arms and back are completely numb. MoJo still coaches him, but the whooping tapers as the fight drags into the afternoon. Talk is sporadic.

"So where are all the mammoth marlin Cecil has killed? Padgett says. I only saw the one you say is Bailey's."

"Caught, I said. Not killed. He kept some in the old days—gave 'em away mostly. Now he tags them—let's them go. Unless he's got a charter. Big dollars get the choice. Up to Mister Cecil, they'd all be released. He knows what I've seen with my own eyes off Australia where he loves the big blackies so."

"What's that?"

"Long-liners," MoJoe says. Japanese commercial boats. They run lines fifty miles long, thousands of hooks coming off one big vessel. Catch everything there is—and I mean everything."

"But it's eaten, right?"

"Eat, sure. But no mind paid to whether the fish are breeding females or what."

"They really take that many?"

"Let's put it this way. It would take twenty years for one game fishing boat like this to bring in the marlin a long-liner gets in a day."

"Damn."

"Damn is right, but that only starts the trouble. The by-catch would break your heart. Dolphins, porpoise, whales, sharks, turtles—die by the tens of thousands. Sea birds dive for the baited hooks and drown. Dirty business. It's all about respect, you know. There's greed and there's respect."

Into the fourth hour there is little talk and the engine grind is nothing but a drone. Cecil stands to the side for a while and whistles his unnerving notes, climbs to the wheel house to look in on Leather Joe every once in a while, checks gauges, but he comes nowhere near the back deck where Padgett sweats.

The fish is drawn closer and closer, wearing down. It almost pains Padgett now when she hurls herself into the air, now that he knows he will win, knows that unless something goes wrong when he gets her to the boat, he has won. When the marlin had first come crashing out of the water, he was in awe. Had never seen a living thing with such power and mobility, its heavy shouldered body compressed into spectacular leaps from the wet mystery of its existence. He'd wanted it, wanted to conquer it. But now the adrenaline has subsided and he is ashamed, unworthy to be dragging this mammoth creature from its world. This gigantic fish that is older than his children.

Five and a half hours into the fight Padgett has a sudden urge to throw up his arms and let go. Part of him longs to jump in and swim toward the strength of the marlin. The other part knows it's only fatigue, his old pal fatigue. Knows he can fight past fatigue, that he's the one in the boat and not the one being dragged through the water behind it.

Over six hours and the fish is nearly close enough to be gaffed. Padgett is dazed, wants the line to pop, wants the fish to get away, wants to go overboard and kill it himself, is uncertain what he wants.

"I don't know if I can do this by myself." MoJo speaks quietly to Padgett as he pulls on his gloves and checks the flying gaff.

Before Padgett thinks it through, he swings his head to where he knows Cecil is standing and says, "Come down here and help us, you old bastard."

Cecil cackles and comes straight to the chair.

"All you had to do was ask," he says.

Cecil's laugh fuels Padgett with anger and he reels with force like he'd had hours before, reels until the fish is where it has to be.

"I shouldn't keep it," Padgett says. "We should tag her."

"Fish is worn out," Cecil says. "Don't know that it would make it anyway."

"What should I do?"

"Everybody's entitled to keep his first one." He slaps Padgett on the back. "It was a clean fight. You did a fine job."

MoJo's whoops resume and Leather Joe appears out of nowhere. Cecil gives clipped but patient commands and the boat and men on it become a smooth running performance machine. As he quiets to gaff the giant marlin, MoJo's handwork is delicate and his concentration intense. Padgett follows every order he's given and although he understands nothing of their techniques he clearly sees the finesse that lands the behemoth within minutes.

MoJo bear hugs Padgett and pounds hand drums on his back. Cecil shakes his hand. Leather Joe nods the slightest of unsmiling nods in acknowledgment if not congratulation, returns to the bridge, and steers the boat toward shore. Beer comes from somewhere, ice cold beer, and the three of them drink—to the fisherman, to the fish, to the crew, and to the vessel. The long ride back is loud and wet and smells like fish and sweat and men and the sea. By the time they make landfall the color has drained from everything, living and dead.

~ ~

Bailey wipes dust from the burnished sextant. She and Padgett boated to May Isle earlier that morning, the morning after the big fishing trip, and have spent hours piddling in the would-be garden and spider-filled dock house. Now they're stuffed on pimiento cheese sandwiches and potato chips and Bailey amuses herself with shelf treasures while Padgett adjusts the door handle.

If the variation is West, the compass is best," Bailey says.

"If the variation is East, the compass is least," Padgett finishes.

"So you know how to use it?"

"I picked up a few things along the way," he smiles. "So much for the noon shoot. Sunset—or wait for Polaris?"

"Let's wait for the stars," she says.

He opens and shuts the door a few times to make certain it closes securely.

"There should be a lock on this door," he says.

"That's not how it works around the Jericho," she says. "Nobody's gonna mess with our stuff."

"You live in a dream world, Bailey."

"Thanks, Padg," she says. "I like it here."

She flips through Merissa's copy of *Chapman's Piloting*, smiling at the intricate side notes, her mother's graceful penmanship always a pleasure to read.

"Want to play Truth or Dare?"

"Padgett, you know I'll do it if you dare. What truth is it you want?"

"You and your dad."

She closes the book, holds it to her chest.

"Which part?"

"The missing part," he says.

"Two hard heads, I guess. I got it from him, but evidently I have natural talent anyway."

She turns to slide the volume into its resting place.

"Okay," he says. "Fine."

"Okay," she says. "Okay, so when Mom died those two hard heads really butted, and it's been easier to just steer clear of each other. But since last fall, these months of watching you with the boys, it's been eating at me. I love my dad and I know he loves me—but for three years I couldn't find my way home, at least not all the way home."

Between the front windows hangs a small carved totem pole. Bailey stands before it and traces the shapes of story with her slender fingers.

"And . . . ?"

"And then I went to Alaska and couldn't stop hearing the echo of my mother's heartbreak."

"There's more to it, Bailey."

"My mom died at home, would have nothing to do with hospitals. When she was too weak to use the stairs we set up camp in the sunroom with the river on one side and the aquarium on the other but when she went on ahead the house smelled like sickness. You've smelled death. You know what I mean. It echoes and echoes."

She paces back to the shelves and absently opens another book.

"I couldn't be around my father's pain," she says. "Or my guilt."

"That's not fair," he says. "I've heard enough to know you took great care of your mom, and I know she was sick for a long time."

"That's true. But I might have taken too much care. That's what Daddy thinks."

The books snaps shut and she wedges it into place.

"We don't need to talk about this."

"It's alright," she says. "I trust you to know it."

He moves toward her but she stands away and is quiet.

She says, "More than Mom wanted to die at home she wanted to be buried at sea. Cecil knew, and he knew all the protocol—old Navy guy—but he wouldn't hear of it. Put his foot down like when they moved from May Isle to the mainland."

She walks onto the porch and stands looking toward the river. Padgett follows and sits nearby but not too near.

"When it got closer she wrote a letter to Cecil and one to me, carefully spelling out how she wanted it to happen, how much she needed us to let this happen. He didn't open his for a week after she was gone, and I already knew what she wanted. She'd been through it with me time and time again."

A kingfisher flies from its perch under the dock with a piercing rattle, setting off a series of clapper rail complaints.

"But I couldn't do it. It wasn't only the burial at sea. She wanted to die in the water—was adamant about it. Pleaded with me to let her die in the water and drift away."

She crosses her hands onto her shoulders and slides them down her arms, rests them on her hips and stretches her shoulders.

"Have you ever watched someone eaten away with cancer?"

"I know who death is," he says. "And I understand about death wishes. Bailey, it's not your fault."

"Wait," she says. "Listen. Near the end, Mom was so weak, but she begged. The hospice nurse had already given us the override code on the morphine pump. The mercy dose. I even went so far as to take her in the boat, to the spot she'd showed me over and over. But I couldn't do it. She wanted me to ease her over the side, administer the dose, and let go. But what if she changed her mind? What if she was only in a coma? She wanted it so badly but I couldn't do it for her—my dying, begging mother."

"It's okay," he says, but makes no move from the chair.

"It is okay," she says. "But it wasn't okay then. The best I could do was take her to the dock. Cecil was in and out, but it was too much for him, all of it. Somehow women are the ones who deal with death in families. She didn't ease out like we hoped. Death came, but it was ugly and brutal. I was there, though, and for that I am grateful."

She says nothing, but there's more to tell. They sit in the Sunday stillness until the words come.

"I held her while she died, and I couldn't let go. I knew I should get Daddy and Retta, but I couldn't let go."

She moves her fingers, lightly, back and forth across the porch screen. How many times had she and Ben replaced ripped and sagging sheets of it? Merissa had shown them how. Merissa had shown them how to turn cartwheels and, when none of the other adults were around, how to do back flips off the dock. How to tie a bowline knot and loosen it with one hand. How to find a dolphin patch. How to keep a secret.

"The night before the funeral I cupped my fingers into her little hands, one crossed over the other, as she lay there in that pillowed coffin. Cecil and I thanked a line of people for paying their respects while my grandparents sat outside under the stars and waited. My father kissed his bride one last time, tenderly on the forehead, and squeezed his big hand over ours, and we closed the casket and went home. More people were at the house, all the food and the chatter, and I couldn't do it. I went back to the funeral home and sat into the night with my mother. The next day they dug a hole and sweet things were said and sung and a box was buried in the soft dirt."

She leans down and pushes her palms hard against her knees, stretches up slowly, leans her head backward, forward, and looks at Padgett.

"My mother didn't want to be in the ground, and she didn't want to be ashes. She made me promise. She held my hand on her chest and made me swear it."

"Bailey, what are you saying?"

"I did what my mother asked."

"You couldn't have lifted her body."

"No, I couldn't have."

"Are you . . . ?"

"The next week when Cecil read the letter, he blasted into the sunroom where I was pressing roses into Mom's books and waved the pages at me. 'Did you?' he yelled. 'Answer me. Did you?' I looked up but what was there to say?"

She walks to the screen again.

"He was outraged. Beyond outraged. I had stolen something from him, and he could never forgive me—except that she pleaded with him in the letter, from the grave, to do just that. I took him to the place, the exact spot, and he dove in the water and thrashed and cursed and swam as hard as he could for as long as he could until he literally wore himself down to nothing. After a very long time, he climbed into the boat and we went home. I sorted Mom's things and left."

"No contact since then?"

"Oh sure, there's been contact—of sorts," she says. "But understand that all my life, every phone conversation with Cecil has gone like this: 'Everything good on that end? Yep. Everything good on that end? Yep. Alright then, see you later alligator. After while crocodile.' I call him on his birthday and I call him on my birthday, like I always have. Since Momma died we've been leaving off the alligator part. And he's home folks. When we talk to Retta and Mister George it's the same as talking to Cecil."

"We?"

"Ben and I."

"Does that fucker call every shot you make?" Growled, before he can catch it.

"Excuse me." Her head snaps as if she's been struck. "You asked for this and I trusted you to hear it." She's out the door toward the river.

He quells his temper and follows, saying, "Bailey please stop, that was totally uncalled for, please finish telling me."

She walks to the end of the dock, sits on the rail and watches a wood stork circling on a faraway drift of invisible wind.

"Then I fell in love with you." Shakes her head. Laughs a single hard note. "And then I went to Alaska this last time. And then it was time to come home, come home to my father I mean."

"And that's that?"

"And that's that. We're odd birds, but we're family."

~ ~ ~ ~ ~ ~ ~ ~ ~ ~ ~ ~ ~

*"I lost her Bailey, and I nearly lost you."*

*"She wanted to be lost, Momma. It was never meant for you to save her."*

*"I almost went too."*

*"But you didn't. You came back for me."*

*"Retta told me what happened, Bailey."*

*"It wasn't your fault, Momma."*

*"What Retta doesn't know is that I came so close to gone. I was so close to gone, but I kept feeling your voice."*

*"You'll always hear my voice."*

*"Look how the tides have turned, child. Your whole life through it's been me telling you I'll always be there—and now listen."*

*"Rest, Momma."*

*"Listen, Bailey. There are many moons in this old world—some to untie and take with you, some to untie and let go. I suppose I've come to be both."*

*"Rest, Momma."*

*"To hell with rest, girl. When have I ever wanted to rest? Hand me my mandolin and take me to the dock."*

~ ~ ~ ~ ~ ~ ~ ~ ~ ~ ~ ~ ~

"Hey Boss."

"Hey Boo."

"Well, what's the report?" she says.

"Cecil said to Retta, and I quote. 'I don't smell it, but I'm not ready to swallow yet.'"

Bailey laughs as she paces around the aquariums in Alexandria. Ben tries to as he leans against the door jamb of Bailey's bedroom in Philadelphia. He can't. She hears it. He knows she does.

"That's all you've got?"

"Retta saw him hanging new rope on the tire swing," he says.

"Good god, it's a wonder he didn't have to replace the tire too as much as you and I wore that thing out."

"You're right about that," Ben says.

"So I guess it's okay to bring Padgett back and invite the boys."

"Seems like it," Ben says.

He takes a photograph from Bailey's shelf—the two of them, one on either side of the same tire swing, in mid air over the bluff, just about to jump into the river. He hears them whooping.

"That was the best peach ice cream in the world," he says.

"Fourth of July—the cousins came and Mister George drove us in the parade?"

"Yep," Ben says. "I'm standing in your room."

"I miss you too, Boss," she says. "Let's you and me go home this Fourth. Padgett will be with the boys at their grandparents. We can bring some of my swim kids."

"Watch the parade?"

"Watch, hell—we'll load up Miss Ruby and that Solid Gold Cadillac and ride."

~ ~ ~

# Another Time

The last time she'd been on Edisto Island was when she'd come down out of the mountains the summer before, high on motion, overjoyed to be in home waters. Now she lies there in a sagging mattress damp from sea spray and rain and waits for Padgett's breathing to harden, for him to edge further into sleep. Then she untangles herself like an insect in reprieve backing its way out of a spider's web and eases to the other side of the bed.

The house is doing the same thing she thinks as she listens to the tide flooding around her—holding itself together in troubled waters. Only with the house it's literal. Forty years ago it sat high and white on its massive supports and looked across dune grass to the wrack line fifty yards away. But the salty conclusion to the story has been coming after it ever since, unimpressed by stout boards and fresh paint.

Helped along by Grace and David the shoreline has now inched its way entirely to the front supports and past them, pushing colossal sand dunes aside on its way. Steps that once led down to the beach now dangle three or four feet over the great mats of storm swept Sargasso and bob haphazardly in the surf when the water's high.

The pilings have held, though, so far, even if the floors slant more and more toward the sea. Even if there's a few inch gap in places between the original part of the house and the porch addition. Even if hermit crabs come up through the cracks and whisper around the mismatched furniture, yard sale bought and dumpster bound.

The house belongs to one of Padgett's buddies who's in the process of losing it in a divorce. The wife, who never used it anyway because there's no air conditioning, has already contracted to bulldoze the place and build something civilized.

Padgett thought it would be nice for them to spend time some place different, just the two of them, and Bailey fell in love with the house as soon as she saw it that morning. Padgett warned her when they planned the weekend that it wasn't exactly luxurious, but he didn't tell her that instead of being *on* the beach, the house is *in* the beach, that people have to detour around it on their search for seashells.

They drove through the night from D.C. When they got to Edisto Padgett unloaded the refrigerator things while Bailey went for her ritual swim, then they collapsed into one of the dozen sagging cast iron beds scattered around the rambling house and fell asleep as the August heat began to creep through windows, listening to the ocean and flies at the screens.

They woke soaked with sweat and swam, the water refreshing but the air hazy now with heat. The beach almost entirely to themselves, they fished in the surf for a while, no luck, then followed the creek path to the back side of the island, pulled off their sneakers and dug for clams with their toes in the sandy shallows.

The tide was already incoming, so that one had to hold the clam in place with a foot while the other dove to get it. They took turns, but Bailey liked diving into the tinkling salt water better than holding the clams, so she let Padgett find most of them.

When they'd filled the rolled bottoms of their tee shirts they swam to the bank with the first load. It was sweltering on the lee side of the island, away from the sea breeze, but a cooling afternoon thunderhead was building in the west while they played in the creek, he bragging about the culinary genius of his renowned clam chowder, she biting him on the ankles when she dove for a clam he'd marked.

They collected enough to throw the big ones back, piled them in the tin bucket, and hiked to the cabin in plenty of time to beat the rain storm. After a cool rinse under the outdoor shower and fresh dry clothes, they opened a bottle of freezer chilled wine and drank to Charlie Wilson, Padgett's pal who'd offered them use of the place.

He left her on the porch reading, with specific instructions not to interrupt the progress of his world famous, not-made-for-just-any-old-body chowder, and went into the kitchen to get started. He cracked the shells with a screwdriver handle and poured out the fresh juice, cut the clams into tiny pieces, then chopped onions and made a roux.

She checked on him more than an hour later and found him dicing potatoes, soaked with sweat, there being no cross breeze in the back of the house where the kitchen was enclosed.

"What are you doing in here?" He looked up with a half-cocked smirk.

"What can I do to help?" she said.

"Nothing, I told you. Scram."

"What's this, matie?" She picked up a bottle with a paper bag twisted around its neck.

"Eye, Captain, the men are in need of a ration of rum." He grinned wide and winked.

She pulled the bottle from the wrapper and saw it was already a third empty. She looked to him, but he held his place hunched over the potatoes.

"Holiday, Captain," he said. "Splicing the main brace, you savvy?"

"Sure," she said, making herself lighten. "By all means."

"Then out with you, Captain, and let the crew get on with their duties."

On the porch she watched the sky darken from behind, from where she knew another thunderhead was mounting. With the rain coming, the temperature had dropped, so she curled into the corner hammock with a cotton spread and opened her book. When it began she shut the book again and watched the horizon disappear. She pulled the spread closer, chilled from all the sun she'd gotten, and closed her eyes to listen to the sleepy sound of raindrops on the battered tin roof.

A clap of thunder woke her, dusk coming on, and before she could orient herself she heard Padgett banging around and yelling. When she walked into the kitchen he was pounding the screwdriver against the counter saying son-of-a-bitch over and over.

"What is it," she asked, still hazy from sleep.

"Salt," he said. "The son-of-a-bitching salt."

"Calm down. What about it?"

"The whole son-of-a-bitching box of it just went in the chowder, that's what."

"How?" she laughed.

"It was caked in the box, so I had to cut the top off. Sliced my son-of-a-bitching hand doing it."

She saw now the blood soaked paper towels wrapped around his palm and reached for it but he pulled the hand away.

"You don't give a damn," he said. "You think it's funny don't you, bitch? You think it's fucking funny as hell."

"I didn't know you cut yourself," she said. "Let me see."

"Fucking funny, huh? You want to see funny. Watch this, you fucking bitch."

He shoved her aside, hard into the refrigerator, picked up the empty rum bottle and broke it across the stew pot full of chowder he'd spent all afternoon cooking, sending shards of glass flying everywhere.

"I hereby christen thee dead," he said, and slammed the bottle into the pot. Then he picked up the whole thing, stumbled through the house, and hurled it off the porch into the big water below.

She followed, trying to reason with him, but when he wheeled around to tell her she wasn't worth the time he'd wasted making it, she saw what was in his eyes, mean and nasty and desperate, and she stopped where she was and watched him through the open window between the living room and the porch.

When the pot sailed out of his hands he lost balance but caught the railing before he went down. Then he froze. He stood there, holding on with both hands, staring up into the rain that he hadn't even heard begin, and pulled himself together, his body and his mind, until he realized what had just happened. Still he couldn't move, insensible to what would happen next.

Bailey watched him, afraid too, and angry, so angry. When he finally unlocked himself he saw the shape of her through the windows. He couldn't see her face well enough to tell what to do, so he offered his hand to her and stared into the shadows until she finally came to him.

Angry, she came. Angry but trying not to be, knowing that if she got him going again things would be much worse, sucking back the cynicism and outrage that did not want to be sucked back. The cynicism and outrage that stood ready to surge, as strong as the tide that ran beneath them.

He stepped cautiously out of the rain and held a rocking chair for her, then sat in another beside her, no words passing between them at all. Even after he rose to get the blanket when he saw her shivering, even after the storm cleared and stars broke through the darkened sky. Even after the moon woke up and witnessed.

Sitting there on the porch with her sucked up anger swelling inside, she thought of how it would be if a trap door opened like on some huge stage and down he went into the deep blue sea. She wondered if she would lean over and look to where he and the chair tumbled, or if she would continue rocking back and forth, calmly watching the horizon to see if he bobbed up anywhere in the distance.

"What are you thinking?"

"You don't want to know."

"Go ahead," he said. "I deserve it."

"I was wondering what I'd do if a door opened and you fell into the ocean."

"You don't mean that."

"Yes," she said. "I do."

"No, you don't. You know you don't. You dream up these crazy scenarios when you're upset."

"Is that it?"

"Sure. You'd throw me a line, right?"

"I don't think so."

"Sure you would."

"Maybe another time."

They got quiet again, both sensing it was best, and said nothing else until he stood and took her hand and walked with her to the bedroom. "Good night," he said. "I'm sorry," and he turned to go to another room.

"It'll be okay," she said, and pulled him into the bed beside her. "But it's got to stop, Padgett. Something's been changing in you this last couple of months. You scare me and you hurt me and it's got to stop."

He held her close and tried to tell her something about his boys and clam chowder, but then he passed out before her heart settled.

Now she lies there in the damp stillness, surrounded by the language of water, watching shadows of the hermit crabs move across the window screens as she listens for sounds of the house falling down around them, funneling all her strength into the hope that the ocean will take it before the bulldozer can.

~ ~ ~

For more than a week Bailey has spent nights on the Martin's dock at Kirk's Bluff immersed in shooting stars. Skies have mostly been unclouded and she's counted hundreds each night, dependable Perseids, streaming across in early evening earth grazers and midnight sprints, showers of silver and gold meteors that illuminate sky and sea alike.

There's no way around August. In the sweltering dog days of summer in the deep South mornings haze with humidity that doesn't end with the coming of dark. Cuts don't heal. Grudges fester. Mold grows on damp sheets and dogs don't bother to come out from under the house and bark. What would be the point? In more cultivated times people closed the shutters midday and sallied forth when the worst was over.

The river is a different story.

And if you are fortunate enough to have a dock with hammocks hanging under it and boats tied at the end of it and all of Jericho waiting to enfold you, not to mention the Perseid meteor showers to keep you company at night, why would you be anywhere else? Especially if you have peaches.

George Simmons says to Cecil aw she'll be alright, but Retta calls Ben and says I think you need to come talk to this girl. She hasn't left the dock since she got here—except to go in the river.

~ ~ ~

"Oh for godsakes," Bailey says when she sees Ben coming across the yard.

"Boo," he says.

"Boo," she says back.

"What are you doing?"

"Thinking," she says.

"Boo?"

"Oh for godsakes," she says again. "Old ladies everywhere—all of you. Cecil comes to drink coffee in the mornings and I see all of them during the day—Retta, Mister George, the Joes. Everybody, every day. I help them when they come in at the big dock."

"So you're just fine?"

"I didn't say that."

"What's going on, Booney?"

They watch a flock of ibis rise in a curve of ink-dipped wings then settle once more into the marsh flats to peck along for lunch.

"You want to hear it?" she says. "You really want to hear it?"

"That's why I'm here."

"Oh, I thought you just happened to be in the neighborhood."

"Funny. You're a funny girl."

An osprey flies too close and the ibis flock tatters. Bailey stretches onto the floor planks of the splintered dock.

"It's fucked up," she says. "All of it's fucked up. When he's a son of a bitch but then regrets it, there's no way to win."

She slams the length of both arms onto to dock and slowly shakes her head.

"Forgiveness, right? Who am I to judge and all that chickenshit. God-dammit. Just when I'm at the edge of fuck it—no more—then he comes back with sorry. Sorry."

She rolls toward the outgoing tide, watches circles of finger mullet swirl in the shadows. Ben stands at the fish cleaning sink and slices one of the last watermelons from Retta's garden in half, a burst of soft-scented pleasantness.

She says, "I love him, you see. He's crossed the line and now he matters. I make excuses for him. If he hadn't crossed that line I'd be out of here, adios. But he crossed it, and here I am."

She wraps her knuckles on the plank beside her in cadence with her quickened heartbeat.

"Unless he crosses back," she says. "Unless he crosses the line again into nofuckingway."

She turns to where Ben has quartered the melon and is flicking seeds in rhythm with her heedless anger.

"And you know what I can do about it?" she says. "Nothing. Big fat zero. That's what I can do about it. Here comes the train, and I can't do a goddamned thing but stand there in the middle of the tracks holding out my sweet lovin' arms."

Ben splits the melon once more but that's all he can stifle. He drives the filet knife into the rind and says, "Listen to you. Just listen to you. Can you imagine what you'd say to a friend talking like that? No, forget friend. Anybody. You'd be jumping up and down saying fuck that asshole—hit the road—nobody deserves to be treated that way. I can hear you now. Why do you do this? Why?"

"I'm screwed, Boss. Don't you think I see that? If I cut out it's the same old thing. Bailey can't make a relationship work. Bailey can't commit. What's wrong with Bailey? Why can't Bailey get her shit together?"

She looks to the river again and he looks beyond her. Oyster mounds become visible as the tide lowers, but it's too hot for oysters.

"You don't know," she says. "You've had no way to know the hide I've hacked away sliver by chunk. But every time I'm ready to go I hold myself back, suck it up. And Jesus, Boss, I could roll on without a trace. That's the easy part for me, moving down the line. I'm great at that—it's the hanging in there that's tough."

She lays her hands flat, speaks in a lowered voice.

"There's a part of me that's missing, Boss. I let myself get pushed around because he matters, because I'm a hard-headed fool that wants to show I can tough it out. I'm so good at rolling. Why can't I stick?"

"There's a part that's missing alright, and I've kept my mouth shut for way too long. Like I forever keep my mouth shut when it comes to you. I wish I had a tape recorder so you could hear what it is you're saying. But this isn't you, Bailey. This isn't who we are. This isn't how we were raised."

"I do wake up next to myself, and wonder," she says.

"Wonder what?"

"If anybody ever really learns anything."

"I don't know, Booney," he says, "but we've still got to make the effort." He softens to her, as he will always soften to her, even as he knows that if he laid eyes on Padgett Turner right now somebody would be going to jail and somebody else might be going to the graveyard.

~ ~ ~

A quarantine of the heart. And yet there is the way his smile cocks to one side and makes her want to lick his teeth. And when his hair is mussed and boyish and his brown eyes dance.

~ ~ ~

It's Padgett's birthday and the day after a dinner that the boys help cook, Bailey drives him to the mountains. She's arranged everything—a cooling get-away—champagne and presents and views to forever. Pleasant in the daytime, downright brisk at night. There's no water, save a poor dammed lake, but there's quite a lot to be said for altitude in August.

She gives him a kite and they're flying it in the parking lot at the inn when a silver haired woman smartly dressed in a summer weight wool suit that's still too hot approaches, asks about the kite, tells them how splendid it is that they're so obviously in love, and says she's never flown a kite, never had a childhood in Poland. Her husband died last year and this is the first time she's been back to this, a favorite place of theirs.

Padgett looks to Bailey and she smiles, knowing what he's thinking.

"Are you sure?" he says.

"It's your kite, remember?"

So he gives the string to the lady who becomes a child right there on the side of the mountain.

And when the lady gets into the big Lincoln with the younger couple who've driven her there Padgett once again looks at Bailey and Bailey once again smiles and nods. He hurriedly reels the kite and gives it to the fine-spun lady in the back seat, but the lady says, "What will you have if you give this to me?"

"I'll have Bailey," he says.

They celebrate in the taproom after dinner and one table, then another and another buys Padgett a birthday round of whisky.

"Let's go check out the campground for next time," Bailey says.

"Why not tomorrow?"

"Stars are out," she says. "Brighter on that side."

They hold hands and walk the evergreen road to the campground. It's mostly quiet and dark but there's a couple enjoying a campfire who invite Bailey and Padgett to sit when they ask about the bear someone in the bar had mentioned. Bee and Arnelle.

Their smoke striped percolator is off to the side but warm and Bee insists they share a cup. No worries about the bears. Arnelle holds a banjo, easily picking notes with barely a sound. Bee brags that he picked with Raymond Fairchild earlier that week, Raymond having called him up on stage, venerable elder. Others call him up as well, as he and the missus ramble around the bluegrass countryside. Part of him has gone on ahead someplace, Bee tells them, but the banjo anchors him to this world for now. He's fine when he's picking.

He's fine when he's not, Bee says, but people can't see it that way. She's good with the what's left, satisfied that the what's gone hasn't gone too far. Since they started sleeping with the banjo he's gotten on better in the world. He likes picking to the rising sun so they camp a lot, for she is partial to a mountain sunrise. He likes picking to the stars even better but after a while people want to go to bed. They're glad for the company.

Bailey can't get Padgett to bed when they cross back to the inn. She tries so hard for them to just sleep and go for a long walk in the morning. A hike in the cool forest where ferns and purple wildflowers spill around the rocks. Yellow bright daisies and broad winged butterflies. All the shades of berries—pink and red, purple and black and lavender—waiting for the bears. They could hike to the ridge and look across fog draped valleys. Not this time.

"Can't you see it, Bailey?" he says. "You're the kite—and I'm what's holding you back, weighing you down. I'm dark and heavy, cast iron, and you—I—I'm bringing you down. You should soar, Bailey. You should be free."

"I don't want to be free, you son-of-a-bitch. I'm not free. The most free I've ever felt has been with you."

"And the most weighed down. Jesus Christ, Bailey. I'm no good. The pain I've caused hangs on me like a millstone."

"And what? You can't help it? You can't do anything about it? You can't be with me out of shame for what you've done, and you can't be with yourself for fear you'll do it again."

Her voice grows more high pitched but quieter.

"So don't," she says. "Stop fucking doing it. Regain my trust. You love me—"

"—Yes. I do. "

She founders into his arms, clinging like the tangled lines of a freighter on the deck of a jon boat.

"You're not a bad man, Padgett," she says. "We just need to heal."

She closes the curtains but doesn't move away from them.

"There's no cure for cast iron, sweetheart." He reaches for her and misses.

"I'm gonna shower, Padg. Let's go to bed."

"No, wait—I know I'm drunk, and I know I'm drunk a lot—and okay, there's nothing bad about cast iron. And the only danger of a kite is it can haul down a bolt from the blue."

She stands in the shower and cries. Cries. He stands on the other side of the curtain.

"But Bailey—together we're a cast iron kite. And that won't get you anywhere. That will break your heart. And I surely have."

She snatches the shower curtain back and wipes water from her face.

"Why can't it be that I soar and you ground me so I don't drift away?"

"Because it's not working like that. I'm trying to find the guts to let go the string and it's killing me. It's killing us. Help me let go, Bailey."

"No, Padgett, I won't. It's too big for that."

He turns to walk out of the bathroom, stops.

"So what do I do about the trap?" he says.

"There is no trap, Padgett."

"Yes, goddam it, there is. The same trap between loving you and my sons that aren't allowed to leave Bethesda. An ex who says she'll cut off visitation if things get any more serious between us."

"What? What are you saying? Why haven't you told me this?"

"Because there's no way it can work."

"There is, Padg. We'll figure it out. She can't call all the shots."

"Yes, Bailey, she can. She's known more darkness in me than I pray you'll ever imagine."

"I'm not afraid of who you are, Padgett. Surely to god you've seen that by now."

The water streams in vapors but she cannot warm. Doesn't even feel wet.

"I'm trying so hard to hold on," she says.

She shuts off the water and reaches for a towel, but she can't make herself do it, can't even get out of the tub. She lays the towel on the edge and sits facing the tile wall. He sits beside her facing the mirror and wraps around her, no matter the awkward shape of them.

~ ~ ~

153

"Hey Boss."

"Hey Boo."

"Remember that place with the grape arbor when I first saw Padgett?"

"I remember you telling me about it."

"He's bought it," she says.

"Okay."

So thin, the stockpile of patience. Threadbare.

"He's bought it for me—well for us," Bailey says. "We're gonna fix it up, and the boys can stay on the weekends."

"I thought that wasn't allowed."

"It's complicated, but Padgett thinks there's a way."

"Well isn't that nice."

"Yes, it is," she says. "Maybe it's something we can build on, Boss. I've got to give it a go at least."

"Why don't you just call things what they are?"

The muscles in his shoulders tighten. The muscles in his chest.

"Maybe because I don't know what things are—or how things are—or why things are. Hell, I'm not even certain *if* things are. But I'm trying to figure it out. Isn't that what you tell me?"

"You've already figured it out, Booney, but you won't listen to what you know."

"The place won't close for a month," she says. "I'll keep you posted."

~ ~ ~

Bailey and Padgett have been offshore fishing all day in the flat breathless scorch of September—always an autumn joke in the Deep South—nothing but chips to eat, beer to drink, and rum, Padgett drinking lots of rum. They take no prize in the tournament, but the cooler is filled with wahoo and snapper. They've returned the borrowed boat and are driving toward the little port south of Murrells Inlet nearest the boat ramp and motor court. She drives. He somehow seems more drunk sitting in the truck than he'd been when they pulled the boat out of the water. Very drunk. She begins speaking carefully, thinking carefully about what she's saying, what he's hearing her say. Mostly she remains voiceless, glancing at him sideways.

His head bobs against the seat rest behind him and she knows she needs to get food in him. When he nods and begins mumbling she speaks of the French restaurant where they will eat, the one they'd chosen the night before when they'd window shopped at the antique stores and smelled butter frying and fresh bread. She reminds him how good the steamed mussels will be.

"I'll drive," he straightens and says.

"It's okay," she says, warily. "I've got it."

"I want to drive."

"We're almost there."

He looks as if he might fade again but then his voice sharpens and he yells how she never does anything he wants her to, about how she has to do every goddamned thing her own way, about how he'll teach her it doesn't work like that. About nothing that makes any sense.

"It's okay," she says, trying to soothe him with the sound of her voice. "We're almost there. We'll get some of that good bread. Everything's okay."

"No, it's not, goddamn it. It's not okay. Not a goddamned thing is okay."

She feels it coming when she hears the shift in his voice, just like the other times. But the other times he'd just shaken her, pushed her down on the bed, hit her once on her legs while she lay with her arms curled around her knees in that hotel where they'd laughed about the velveteen bedspread.

She told him then the next time would be the last time. And then she prayed to all gods there would be no next time. That she wouldn't have to square off with what to do if there was a next time. Then she'd simply put it out of her mind. There wasn't going to be a next time. For weeks she's steadfastly reminded herself there wouldn't be a next time.

But here it is—the force of his balled up fist pounding her face, the side of her head. Blows to her shoulder when he misses. Instinct begs to protect her face, but she can't. She dares not raise her arm in challenge. She has to keep the truck on the road, slow the truck down to steady, steady. Again. Again. Teeth cracking. Blood in her mouth, leaking out of her mouth. Again. Somehow thinking she's lucky he can't reach back any farther with his swing, that if they weren't in the truck her jaw could be shattered into a million slivers.

She keeps calling his name, saying, as calmly as she can, "Padgett, it's me. Padgett, it's me. Look at me Padgett. It's Bailey." Crying, "Please, Padgett, it's me." Trying not to cry. The instant before each strike slows in her periphery.

He hears nothing. Pounding, crazed. Skin on skin. Bones, his strong bones, barely covered with skin striking tender skin, the tender bones of her face. Blood from the bone of her eyebrow, from her nose. Blood on his hands, both hearts exploding.

On the outskirts of the little town there's a shopping center with a grocery store. It will be safe where there are people. She can get there. She can do this.

When lights from the strip mall blast his eyes he stops. Snaps out of the rage and into awareness with a jerk of his own head, as if he's been coldcocked.

And as he does, he says evenly, "I'll kill you, you sorry bitch. Caca Dau. When I get you where I can do it, I will take you down."

She believes him. She knows that no matter what else, at that moment he means it.

She pulls into the parking lot, into a space under a big silver street light with clinging moths and says in a faraway fairy tale voice, "We're at the grocery store, Padgett."

He looks at her, dazed, some dangerous animal in dark and distant speculation.

"I'm going in for the ice and freezer bags," she says calmly, softly, tasting the blood, her head ringing. "I'll be right back."

She isn't sure he'll let her out of the truck, isn't sure if she'll scream or not if he tries to stop her, isn't sure if the sound of her opening the door will set him off again. So she lifts the latch as gently as she can and he slurs something in a voice that isn't harsh and leans back with his eyes closed.

Out of the truck, she wants to run to someone, anyone, everyone, put her arms around them and cry and cry and cry and say please take care of me. But of course she can't. Of course she can't walk into the grocery store and scream for help either. She can't cry out at all, can't attract attention. So she walks into the store and places her hands on a buggy to steady herself and starts down the produce aisle. Her right eye is swelling, and that deep down, past the first punch throb settles into her jaw.

Keep calm. She knows that. That's what has brought him around the other times, the other times when he'd explained later how she makes him crazy, how the fever she stirs gets out of hand sometimes and makes him lose control. He'd never lost it like that in country. Never hit a woman before. But there she is in the reflection. Right eye swollen shut now, hair matted around her temple. The blood. How can so much blood come from an eyebrow? She pads her forearm against her face and pulls her ball cap farther down. Winces.

She imagines what it would be like to call the police, yet there's no way she would go with them and sign a statement. Maybe she could make an anonymous call to say there's a man passed out in the parking lot—that she doesn't want to cause a stir, but maybe somebody should see about him. She knows they'd come get him and keep it quiet. She's seen the security clearance. She's seen the badge.

But she'd still have to get to the room and get her things before they came back there with him, which would never happen because pop at the Mom & Pop motor court has a police scanner in his office and would call in immediately to say he recognized the vehicle.

Too much thinking. She leans on the buggy, reeling, talking inside herself about standing up, about not fainting, not calling attention to herself. She mops her face with her shirt sleeve, good that the cloth is navy.

Halfway down the canned goods aisle a woman with sunburned shoulders looks at her funny, and she tries to concentrate harder on not having anybody stare. She starts toward the rice and pasta, turning her face into the shelves when she crosses paths with anyone.

The zip-lock bags are on the next aisle and when she moves to reach for them she sees the white of her fingers from clenching the buggy, the blood. Tries to focus on whether they need quart or gallon size but the answer won't come. She nearly panics at her own confusion, so she places both boxes into the cart and keeps rolling.

She remembers the fish hook tear on Padgett's thumb and backtracks to the toiletries, bright lights beaming down on her, everything bright and buzzing from the fluorescent spans and from her eardrums. She stands in the same spot staring at the antibiotic ointments and peroxide and merthiolate and iodine and gauze and tape and bandaids until a stock boy finally walks by and asks if he can be of some help and she recognizes that she'll have to keep moving. No thank you, she tells him, and reaches for the Neosporin, for what her mother put on her cuts.

She's been in the store for twenty-six minutes from when she first thought to look at her watch and planned to give him plenty of time to fall into the deep snoring sleep of his hard drunks. Or for him to wake and come after her. Or for her to figure what to do next.

The numbness in her nose prickles and her fingers come away with caked and fresh blood both when she rubs it. There's a restroom where she wipes what she can, straightens what she can, pulls her hair back as best she can.

The lock box of her memory opens dirty and ashamed to the old black and tan cur dog she had seen a man kicking in a Savannah alleyway. It kept whimpering, blood spurting from its mouth, but it kept coming back, and the man kicked it harder and harder. Still the dog came back, whimpering, confused.

She braces herself against the buggy every time somebody comes near her, waiting to be kicked. For someone to make her get down on her hands and knees and feel the glassy dirt from boot bottoms grinding into her cheek. Dear god, she says to herself please let me get far enough away from here that I can whimper out loud with no one to hear me.

The lights are more and more intense. She pushes the buggy where she can discretely look into the parking lot and tries to see him in the truck, but she can't tell if it's his head or the seat rest. She can't tell anything.

The last aisle is cookies. Usually she goes straight for the Oreos, but now she starts at one end of the row, picks up every package and reads them all. Every one. She's seen women do this with different things, read about calories and fat content and carbs, so she selects one of each kind and acts as if she's studying the label. Tries to concentrate with one eye salty blind.

Each time she repeats the number, not quite out loud, until she sets the package down and picks up the next. Thirty-seven she says over and over, holding on to the graham crackers. Thirty-seven. And then she puts them down and goes to the ginger snaps. Thirty-eight. Thirty-eight. Thirty-eight. An on to the next.

There are eighty-three different kinds of cookies in that particular Winn-Dixie. She thinks about counting the cereals but knows she'll scream, that she's come to the end of how long she can spend buying time with preposterous colors and shapes and tunneled aisles—all of it pulsing and way too bright.

At the checkout counter she tells the cashier she needs two bags of ice and stares into her change purse while the girl rings her total. When she pays, the bag boy gets ice from the freezer beside the manager's office and sets it in the cart. No thanks, she says, when he asks if she needs any help.

She walks to Padgett's side of the truck and opens the back door to where the cooler sits on a flattened cardboard box. He flinches when she sets the bag of hard ice inside it.

"It's me, Padg," she says. "I got the ice."

He mutters something she can't understand but she hears no malice in it so she shuts the door and comes around.

"I got the zip-locks too," she says as she opens the door to the driver's side and gets behind the steering wheel.

He lifts his head from his chest where it has been hanging and looks straight at her.

"Did you call the cops?"

"No."

"Sure you did. I've been sitting here waiting for them."

"I don't know what you're talking about. Here, I got this for your hand."

Bailey reaches for his finger and rubs the ointment into it, glad she didn't get anything that would sting.

"Can you hear me now?" she asks him.

He says nothing.

"I'm going to drive us back, okay?"

Nothing.

Her stomach twists as she pulls out of the parking lot, away from the lights, but she drives, slowly, hoping they won't meet many cars on the way to the motel, hoping headlights won't blare and wake him. At the motor court she parks away from Blue Ruby and considers leaving Padgett in the truck, but when they stop he comes to as she opens her door.

"We're here," she says. "Let's go in."

He murmurs something.

"I'm really tired," she says. "Let's come on in and go to bed. Aren't you tired?"

He turns and studies her but says nothing.

"Come on," she says. "Let's go in."

She leans in at the passenger door and places his arm around her shoulder, saying over and over we're back, it's time for bed, everything's okay. She walks with him to the room door, bracing him, trying to remember where her own car keys are. Inside, before she gets him to bed he spots the rum bottle on the dresser and goes for it. She catches herself before she speaks, manages to say instead, "Why don't you lie down and let me rub your shoulders. It's been a long day."

He swivels his head in confusion, but she helps him with his shirt, sets the rum bottle aside. He lies on his stomach and she switches off the lamp beside his head and massages him until he passes out. Massages the muscles of the back that supply the shoulders that supply the arms of the fists that hit her. Rum seeps from his sweat in the smothering room.

In the near dark she stuffs her clothes into the open weekend bag as she searches for her car keys, finds them in her shorts pocket from the day before. She almost grabs them and runs out the door, but instead gathers what she can, waiting for him to be totally crashed. When she's almost done he sits up in the bed and says, "I need to get some things out of the boat."

"I'll get them," she says, standing away from the bag. "What do you need?"

"Before somebody takes them," he slurs.

He veers through the door and she waits, nearing her bag to the curtains, watching him through the smudged window. She cranks the window unit as high as it will go and spits on her fingers to wipe the blood that keeps coming from her eyebrow. He comes back with a net in one hand, tackle box and a filet knife in the other, and for a wisp of a second she wonders if he's about to kill her. Then she remembers the gun. My god, the gun.

But he sets the knife on top the tackle box and sprawls across the bed. She's careful not to expose the right side of her face to light from the bathroom, but he only glances at her. She rubs his shoulders until he's gone again, hides his truck keys in the toe of his boots where he'll find them, but not for a while, then slips out of the room and eases the door shut.

Miss Ruby's heavy door would need too much of a slam, so she eases that shut as well, closed but not quite secure. She turns on the ignition and forces herself to wait while the engine warms, knowing if Padgett hears her she'd better be sure she can get away.

She exits the parking lot on the side where Pop might not notice and builds speed, pausing once as she drives faster and faster to reach behind her and push the top down, away from the mom & pop, away from the little town, away from the filet knife and the love and the hate and the shame, down a straight black road that she wishes would go on forever.

And when she's moving with enough speed to numb her entire face and not just her eye and cheek and jaw, she looks to the stars in the huge black sky and wails, aloud this time, wails until her throat is numb too, wails but does not whimper. Refuses to whimper.

# PART III

# Diligent River
# September 1989

# Slow Curving Destiny

A last strand of self dials the telephone. There is no Hey Boss. There is no Hey Boo.

"I'm in Charleston at the Mills House," she says. "Come see about me. There's a key for you downstairs."

~

She won't come to the door. He knocks lightly and waits, hears her dragging furniture and knocks again. Nothing. He unlocks the door and speaks softly but the chain's on and she won't trust her ears.

"Boo," he says, "I'm going to walk down the hall and call you on the house phone. It's me, Boo. Pick up the phone when it rings."

In the elevator alcove he stands with the guest phone in his hands, trying to stretch the chord far enough to reach the hallway. The phone rings and rings but he dares not set down the receiver.

When she finally answers she hears his voice, and when he knocks again she slides the chain open and cowers back into the hiding place she's made between the bed and the wall with all the covers and linens and pillows in the room, a pile of gold tasseled brocade in deep reds and blues. The room chairs, one for the desk, two for a table, a small easy chair, all upholstered in fabrics that match the bedding and drapes, line the wall between the entrance and the bathroom. The lights are off but he sees her mauled face when she cracks the door.

"Boo," he says tentatively.

"Boo," she whispers blankly in return.

"Booney," he says, "I've come to see about you. Listen to me, Boo. I'm turning on the bathroom light so I can see the telephone, okay. I have to call the pharmacy and get some things to take care of you."

She slowly shakes her head no.

"They can bring what we need here to the hotel," Ben says. "I'll go to the door but nobody will come in the room. I'll leave the chain hooked. I'm right here. I'm not going anywhere, but I've got to see about your face."

She rocks slowly side to side while he calls the pharmacy and room service, cautioning both to knock quietly, someone isn't feeling well. Ice and ginger ale arrive within minutes and Ben crushes the valium and Percocet he's brought with him into sips of the drink. She won't let him touch her, but she takes the cup and manages to swallow. When he makes the icepack and wraps it in his handkerchief she holds it to her face as she rocks in her haphazard shelter.

As she calms, he hands her warm wash cloths that come away blood soaked, and when medications are delivered he gives her the antibiotic and antiseptic soaked gauze to clean the lacerations. The slash over her eyebrow could use a few stitches but he can work with that when she'll let him. He first thinks her jaw is broken and he'll have to totally sedate her, but he makes more ice packs and prays for the swelling to ease, knowing the emergency room would fracture her more.

Two hours later he gives her another Percocet and a sleeping pill and waits until she appears to be resting. He unlaces his shoes and stretches on the stripped bed above where she lies. He has driven through the night from Philadelphia, stopping only for fuel and caffeine. Staring into the darkened ceiling he is filled with tenderness and overladen with outrage. One would have to come first.

Later he calls Retta and has her guess at much of what there is to tell. He doesn't want Bailey, if she's listening, to hear the words it would take for anyone other than Retta to understand.

"I've given her what I can for now," he tells his mother.

"She's shut down," Retta says. "What she needs is some open up." She tells him what to ask for, who to ask for, and where to find her.

When Bailey is lucid enough, Ben explains several times over that he has to go out for supplies. He gives her his watch and promises to be back in an hour. Bailey closes her hand around the watch, unfastens her own, places both of them carefully on the stained pillow and draws the covers around her head.

In the Market Ben asks for Fosstine and is directed to a sweetgrass lady on the corner at Church Street. The coiled fruits of her patient labor surround her, as do the raw materials—strips of palmetto fronds and long leaf pine needles, bulrushes and sweetgrass. When she reaches for Retta's list it is with long fingers, nimble and gnarled. She squints at the note, folds it thrice, tucks it into a leather pouch that hangs from her neck, and asks about the color of the bruises and exactly what Bailey has said and done since his arrival.

She asks for Bailey's full name and his full name, then she bends from the basket in her lap to another filled with packets of herbs, selects one, reaches behind her for a rumpled sack of unlabeled powders, opens two waxed paper bags, and pours a mixture into each.

"Some of this must be sent for," she says. "This is arnica—use it with the ice. Make a strong tea from this comfrey and buchu and apply it as a warm poultice. This one is mullein—have her drink a small cup each time she wakes. I'll have the other things tomorrow."

In the early evening Bailey props against the plaster wall and holds the two watches, one in each hand.

"I'm hearing in echoes," she says.

"It's tinnitus, Booney. It'll pass."

She arranges the watches on the edge of the bed, both faces toward her.

"The water calls me, Boss—always. Just like it called to Momma, but it never called as loud as last night. I wanted so bad to crest the Cooper River Bridge and sail right off the top, land in the river and never stop—me and Miss Ruby out to sea."

She turns the watches over, lines them end to end, then sets them back like they were.

"I thought about it all the way from Georgetown, how good it would feel to fly those fifty yards and then keep on flying, look up and see Mom's stars and keep on going."

Her watch slides off the bed and she picks it up and buckles the band of it into Ben's clasp.

"I belong to that ocean, Boss. I wasn't meant to walk in this world. The one thing, the one and only thing that kept me from doing it is you. I knew how mad you'd be—you'd probably fish me out anyway."

She fastens the ends of the tang-buckles together, tucks the leather tips into both keepers.

"It took strength I didn't have to steer straight across the bridge and not over the side. I coasted down East Bay and somehow got myself here, had enough sense to remember the parking garage, knew I had to keep Miss Ruby off the street. Pulled a scarf around me to check in downstairs."

"Did he follow you, Booney?

"No, he couldn't be following me, but I felt like he was. His best guess would be I'm driving to you."

"Where was he when you left?"

"Passed out in the motel room. He has no idea how bad it is, Boss."

She sets the watches down and looks up at Ben.

"He was in another place," she says, "that dark, dark place. I've seen it before, but last night he was locked into it—a machine, like he must have been in Vietnam. I don't know what he'll do to himself if he remembers—except that he'll think about the boys. I hope."

Ben bites his tongue and listens.

All is still, yet the stars are a fury.

"I know I'm somewhere inside here," she says. "But I can't find me. My head reels but I don't know where I am. And it hurts, Boss. All of it."

"I know it hurts, Booney, but you've got to untie the moon and walk on."

"These legs won't walk me," she says.

"Then swim," he tells her. "But untie the moon and move on. Sail on. Float on. Fly."

With her index fingers she circles the watches round and round like a leather buckled ferris wheel and stares past him.

"Listen to me, Booney," he says. "You can't assume anything's the edge just because it looks like the edge."

~ ~

It is a troubled night but rivulets of sleep trickle through the hours. In the morning she's able to sip broth and allows Ben to examine her face and shoulder more closely, but she still won't let him touch her. He hears the housekeepers and steps one foot into the hall to ask for fresh sheets and towels and makes the beds while Bailey's in the bathroom.

He's brought no clothes save those on his back, so when she's comfortable enough Ben reassures her of his return within the hour and walks around the corner to Berlin's. From there he hurries past the shops and restaurants of bustling King Street, glancing sideways with a jolt of vengeance at every stocky guy he sees, craving a blood reckoning. At Market Street he turns right and crosses Meeting, past the old slave market and all the rows of trinkets.

At her Church Street post Fosstine sits in the morning shade humming. She wears a bright yellow blouse today and a red skirt red with bold indigo strips on the bottom. The hemline flows around her and makes a vivid island of color. She's woven a little basket with a wingback handle that she places in his hands, then reaches behind her for the same rumpled sack.

"Life everlasting," she says, and drops a ribboned bundle of fresh leaves into the basket. "Make a tea and also use it for bath soak. Some call it Rabbit Tobacco. You drink some too."

Next she holds a small corked bottle and says, "Same thing, but this is fresh juice. Half for you and half for her." When she sees the question in his eyes she says, "Mus tek cyear a de root fa heal de tree."

"Yes, ma'am, I've heard my mother say that many times—take care of the root to heal the tree."

"Soon she will be able to eat," Fosstine says. "Sprinkle these on all the food—basil, coriander, ginger. This ginger root can be used in the teas as well. Steep it with this last one. Vervain—herb of grace—good for everybody."

Before he can ask, she rests her hands onto his and her mouth forms a sly smile. "These are gifts that cannot be bought," she says. "I know your mother well, and she has done for me."

On the way back to the Mills House Ben stops at 82 Queen for a takeout menu, then calls Retta from the guest phone downstairs.

"I can treat abrasions and swelling. I can treat shock. But I can't treat the heartache."

"Yes you can," she tells her son. "You always have. Did you find Fosstine?"

"I just came from there and got what she didn't have yesterday. Bailey's sipping the teas."

"Something bigger than tea is brewing, son. Are you hearing the hurricane talk?"

"On the drive down, but I've hardly left the room since before daylight yesterday," he says.

"Hard hits in the Islands. People dead. It's Cape Verde—if it turns we've got trouble. Domfe Kurumba is stirring it up."

"I'll talk to the desk clerk," he says. "Call if it gets bad. The room's in your name, by the way."

"Day is jes an arm long, Benjamin. You can reach clean across it."

The hour is nearly spent so he takes the elevator upstairs, heats water in the coffee pot for the tea, and explains to Bailey he has a few more errands, that he'll only be a little while.

"Check the watches, Boo. I won't be more than an hour."

At the Meeting Street Pig he buys what he can—water and fruit for now, nonperishables if it comes to later—snacks, boxes of chicken soup, flashlights and batteries, chocolate for when Bailey makes the turn. Candles. He fills his car with gas and parks it near Blue Ruby on the fourth level of the garage.

Late that afternoon she has appetite. Ben reads the menu aloud and waits to see if she'll answer.

"It's right across the street," he says. "I'll only be a few minutes."

"Shrimp and grits," she says. "And crab cakes."

Before he closes the door she asks him to take the car keys and bring her quilt from Miss Ruby's trunk.

"There's no telling what else needs to come from there," she says. "I can't even remember where I parked."

"I've already found her, Booney," he says. "It's alright."

"No it's not, Boss." She drags the words, trying to focus.

Since the night before she's said very little and all of it lags. If he makes an unannounced move she cringes and if he comes too close she shields herself mechanically.

"The spinning slows for a while," she says, "but then it swirls again and I can't hold on."

"Yes you can," he says. "I'll catch you if I need to, but don't let go."

He doesn't want her to fret about the storm, but news while he waits in the restaurant lounge isn't good. Hugo has pummeled Puerto Rico with winds over a hundred miles an hour and there's a chance it will hit the Carolinas. More than a chance.

"I'm not leaving here," she says when he tells her.

"We may have to," he says. "They may not let us stay."

"They'll let us stay," she says, and will say nothing more.

Downstairs Ben speaks with the manager and is surprised that, for the time being, they remain welcome. Most guests have already checked out, but the hurricane track is erratic.

~ ~

That night she bathes and sleeps in a bed, restless but not fitful. In the morning as she slowly chews the room service grits and eggs Ben can see that healing has begun around her eyes, but what he sees in them is troubling.

Television would be too much, so Ben listens to updates downstairs whenever Bailey is okay for him to leave for those minutes. At noon Mayor Riley says it's time to board up and get out. Never mind the sunshine. A skeleton crew has volunteered to stay on at the hotel and a few downtown restaurant managers are now among the handful of remaining guests.

Next news is that watch has turned to warning. Logjams build in hardware and grocery stores. Traffic on the few roads out of Charleston crawls by mid-afternoon. Over a hundred thousand people stuck on meager evacuation routes—the truth of a peninsula. Ben makes a last run to the Pig, stands in line at the bank, and calls Kirk's Bluff to tell the home folks not to look for them.

~ ~

Thursday morning the governor orders mandatory evacuation of barrier islands. Most have already long gone. Through the day Bailey gathers strength, but Hugo gathers strength as well. Predictions worsen as the hurricane is upgraded once more from Category Two to Category Four. At six o'clock the sun shines on a ghost town.

Then comes the deluge—instant inches of torrential rain that will mix with many more feet of tidal surge—followed by the wind. Ben hurries for a last report and takes the stairs when he sees rain from the roof cascading through the elevator shaft.

Front doors of the hotel have been roped shut against the wind, but the Mills House has held its ground through much harsher history than this. Around 9:00 pm Ben and the other stragglers stand in the First Shot Lounge studying the weather channel. The power flickers and is gone. Gone.

He follows the flashlight beam up five flights of stairs and along the hallway to where Bailey has already lit the candles. Her hands move with purpose once more, and the two of them play gin in the pale light while windows bulge and break in the city around them.

Ben knows the home folks will be watching the eleven o'clock news so he picks up the phone to check on them and say he and Bailey are safe. Circuits are busy and when he tries again the receiver is soundless.

All is silence as the eye of the storm opens and an exhilarated Bailey lays her cards on the table and says let's go see. They pick their silent way along the hall and down the back steps, through the cloistered courtyard, out the side entrance onto Queen Street and over to King.

Stars.

In the hushed miles between hurricane walls skies open and seabirds caught in the vortex call in calm and confusion. Petrels and skuas, jaegers and shearwaters swoop the saturated streets. Bailey picks up a storm feather and puts it in her back pocket.

"Beautiful," she says and leans back to look, both hands outstretched high above her head. "Stunning."

She closes her eyes and opens them. Closes her eyes and opens them.

"Delphinus is there," she says, "but you're the only star I have to fix on in this world. You're all there is that shines true."

Then she takes his hand, not like the hand of a brother but as the hand of a man, and they make their way through the darkness together, Bailey and Ben, pulses swelling in the unearthly eye of the storm.

The back side of the hurricane wall hits with ferocity around midnight and the tide surges with two more hours until high. Centuries old live oaks are uprooted and pines by the tens of thousands double and snap. Winds gust to 135 miles per hour. Consider that.

The candles dwindle as the night wears on but neither moves to replenish them. Each is stretched across a bed listening to punctuations of the relentless tempest.

And then she gives voice to his name.

"Ben," she says.

She bridges her hand between the two beds, reaching for his. Fingers touch, clasp, draw one to the other as she crosses to him.

"Help me know my body again," she says.

With longing from the marrow in his bones he enfolds her, careful of her healing places, but he holds her as a woman nonetheless, holds her long enough to make certain this is the path they will travel.

She is fragile, but she is Bailey once more and she offers herself to him entirely. When she stands to undress he says I'd like to do that, but let me light the candles first. Sweet illumination. They lie side by side in the dancing candlelight and he smoothes his fingertips over the golden form of the woman who was the girl who has awed him since the day of her birth.

Gone are the childhood nicknames they have used to buffer intimacy through the years. They are Bailey and Ben granting themselves the long withheld privilege of one another. Passion concealed in prudence is laid bare. Desire stymied by duty flows free. Hurricane Hugo careens into Carolina as she moves over him and licks his eyelids, his earlobes, the nape of his neck, the cup of his navel, the swell of every muscle that quivers in his powerful athletic body. Marathon man.

And after the first surge he rolls atop her and with the feather she found wisps the shape of her, every curve, every angle, slowly outlining the features of her fullness. Ever so slowly he coaxes chill bumps on her sweat glistened skin until she draws him to her with trembling hunger. Then he kisses the sweat from the back of her knees, the crook of her elbow, the swell of her breasts. Kisses the scars of childhood mishaps, the marks of recent wounds as well. Hurricane or not, they are heedless of all else in existence but the rhythm of their bodies sounding one another without guile.

He dampens a soft white wash cloth and freshens her, blows long un-hurried breaths for her to dry. In the last hours before daybreak they sleep entwined as Poseidon and Zephyros gather water and wind and gaudily with-draw to the west.

~ ~

At first light Bailey stands at the curtains, massive damask curtains that have shut out the light for four days. She opens them enough for her long elegant body to silhouette in an image Ben will carry to his grave. Aphrodite as she looks to the sea that spawned her.

"My god," she says. "The river is there. And the bridge. What day is this?"

"Friday—the twenty-second."

"The equinox," she says. "Grand Mère's birthday."

She turns to where he lies and smiles a real Bailey smile, opens a window to the fresh sea breeze.

"Get up, Bossman," she says. "There's work to be done."

~

By 7:00 A.M. Hugo has been downgraded to a tropical storm and passes over Charlotte with sixty mile per hour winds. In South Carolina everyone east of I-95 is without power. Hundreds of thousands. In Charleston there is no elec-tricity, no running water, no phone service. Trees and power lines barricade the streets.

Bailey and Ben pitch in with the already hustling Mills House staff. No one pays attention to bruises. The second floor pool deck is converted to an outdoor kitchen and by lunch time National Guardsmen are treated to cheeseburgers. In the next days the refrigerators and freezers are cleared and many meals are shared before the food can spoil.

Downtown Charleston is a world unto itself for those like Ben and Bailey who have no option to exit, and help is needed everywhere on the peninsula. Hundreds of workers from out-of-state power companies are welcomed. Red Cross and other volunteers emerge and neighbors look after one another.

Tammy Barnes helps care for the 850 people who have taken shelter at Gaillard Auditorium where the roof is gone and windows are shattered. David Johns hand pumps fuel to keep the hospital generator going. In the full force hurricane winds Gary Fulford and Benjamin Green have run backhoes to res-cue three old ladies and four kids trapped in a collapsed building. Down the street Leroy Mosely unlocks the doors to the grocery store before meats and produce go to waste. Heroes of Hugo. The news is filled with their stories.

In Awendaw Fire Chief David Phillips helps evacuate twelve people from a fallen building and opens a relief center to distribute food and clothing. Principal Jennings Austin and Deputy Charlie DuTart are in charge of the shelter in McLellanville where the storm has surged twenty feet. Heroes all.

~ ~ ~

By Sunday Hugo crosses the Ohio Valley and dissipates in the North Atlantic, but stories and statistics, good and bad, take center stage in the days that follow. In Francis Marion National Forest 8,800 square miles of trees are down. In Montserrat alone 60,000 people are homeless—100,000 in the Caribbean and Carolinas combined. Thirty-four people have died in the islands. Twenty-seven in South Carolina. Martial law is in effect—no one is allowed out after dark—but even Chief Greenberg is unable to stop glass from shattering. Looters now, not the storm.

Crews, paid and unpaid, work around the clock to restore services and provide food and shelter. Truckloads of water, canned goods, diapers, bread, ice, roofing shingles, nails, radios, even generators are received from donors near and far. People at phone banks coordinate help for displaced animals. Once the roads are cleared, a swarm of volunteers lights daily with their own tools and the sounds most heard throughout Charleston county come from hammers and chain saws.

Bailey and Ben help cook and ladle, saw and stack wherever they are needed. In the weeks that follow they car pool with others from Kirk's Bluff up and down Highway 17. Ben takes leave from his practice and rents a carriage house on Tradd Street, calling up every trick he learned in medical school at short-handed clinics around the Lowcountry.

~ ~ ~

The day after Hugo hits Padgett lets himself into Bailey's loft in Alexandria and removes all evidence of his presence. Music, books, clothes, photographs. The rum only he drinks in the freezer. His sweatshirt in the hamper. He seals the key in an envelope with no return address and mails it to Ben in Philadelphia. A typed note says, "No duplicate made, but go ahead and change the lock."

As if he needs a key. The following week when no one has come he lets himself in on the night guard's break and rearranges most of it exactly as it was. He'd missed an album on the turntable. Slack, Turner. He clicks off the penlight, sits in the chair that was once his and hears words about losing your senses. Knocks back a shot of añejo. Words about making your own prison. Another shot. About being too far gone to hope for what you've lost. Another. He doesn't have to play the song—he is the song. There's not enough booze in the world, not even to numb it. Desperado.

And he doesn't need the light to find the pillow where he's lain with his head turned to hers and tried to tell her. Now there's nothing to tell. Instead he gathers his things again and flees. Holes up in his lair with no way to lick the self-inflicted wounds. But he cannot stay away. One night he takes the towel she'd hung on the shower bar, the thinning bar of soap, strands of hair from her brush. Another night his plunder is the white skirt she wore that first day in the arbor, then a small piece of blue beach glass, a paint brush long set aside and a strip of canvas where she's haphazardly wiped the brush of color.

Night after night in pockets of darkness he organizes her music alphabetically, takes every book from its shelf and holds it. Each time he begins a letter that he crumbles and carries away, makes himself remember that his sons have birthdays and soccer matches. His sons who keep asking about Bailey.

~ ~ ~

As life settles from the hurricane, Retta tricksters Bailey into staying near Kirk's Bluff with veiled hints of some health concern. Says she needs Bailey to drive her to Savannah or Beaufort or Charleston for various appointments. Mentions that she's feeling a bit lightheaded and isn't as young as she used to be—nothing to worry too much about but she sure does appreciate Bailey being there with her. And while she's at it Retta eases Bailey into prenatal care, makes the first appointment herself.

"This is *your* baby," Retta says. "Never mind about the rest of it. Your child and my grandbaby—that's what I know for sure and that's all this baby needs."

~ ~ ~

The lease doesn't expire on the loft until January but there's no point. Thanksgiving Sunday Bailey and Ben drive to Alexandria and she sits cross legged listening to the Eagles as she packs boxes for Kirk's Bluff and boxes to give away. Padgett is unmentioned but Ben smells the loathing and anguish.

Once again she gives the aquariums, this time to her landlord who's replenished the fish feeder and checked the balance of the tricky saltwater tank. Laborers are there Tuesday morning to load the pieces for Kirk's Bluff in the front and the pieces for storage in the back. Ben drives the U-haul to Philly to offload what Bailey doesn't need and pack the rest of what they're taking to Carolina.

~ ~ ~

Two days before Christmas, exactly three months after Hugo, a winter storm spreads a soft layer of snow across the Lowcountry. Real snow. Birds around the feeder: Cardinal, Northern Junco, Carolina Wren, Yellow-Rumped Warbler, Tufted Titmouse, Chickadee, Red-bellied Woodpecker, Mourning Dove, Swamp Sparrow, Song Sparrow. Their cross-hatched patterns in the wet ground can be witnessed even after the snow has melted.

Some people live their entire lives without marvels.

~ ~ ~

March comes in tangles of jessamine and wisteria, azaleas and dogwood lace. Bailey's birthday means three months before the baby's due. She tries to shut the box on forbidden sorrow but finds there's no such thing as forbidden sorrow. The pull to Padgett is excruciating. Until she forces herself to slow down and remember. Even then.

Desire leaves long trails in a bygone heart.

~ ~ ~

Leather Joe has designated himself watchman of the property. He's pleaded with Cecil to let him work at the dock and made a deal with George to help farm the Simmons' crops. He keeps guard on the road and both houses—wherever Bailey is. He sleeps on the boat and if Cecil stays offshore he sleeps in his truck.

"He won't hurt me," Bailey says to Leather Joe one hot afternoon. She's made corned beef sandwiches for the crew and hands him a jug of tea.

"No ma'am, he won't," Leather Joe replies.

~

Retta knows this too, but she's also aware that Padgett has been in the woods watching Bailey—and him. Too stealthy for the dogs and far too stealthy for Leather Joe, but the birds confirm what she's already been told.

The eyes of Henrietta Simmons reach deep into the Lowcountry. Whether strip mall parking lot or logging road cut-through, automobiles with Maryland or Virginia plates are made known to her—the unmarked ones even more quickly. As if she needs spies to verify. He can slip around the underbrush all he wants, stand on the roadside with a gas can, but she is full aware each time he sets foot on Martin or Simmons property. Full aware that whatever happens on the bluff stays on the bluff. If she needed Cecil or Ben she'd let them know, but she can tend to this. She and High Sheriff Henry have a non-negotiable understanding. You don't mess with Retta, son.

~ ~ ~

Late into the night on the third Friday in May Retta sits on the porch shelling butterbeans in the dark and hears a heron scold its way out of the creek. She has been waiting. As she walks to where he's braced himself into a moon-shadowed pine she stops and he steps forward. Cicadas drum thousandfold in the thicket around them. She reaches toward him with the package, simply wrapped—the last violet handkerchief—farewell gift she gave him the day they met. She says nothing, regal, but doesn't look on him with disgust. The note that he will later tape inside his foot locker says,

"People don't change, son, they only become who they are.

You've known who you are for a long while, but she is still becoming. Let her."

In the house Retta refrigerates the beans, readies for bed, and eases into the sheets where George lies with his arms behind his head gazing into the pressed tin ceiling.

"This little hitch in my giddy up is all I've got to show for my time overseas," George says. "You can't even see what that boy's got to show for it."

"Not for us to cure," Retta says.

"Not like we could," he tells her. "I never stop praise for the birthday that kept Ben out of that mess."

"I'd have had two chances to remedy that," Retta says.

"The draft?"

"Yes sir," she says. "His left foot and his right foot."

"Those that don't know you might think you jest."

"But you've been around long enough to know better," she says. "And I'm glad about that. Sweet dreams for you."

"Sweet dreams for you, proud walker."

~ ~ ~

Mariel Asherah Martin is born 11:36 A.M. on the twenty-first of June, 1990. Eight and a half pounds, just over twenty-one inches long. She is born on May

Isle, surrounded by water, despite Cecil's months of protest. Bailey agrees for Ben to help Retta but won't budge on her insistence to bear the child as she wishes.

Cecil is the first to call her Curly. And so she is—a curly blend of African features descended through her father's lineage and her mother's Anglo-Eskimo bones. Crystal blue eyes. Bailey's baby. And Ben's. Retta's grandchild, just like she said. George and Cecil are suspended in disbelief—but not for long.

"How 'bout them apples," George says as he and Cecil look at each other and grin, look at the baby and grin.

~ ~ ~

For Bailey the weeks flourish with newborn details and a hunger to paint. She spends hours at the sunroom easel, Mariel snugged into the body wrap carrier or nestled into the "Moses" basket Retta has woven with rushes from the creek bank. The work explodes with spontaneous color that comes too quickly for oils so she's turned to watercolors—bold vibrant strokes with surges of bird shapes and fish shapes. Arcs and angles, shifts of time and water. Ben brings reams of paper and one of every paint tube the Charleston art store stocks. He brings whatever he can think to bring from every baby store he can find. He brings flowers to both houses and anything else any of them need. He's overflowed and unbound.

~ ~ ~

All of them are absorbed with the baby, but Retta doesn't forget. When Padgett comes, as she's known he would, Retta waits for a time between feedings when Bailey's busy painting in the late afternoon light, swaddles the baby in a thin blanket against the mosquitoes, tells the dogs to stay, and follows the seldom used path through the pine patch to the far fence.

"Come out," she says, "and see for yourself." When he does, Retta peers hard into his eyes that cannot hold hers and says flatly, "This is the last time. No more."

She cradles the baby to her chest and stands for a moment to listen if he has words, but there are none.

"Find a way to live with yourself," she says, then turns and walks to the house, knowing he'll not be there when she looks to the woods once more.

As he retraces his steps Padgett sees the old hound dog move like an apparition through the lengthening shadows and knows that other eyes are on him.

He smells the danger before the form of it is manifest, then there it is. From the layered bark of a tall pine beside his pickup the limp snake hangs, lifeless. Impaled by Cecil's hunting knife. Rattler.

It will surely strike no maidens.

He backs out of the thicket, assessing. Proceeds. A hundred yards down the dirt track the familiar truck pulls in behind him from a brambled logging trail, follows at a dead serious distance. In the rear view mirror there are two shapes. The one he knows to be Cecil. The one he knows to be Ben.

Everything solid begins slipping and he's not certain he can catch hold again. Not sure if he should.

The prospect of settlement. Conclusion. Here and now, on this dusty strip of backroad. At their hands or his own.

He slows. Brakes. Stops. The truck behind him follows suit. He reaches under the seat but the leather he withdraws is not the holster, it's the baseball glove Danny couldn't find last week. The gun is there too, and the thought of his son handling it buckles him.

Enough.

Brake lights lift and the two trucks recommence in measured tandem toward the hardtop where one recedes and turns for home and the other continues down the lost highway to a place of further reckoning.

~ ~ ~

# Further Reaches

C urly's third birthday festivities don't end with the party. That Monday three suitcases and a picnic basket are ready to roll.

Retta won't travel farther west than New Orleans but that means Nashville's within range. Blue Ruby's been freshly tuned but Retta says no, she'll chauffeur the Solid Gold Cadillac since she won't be driving to Alaska next summer for Curly's first cross country trip. Ben can accompany them on that excursion.

"Alrighty then," Bailey says, "but that means we need a cooler."

Never mind about Atlanta. They take the back way through the mountains, veer off to Cherokee and Chattanooga, and two days later wheel up to the front door of the Hermitage Hotel, the three of them with their matching straw hats and a car full of road snacks. Their room overlooks the State House, but the room can wait.

Chet Atkins is playing a surprise set at Robert's Western World and they squeeze into a table near the door and order fried bologna sandwiches and onion rings while they listen to the sounds of honky tonk heaven. Curly and her mother twirl on the miniature dance floor and when it's time for a break they buy red cowgirl boots and wear them next night to the Grand Ole Opry.

The Ryman is under renovation so they drive out to Gaylord Opryland and Curly is mesmerized by Marty Stuart and the lights and every detail of what happens on and off stage, where the inner workings of show biz can still be seen. She doesn't understand why they can't dance like they did at Robert's, but she sings words that don't match the songs in a voice sweet enough that nobody minds.

"Looks like we've got us a star in the making," Bailey says after the show on the ride back in to Nashville. "We might as well head on to Graceland from here."

It's the Peabody ducks that Mariel will remember most about Memphis, but when the three of them pull into the driveway at Kirk's Bluff the Solid Gold Cadillac is packed with enough Elvis souvenirs to make the King himself proud.

~ ~ ~

Fourth of July is the next week, and Bailey's swim kids from D.C. and Philadelphia arrive for what's become the fifth annual Fifth of July Mullet Jamboree held on the Simmons-Martin part of the bluff. Each year different ones of the kids are able to make the trip, and this time four come from Philadelphia and three from Washington, with a chaperone mom for each group. Both convertibles await them at the station in Yemassee, and they wave at everybody on the road to Kirk's Bluff—practicing for the parade.

The whole gang pitches in to decorate the cars for the Kirk's Bluff Independence Parade and *Miss Merissa* for the Blessing of the Fleet afterwards. *Sonny Girl* will take her turn again next year. Posters on the sides of the cars say "BAILEY'S KIDS" and the seven of them switch back and forth between front seat and beauty queen spot in the rear. Curly stands beside Bailey for the first shift in Miss Ruby then trades to Ben in the Solid Gold Cadillac for the last leg of the parade.

In the Jericho River after the car parade *Miss Merissa* blazes in red, white, and blue banners and bows. Fourteen of them onboard blow kazoos and wave Lady Liberty mermaid streamers Bailey's made, each streamer splotched with Curly applied glitter. Cecil pilots the boat and Leather Joe patrols the decks but the rest of them—Retta, Mariel, Bailey, Ben, MoJo, seven teenagers and two of their moms—make the Martin boat the envy of the river. George Simmons was pulling nobody's leg when he said he's had his fill of seafaring and cheers them on from the dock.

~

As is Jamboree tradition, they camp on May Isle, young people in tents, others in the cabin. They run and squawk and play soccer and softball and hacky sack, and there are contests for everything—farthest watermelon seed spit, most jumps off the dock, biggest water balloon splats, longest breath underwater, scariest ghost story. They catch crabs with chicken necks and practice casting the shrimp net. Whoever sees a dolphin gets to ring the bell, and it tolls intermittently all through the day. They whoop and holler and sing and are the silly selves unknown on urban streets back home. This is the first year Curly is old enough to be in the thick of it, and indeed she is.

~

Biggest event of all is the After the Fourth Float. Everyone gets an inner tube and everyone gets two tangerines. They plunge off the May Isle dock exactly an hour and a half before high tide, float past Heyward Cove and their Simmons-Martin bluff almost half an hour later, then past the public dock and the village of Kirk's Bluff itself, past the oyster factory. When the tide turns they ride the hour of it back to the bluff for the customary shrimp and crab boil. Keeping tabs on the tangerines is as much fun for the city kids as it was for Bailey and Ben, and when the dolphins surface around them they're wild with joy.

The weather forecast is the same as they've had for days—partly cloudy, chance of isolated thunderstorms—hot July weather cooled with occasional rain showers. Distant thunders grumble as they eat breakfast but blue skies prevail and when the time comes they pile their clean clothes into the dry bag for Bailey to bring over in the jon boat. She'll ferry the rest of what they need for the party, then float with them from the mainland dock in a few minutes.

Ben sets out with the inner tube flotilla and as Bailey waves them off she sees the mermaid streamers across the river where Retta and Mariel and the granddads make ready for the cookout.

"Be there soon," she says.

~

Ten minutes into the float trip a thunderhead forms to the west and the rain begins before Ben and the kids can cross the river, only a light shower but Ben herds them splashing to the mainland dock. They'll let the rain pass and wait for Bailey—good call since the wind kicks up before everyone's in the back door. They wrap themselves in warm towels and stand on the porch watching the sky blacken. The dogs pace and Retta decides everybody gets an early cupcake.

It's one of those biblical thunderstorms—teeth rattling thunder, white capped waves, relentless wind and fierce bolts of frayed lightning. On the island, tent flaps snap and cedar branches swirl. Bailey chases cushions and secures the jon boat. A stray bag sails off the dock table and bits of potato chips scatter into the swelling river. Bathing suits and tee shirts blow helter skelter on the clothes line. The electric air sparks, charges, trips, and Bailey is the only one at ease.

Rain pelts in big hard drops, half an inch in the rain gauge before the front passes twenty minutes later and hot blue skies open again on the river. Summer. Cumulus clouds billow white and fat and the marsh grass is especially vibrant in fresh light. Green glistens from palmetto fronds and pine branches and the effect is cinematic. The birds concur that the storm has passed and a pod of dolphins blows and dips in the calmed water.

Bailey gathers the last few supplies and rings out the soggy clothes. On the bluff side Cecil and George talk about whether or not they'll steam the shrimp in the same pot with the crabs, and Retta slices peaches with the swim moms. The Joes are coming across the yard with a wheel barrow full of ice and Ben is folding Curly into one of the bright striped hammocks they brought home from Belize. Most of the city kids are hanging out on the dock arguing over who'll take the lines from Bailey to secure the boat when she gets there.

She's more than halfway across the river when the slightest zephyr gusts a serpentine pattern of wind on the surface of the water. The sky shadows and a sudden cannonade of nearby thunder explodes with the simultaneous fire-blaze that jolts her from the jon boat and into the dreamy deep. All of it in the twinkling of an unforeseen instant.

On the mainland they refuse what their eyes tell them, refuse to let go the path she takes toward the dock, refuse the boat that continues without her. Every pulse of energy from every being on that bluff surges in resistance. This cannot be.

All of them wailing Bailey, Bailey, Bailey . . . and in the chorus of voices there is her own calling Momma, Momma . . . and the voice of another daughter calling, crying . . . a daughter who will one day learn to fly as

Sheets of prismatic fallout return to
    Moonswept worlds
        Known and Unknown
       Upward, inward
    Outward, under
  Like diamonds dancing
In a slow wake of
  Elegant weaving
    Astral knots untied
      Each a transgression
        Each transcendent
          Birthright
      Streaming
    Streamlined
   Elements of starlit grace
 Dreamscapes of reconciled motion

Time circular and sacred once more
  Closer to the mainland

Farther from the shore
She curves in the arc of a seeker.

The diligent river folds into itself as stars settle into seas, into skies,
and the moon takes her place in both realms.
Follow that path.
Out of that path she rises.

# ACKNOWLEDGMENTS

This book has been a long time coming. Were it not for the diligent pestering of Pat Conroy, it might yet be a work in progress. He is my treasured brother-in-Dickey, and I offer him my heartfelt thanks. To the remarkable Jonathan Haupt, my masterful editor, I also offer thanks and praise. He is my comrade-in-letters, and his mark is on this book.

My mother gave me words and my granddaddy gave me magic, and James Dickey more than anyone showed me how to make something of those gifts. I have also been fortunate to learn from other generous mentors—Bernie Dunlap chief among them. Also Allen Wier, William Price Fox, John Mac-Nicholas, and Ben Greer. Then there are Steve Lynn, Keen Butterworth, Kevin Lewis, and the incomparable Don Greiner. Charles Wadsworth and Byrne Miller.

For the enduring allegiance of my family I am grateful, not only for Mom—Patricia Ann Lowther Malphrus—and Andy, but also for Sarah, and for Dad—J.N. (Jody) Malphrus—and Joey and Deborah and Andrew and Sara and Brann and Willy B. For Cheryle and all my Lowther family. For my Malphrus family and my Fishkind family. For my special sisters Holly and Heather (Caitlin and Emma) and Susan and Sheila and Martha and Karen.

I am grateful too for the encouragement of friends near and far—Andrew Geyer, always. Diane and Anthony. Matthew. Lil and George. Rainbow Sarah. Babbie and Nancy and Patsy and Jacob—all my Bluffton people, Beaufort too. Schatzie and Ed and all my Montana people. My very own Ridgland people, so many who matter so much. There are others—you know who you are.

To everyone at Story River Books and the USC Press I extend my thanks. For those who generously offered insight and advice during the revision process, especially Valerie Sayers and Ann Hite, I am sincerely appreciative. For unwavering and continued advocacy, I express gratitude to my colleagues at USCB.

Above all I am grateful to my loving husband Andy who has accorded me steadfast support and the unselfish gift of solitude to get my work done. To him I offer my abiding devotion.

## ABOUT THE AUTHOR

ELLEN MALPHRUS lives and writes in her native Carolina Lowcountry and the mountains of Montana. Her fiction, poetry, and essays have appeared in *Southern Literary Journal, Review of Contemporary Fiction, William and Mary Review, Georgia Poetry Review, Haight Ashbury Literary Journal,* and the anthology *Essence of Beaufort and the Lowcountry.* She was a student of James Dickey and teaches at the University of South Carolina Beaufort.